She felt raw and exposed,

too aware of her own mixed feelings about this enigmatic stranger.

Without warning, he caught her wrist and she winced. Christian raised it up and examined the bruise. His voice was filled with regret as he spoke softly, "I did this last eve when I grabbed you, did I not?"

She nodded hesitantly, "I... Yes, you must have."

He grimaced. "I am very sorry, Rowena. It was never my intention to cause you pain of any kind."

Rowena could no more look away from that earnest and compelling blue gaze than she could fly. His hand seemed to near burn her where it rested on the delicate skin of her wrist. But when he broke the contact of their eyes to place his warm mouth against the spot, she gave a start at the streak of heat that flashed through her body....

DRAGON'S DAUGHTER

CATHERINE ARCHER

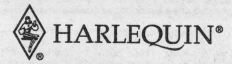

HARLEQUIN®

TORONTO • NEW YORK • LONDON
AMSTERDAM • PARIS • SYDNEY • HAMBURG
STOCKHOLM • ATHENS • TOKYO • MILAN • MADRID
PRAGUE • WARSAW • BUDAPEST • AUCKLAND

ISBN 0-373-29241-4

DRAGON'S DAUGHTER

Please address questions and book requests to:
Harlequin Reader Service
U.S.: 3010 Walden Ave., P.O. Box 1325, Buffalo, NY 14269
Canadian: P.O. Box 609, Fort Erie, Ont. L2A 5X3

This book is dedicated to the most recent additions
to my family:
Steve Krug, Justin Bennett, Jimmy Bennett,
Marty Brace, Diane Brace, Kailynn Brace
and Christopher Brace,
with love and gratitude for you all.

Chapter One

With a frown of pity, Rowena looked down at the man who lay on the windswept beach. His face, which she imagined might normally be handsome enough, was gray and lifeless. His dark hair was matted with seaweed and sand. His garments were in tatters, though because the fabric was a rich, dark blue velvet, she knew they once had been fine.

He was indeed breathing, as young Padriac had said when he came bursting into her cottage with the wild tale of finding a stranger on the beach. But just.

Urgently Rowena turned to the boy, who looked up at her with wide, fawn-colored eyes, his round cheeks flushed with concern and excitement. She spoke with deliberate calm. "We must get him to my cottage."

But how? she wondered. The very reason Padriac had come for her was that all the men, including his own father, had already gone out in their fishing boats for the day. They were not due back for many hours.

The trail up to the village from the shore was steep and slippery. It would not be possible for Rowena and Padriac to move the man without assistance.

"We canna carry him." The round-faced child echoed her thoughts.

Again she looked down at the stranger. There was no telling how long he had been lying here, but surely it could only have been since this very morn, for someone would have seen him the previous day. 'Twas a deserted stretch of coast indeed, with rocky cliffs jutting steeply above the narrow shoreline, but the village children did roam it searching for gulls' eggs, as Padriac was surely doing when he found the man.

Rowena said, "Go to Hagar and tell her to bring some of the women here to help us. He is a big man, but methinks together we can move him."

It was the way things were done in Ashcroft. The village being so remote and small, its occupants were more family than neighbors, for the most part. This fact had helped Rowena to get through the grief and loneliness of losing her mother some three years before.

As Padriac scampered off, Rowena felt a tug of melancholy. Her mother, sad and bitter as she was, had been the center of Rowena's world. She had hardly a clear memory of anything before the two of them had come here to Ashcroft, when Rowena was not quite four.

One of the two memories she did have was of looking up at a high stone wall. So vivid was this recollection that she could almost feel the rough, cool texture of the stone against her fingers. The other was less clear a vision, but more compelling. She believed it was of her father, for she had a sense of being held close to a broad strong chest and hearing the steady and comforting beat of a heart as she inhaled the combined scents of sweat and leather and fresh air. The warmth she felt at the recollection brought up such feelings of love and safety that she was sure it could only be of her father.

The fact that her mother had become so disturbed each time they'd spoken of him, of the fact that he had been a knight, and in the business of making war to protect lands, always kept Rowena from asking about it. Agitated and distraught, her mother would lament the fact that he would still be alive if he were a common man, concerned with no more than his livelihood and family. When Rowena had grown old enough to wonder why they had come to Scotland rather than go to other relatives upon his death, her mother had become hysterical, blurting out that her family were all dead and her husband's family did not want them. She had never been more than a servant in his home, she'd said, never his wife.

She had begged Rowena to let the past remain there. And she had seemed more disturbed by his position as a noble than by the one detail that troubled Rowena most: his failure to legitimate her.

Leave it in the past was what Rowena had done, though in her deepest heart she continued to wonder about the man who had fathered her. In spite of her own anger at his refusal to wed her mother, Rowena would have given much to know him. She wished to know if the memory that lived in her heart was truly of him. For it was the one thing she could not set aside. He may have been mistaken in his loyalties, may have failed to give her his name, but perhaps he had loved her to some extent.

That question would never be answered, for all who might have known had gone on to the next world, or were lost to her because of her illegitimacy.

Rowena looked down at the man before her. He might have someone, somewhere, who would grieve should he fail to return. Perhaps even nobles like her father, if his clothing was any indication. 'Haps it was this that had brought her these unwanted thoughts of things best left forgotten.

With determination, she knelt to run her sure hands over the man's large form. There was an unnatural coldness to his flesh that told her he had been exposed to the elements for too long.

She knew he must be warmed, and without delay. More than one death had been brought about by extended exposure to the cold.

Hurriedly she continued to run her hands over him, searching for injuries. She found nothing more than a prominent lump on the back of his head. And though she tried not to think on it as she slid her fingers over the smooth skin beneath his woolen tunic, she had an unaccustomed awareness that the man's body was hard and lean, the muscles well developed. Rowena felt an odd stirring, a sense of him as a man that was far different than what she usually experienced in her work as a healer.

Even as uncertainty coursed through her, he groaned and opened his eyes.

Starting, Rowena looked up at his face, into the most unusual blue eyes she had ever seen in her life. They were an oddly compelling shade, light and yet dusky at the same time, like periwinkle blossoms.

Rowena's heart thudded in her chest.

As she continued to return his gaze, she noted that although the man was looking directly at her, he did not appear to be focusing. He was seeing but not seeing, his expression troubled by some inner vision. Even as she noted his distress, she saw that it was softened by compassion and yearning.

He opened his pale lips, murmuring, "Rosalind." His lids drifted closed once more.

Rosalind? For a brief instant Rowena felt a stirring of familiarity in hearing that name. She quickly dismissed it. There was no one hereabouts named Rosalind.

Clearly this unknown woman meant something to the man with the unusual and compassionate blue eyes. What an enigma he was. Unless she was completely mistaken, her examination of that powerful, lean body told her he had been in the best of health and vigor ere he had washed up on their beach.

Though she wondered once again how he might have gotten here, the way to Ashcroft being arduous and seldom traveled, Rowena knew that would be determined only if the man regained consciousness. He could have fallen from a passing ship, but few ships sailed this close to their treacherous shores, for the sea was far too shallow for any vessel larger than a fishing boat.

She stood, looking up along the cliffs, as the sound of voices came to her. A group of women led by Hagar, who had become something of a mother to Rowena when her own had died, and the excitedly prancing Padriac, hurried along the path. It looked as if most of the women in the village had come to her aid. They picked their way carefully down to the beach, continuing to ply young Padriac with questions about the man he had found.

Rowena smiled with gratitude. As always, there would be enough hands to accomplish the task. Here in this quiet village were folk who cared for one another. They did not value land or position above life or family.

In a relatively short time, Rowena and the other women had the stranger on the bed, covered with blankets, in Rowena's small but tidy cottage in the wood. He had begun to moan and murmur under his breath, but his words were indecipherable, though the distress behind them could not be mistaken.

It was Hagar who finally stood back and surveyed the man with hands on her narrow hips. "I can make out none o' that. Where do you ken he might come from?"

The elderly widow Aggie answered, "I canna reason it, neither. 'Haps his mind be addled." She sighed. "We won't be finding out, if he dies. And he may indeed, for he's got the look of one not long for this world."

Rowena knew a renewed sense of disquiet at the thought of this powerful man having lost his mind. But she made no mention of the name he had uttered with such clarity. She wished to give them no false sense of hope for his recovery. "'Twill be Rowena who brings him 'round if anyone can," Hagar replied with some uncertainty. "Ye mun recall how bad off was young

John last fall when he fell overboard and breathed in all that seawater.''

There were nods of agreement as all eyes turned to Rowena. She knew not what to say to this, and covered her disquiet by addressing Padriac. ''Pray fetch me an extra bucket of water from the stream.''

She then began to clear the table of the roots she had been preparing for drying when Padriac came to fetch her. As she did so she listened as the women continued to discuss the stranger and the severity of his condition.

They might indeed have great faith in her, but their very likely accurate assessments of the man's chances of recovery were trying Rowena's self-confidence. As soon as Padriac returned with the water, she stated gently, ''Thank you all so very much for your assistance. I am certain you must all have more pressing duties to attend than this. I do promise to let each of you know if there is some change in his condition.''

It would indeed be best if they all went back to their own work. Except for Hagar.

Rowena stopped the older woman with a hand on her arm. ''Pray, would you stay and help me to tend him?'' The request had nothing to do with the odd awareness she had had of the man as she examined him on the shore, she told herself. ''I would greatly appreciate your doing so, for there are some plants I must gather in order to treat him.''

The older woman nodded and said, ''I will warm some water whilst you are at it and clean him up, lass. He's needing a bit of a wash.''

''I...yes, he is.'' Uncertain as to why the thought of

washing the man was so very disturbing to her, when she had seen many a man in various states of undress while treating them, Rowena put water on to heat. She then hurried out into the wood to gather some fresh mandrake. Only when she had gathered what she required did she return to the cottage.

Giving Hagar a brief nod as the older woman looked up from the large wooden bowl of water and the cloth she held, Rowena could not help taking in the long form on the bed. Quickly she set about brewing an infusion that would help to strengthen the stranger's blood as well as calm his unrest.

As she did so, Rowena was infinitely conscious of the fact that Hagar had removed the man's wet and bedraggled clothing, for it lay in a filthy heap upon the floor at the foot of her bed. The sounds of her wetting and wringing out her cloth could not be mistaken, nor could the soft but incoherent sounds he made as he stirred restlessly from time to time.

Rowena did not allow herself to even glance toward the bed again, though she was not certain why. As she had told herself earlier, she had examined and treated more than one man, despite her somewhat tender years. It had been her mother who had taught her about plants and their medicinal properties. Yet she had soon confessed that Rowena's natural aptitude far surpassed her own abilities.

Fascinated as she was with trying new and varied combinations of plants, Rowena had taken what her mother had taught her and expanded her knowledge by trial and error, as well as by searching out every other healer in the surrounding countryside.

Rowena's knowledge and skill had grown until she was often called upon to minister to those in nearby villages. She took great satisfaction putting her life to some use in the community that had taken in a bastard child and her English mother, making them their own when they had had no one.

After what seemed a very long time, Hagar said, "You can get a better look at him with all that muck washed away." She stepped back, the bowl of water held before her, murmuring, "What a pity," as Rowena drew near.

The man was so pale without that covering of sand and dirt that his tenuous hold on life was obvious. As Rowena stopped beside the bed, it seemed as if his incoherent muttering had grown louder, though she still could make out none of what he was saying. Again she felt a sense of regret. At the same time she could not help acknowledging that the face was undeniably a strong one, the features quite pleasingly formed.

She remembered the expression in his eyes when he had opened them on the shore. Rowena realized that those eyes would soften that broad forehead, proud nose, high cheekbones and lean jaw. His face would be a compelling mixture of strength and gentleness.

Hagar distracted her from these thoughts, saying, "I'll warrant there's a broken heart that will never mend, should he die."

"Rosalind."

The name flitted through Rowena's mind and she did not know she had said it aloud until Hagar replied, "What say ye?"

Rowena shrugged. "Just a name he said."

The older woman frowned. "Ye spoke with him?"

Rowena did not look at Hagar as she recalled how the concern and compassion in his gaze as he'd spoke that name had moved her. "Nay, he came 'round only long enough to say that one thing. You see how he has been since."

The older woman moved to the door with the bowl. "I've heard naught of a Rosalind."

Rowena answered softly, "Nor I. He seemed so... If I could I would find her and bring her to him, for there was such a look to him when he said it. Her presence might help him to come through this alive."

Hagar's gaze was kind but measuring. "Aye, love will do such things." She went outside to empty the bowl.

Quickly Rowena returned to the hearth, where the medications she was preparing would soon be ready. In one bowl she had mixed rue with wine she obtained from a monastery some miles away, for any pain he might be having in his head. She had also made another concoction of the mandrake to further aid in relieving any pain, as well as aid in sleeping, though the man had not fully regained consciousness thus far. Lastly she had prepared another bowl with a mixture of rue and vinegar, beside which she'd laid a scrap of clean white cloth.

Hagar, who had now returned, said, "You will bathe his head in rue?"

Rowena nodded. "'Twill perhaps help him to regain his wits."

The older woman nodded in turn.

When Rowena was ready she moved to the bed and,

trying not to show that she felt strangely self-conscious about touching this man, put her arm under his head and tipped the first bowl to his lips. To her relief he took it easily enough, swallowing whilst not fully rousing.

When the second bowl was empty, and Rowena had rubbed the rue and vinegar across his wide brow, Hagar said, "Now all we can do is pray."

Rowena sighed. "Aye. Though I will continue to give the medicaments."

Hagar answered softly, "May God's own hands be with ye, lass."

Rowena bowed her head humbly. "I pray that it be so."

The older woman sounded weary as she sighed and said, "I mun go home and get the meal ready for my Sean now, if you've no more need of me."

Rowena nodded quickly, feeling guilty for keeping the older woman from her work for so long. Hagar's son was Rowena's closest friend and had been since the day Rowena had first wandered down the forest path to their cottage. Of late Sean had seemed somewhat agitated and demanding, wanting her to take long walks and such when she was quite busy. He was wont to talk endlessly of a lass named Berta, whom he had met while delivering fish to a village farther inland. Rowena had no quarrel with his preoccupation, only his insistence that she hear his every thought. But she loved Sean wholly, and he would be hungry from his morning's work. "I will keep you no longer. Thank you so very much for all you have done."

The older woman shrugged as she moved to the

door, her face filled with affection and approval. "I've done no more than yersel, my lass. You've a good heart in ye. If ye have need of me I will come."

Rowena felt a rush of both happiness and self-consciousness. She whispered, "I love you as well."

Hagar smiled, flushing with pleasure, and nodded, closing the door behind her. Her cottage was just a short distance away and close to the main path through the village. It would be no great effort to fetch Hagar if she was needed, but Rowena was determined to manage on her own.

No more than an hour had passed when Rowena was given cause to put her skills to the test. The man in the bed had begun muttering to himself again. By the time a new batch of potions was ready he had grown far louder, tossing and turning as she moved toward the bed to give them to him.

When Rowena reached out to put her arm around his neck to lift him up, he shocked her by grabbing hold of her wrist and rearing up in the bed, those blue eyes flying wide. The bowl fell, spilling the contents upon the coverlet, even as fear raced through her.

Her terror grew as the man cried, "Ashcroft…must find Rosalind…." He shook his head violently. "Dragon dead…the babe dead…not dead…"

Ashcroft, for the love of heaven—the stranger knew of Ashcroft and clearly connected it to this unknown Rosalind. But the references to dragons and dead babes were utterly incomprehensible. Desperately Rowena forced herself to break free from the terror that gripped her. Yet it took all her strength to pull her arm away from his.

Just as suddenly as he had risen up the sick man fell back upon the bed. His eyes were closed now, but the ravings continued, as did his thrashing about. With shaking fingers, Rowena grabbed the bowl and clutched it to her, backing away from the bed.

Calm, she told herself over and over again, she must be calm. Breathing as evenly as she could, she moved to the table to refill the bowl.

And all the while she could hear him repeating the same disjointed phrases. Her chest ached as she realized that he had obviously gone mad, as the other women had feared. It was such a pity for one so strong and virile to be brought so low.

How much of his mind might return when, and if, he recovered, she could not say. All she could do was attempt to keep him quiet, not only for his sake, but for hers.

By the time Rowena had returned to the bed with the bowl and a spoon with which to feed him the liquid, the sick man had quieted somewhat. That strong, tanned forearm lay across his brow, and though she was watchful, he made no effort to take hold of her again as she fed him a strong dose of the mandrake potion.

That done, she rubbed more of the rue upon his forehead and placed a bag of dried rosemary beneath his head to ward off anxiety of the mind. Finally he fell silent once more, his arm dropping to the coverlet.

Rowena stood for a long moment looking down at him. As when she had first seen him on the beach, she felt a deep sympathy for those who loved this man. Who would grieve for the loss of him? Did they even know that he had come to Ashcroft, and thus know where to search for him? If he died having never returned to his right mind, she would not know whom should be sent word of his passing. His people would never know what had happened to him.

He might have a young child—a daughter who would always...

She stopped herself there. She had no reason to think he had anyone, even this Rosalind, who could be as much a product of his addled mind as the dragons he raved on about. Rowena would be far better served by not getting overly involved in what happened to this man. She would tend him, as any other, and accept what came.

Rowena barely glanced up as the door opened without ceremony some time later and she heard Sean's voice say, "What is my mother on about? A stranger washed ashore? And you tending him?"

She spoke with deliberate calm. "Aye, Sean, 'tis true. And here he is."

Hagar's voice was filled with exasperation as she spoke from behind Sean. "As I told ye." Obviously his mother had accompanied him.

Rowena kept her gaze on the strong column of the stranger's throat as he swallowed without fully rousing. She felt strangely self-conscious about holding his head against her breast as Sean moved to stand beside the bed, exclaiming, "Dear God, where could he have come from?"

She shrugged and sighed as the man took the last of the liquid, and allowed his head to fall back against the pillows. She met Sean's gaze briefly, seeing the agitation in his strong but sensitive face. "That is as much a mystery to me as to you. Has anyone sighted a ship?"

Sean shook his dark head. "Nay, there would have been some mention of it amongst the men." He cast an assessing glance over the sick man as Rowena placed the small wooden bowl upon the table beside the bed.

Sean scowled as the stranger passed an agitated hand across his brow. "Why have you brought him here?"

Rowena shrugged again, meeting his green gaze with surprise. "To minister to him, of course. Where else would he be taken?"

"Why, anywhere. To our cottage. To…"

Rowena felt her brow crease with puzzlement as she looked to Hagar, who was frowning. Clearly this notion hadn't come from her. "Why would I have him taken to your cottage when everything I need to treat him is right here?"

Sean's scowl deepened. "You must see that this man cannot stay here with you."

"Others have done so."

He took an exasperated breath. "Those others were known to you and us. This man is a complete stranger. He could—"

Rowena laughed in spite of her irritation with his overprotective manner. They had been struggling over things like this ever since they were children, Sean telling her she could not climb trees and the like, Rowena ignoring his every directive. "And pray, what could he do? The man cannot even raise his hand to wipe his own brow, let alone harm me in some way." She recalled just how strong he had been in that one moment when he had grabbed her wrist, but she would be much more careful to keep him from waking to that degree until he showed some signs of improvement.

Nonetheless, she did not meet Sean's gaze as she said, "You can see the state he is in. I have given him medicaments to quiet him and will continue to do so."

"He could awaken fully at any time."

Rowena said, "I will certainly keep that in mind, and should he awaken with the intent to do me harm, I shall hie myself off to your cottage with all haste."

Sean placed his hands on his lean hips. "Ye canna stay here alone with a strange man, Rowena. I forbid it."

Rowena frowned, feeling a shaft of rebellion race through her. She knew he wished only the best for her, but she would not allow him, nor anyone else to dictate to her.

She placed her hands on her own hips. "What say you, Sean?"

He glared at her even as chagrin registered in his eyes. "Now, Rowena, I did not mean to sound so... I am only..."

She raised her chin. "And have a care that you do not. Now be off with you so that I might get on with my own business here."

"Rowena..." His tone was cajoling now, but she would have none of it.

"Go on, I said. You may stop 'round in the morning if you are truly concerned for my safety." Though her determination to do as she would was still clear, the edge was now gone from her voice. 'Twas impossible to remain vexed at Sean for long. They knew one another far too well. Although she had never had a brother, if she had he would have been just like Sean, bright and handsome and protective.

The fact that she had no brothers, no sisters, no family of any sort besides her mother, made her hold Sean all the more dear. She didn't even know her father's name, having been told that it was for the best. Even on the day she had died her mother had refused to utter his name.

Telling herself that such thoughts could gain her nothing, Rowena watched as her friend moved to the door with obvious reluctance. Yet he said no more, glancing back over his shoulder only once before making his exit.

Rowena then turned to Hagar, who had also watched her son leave the cottage. The older woman suddenly cast a sympathetic, yet distracted glance at her and said, "Is there anything I might do?"

Rowena shook her head. "There is nothing to do but wait." And suddenly she found herself confiding in her friend about those troubling ravings. "He has come around more fully, rambling wildly about dragons and dead babes. I fear his head injury may indeed have left the man addled."

Slowly Hagar came forward, placing a covered container on the table, her dear face fearful. "Those do sound like the ravings of a madman. 'Haps Sean is right in this. The stranger could be dangerous, Rowena."

"Pray do not worry. I have given him sufficient

mandrake as well as other sleeping herbs. He will not waken.''

The older woman shook her head, glancing to the door through which her son had gone. "Sean and I...we love ye, lass. And only wish for ye to be safe.''

Rowena noted the odd catch in Hagar's voice as she spoke of Sean's and her own love. Rowena was more moved by this concern coming from Hagar, who had sought to guide her only in the gentlest ways, than she had been by Sean's demands. Perhaps she should take heed here. Her mother had always told her to be wary of strangers. Heretofore there had been no reason for wariness, as she had never come into such close contact with a total stranger. But she should not allow her stubbornness to make her forget her mother's advice.

Rowena took a deep breath. "I will have a care. But truly, I do not feel there is cause to worry for the next few hours. As I said, I have given more than sufficient of the sleeping potions to keep him docile. In this state he would be near impossible to move, and it would be unfair to call out those who have already sought their beds to aid us.''

Hagar watched her for a long, silent moment, then nodded, indicating the container on the table. "I've brought ye this broth, and will be back when the sun rises.''

Rowena bowed her head in acknowledgment. "Thank you. I am grateful for your care.''

Hagar left the cottage without further conversation.

Rowena sighed. Since her mother died she had spent much time alone. Though she loved the villagers who had taken her and her mother in, she was also fond of her solitude.

She glanced back toward the bed. She tried to tell herself that the sick man would give her little trouble, but knew it was not true. Although she had decided that she would not allow herself to care about the outcome of his illness, she did indeed care. Again she told herself it was because of those who might await him.

It was with a decided determination to think of something besides the sadness engendered by this thought that she began to make herself a pallet on the floor near the fire. She did not mind so very much, as she had also slept there in the last few weeks of her mother's wasting illness.

The task was too soon completed, as well as her other preparations for sleep. Cocking her head, she listened for any stirrings from the bed. There was nothing but the sound of the man's deep breathing, which seemed to have grown somewhat raspy.

Rising, she went to peer down at him by the light of her candle. Though his face was very pale and drawn, that was no change from before. His forehead was cool to her touch.

The sound of his breathing had definitely changed. Determinedly she told herself not to become alarmed, for it could be caused by nothing more than a dry throat. When she fetched and spooned a bit of cool water into his mouth, the harshness did seem to improve somewhat.

Slowly she sank down on the bench beside the table and took a bit of the rich broth Hagar had placed there.

Although it had grown cold, the flavorful liquid was welcome.

Several times Rowena reached up to rub her eyes, which felt gritty and tired. It had been a long and wearisome day.

Once the cup was empty she rose and went to her pallet. There was no telling what tomorrow might bring, and she would be well served to try to get some sleep.

She knew not how long she had actually been asleep when she opened her eyes again. Wondering what could have wakened her, she became aware of the fact that the man's breathing was ragged again. That soft raspiness seemed to have grown harsher, shallower. Frowning, she rose and moved to look down at him.

That handsome face was flushed with heat, and though he slept on, he moved his head restlessly from side to side.

Rowena put her hand to his forehead. It was hot—too hot.

Chapter Two

Fever.

Rowena quickly went to the fire and put the water back on to heat. Because of the likely inflammation in his lungs, she made a mixture of horehound and honey. Then she placed a combination of sorrel and marigold into her mixing bowl to treat the fever. While she waited for the water to heat, she fetched a shallow wooden bowl, filled it with cool water and removed a soft clean cloth from the chest beside the foot of the bed.

Then she stepped toward the bed, placed the bowl upon the narrow table and dipped the cloth into it. When she'd wrung out the cloth, she hesitated, her gaze fixed on his face, handsome in spite of the illness that had robbed it of color and animation. She should not have told Hagar to go.

With a sigh of impatience, Rowena told herself that this was completely foolish. She had performed this very task more times than she could count. To hesitate with this man was madness. He was nothing to her, and utterly unaware of her at any rate.

Her suspicion that he might be a noble, a man who came from the world of her father, made him no different from any other man who lay ill in her care.

Nonetheless, she took a deep breath as she smoothed the cloth slowly across that wide brow, her fingers brushing the thick, dark brown hair Hagar had washed. The stranger stirred slightly and Rowena stiffened. But he did not open those blue eyes and she forced herself to relax.

Yet as she ran the cool cloth over his high cheekbones and lean jaw, she found herself thinking that this man was the most handsome she had ever seen. There was a deep strength to his face that was belied by that one look she had had of his blue eyes, eyes that had seemed so surprisingly gentle. That gentleness was echoed in the softness of his mouth, which was now parted as he took in quick, shallow breaths.

Suddenly she realized that though this man was a stranger, completely unknown to her, she wanted to know him. To know something of the world he came from, the world of her father. It was a world she and her mother had lived in, at least for a time.

She wanted to know why the stranger had come to Ashcroft, and whence he would be going when he left.

Her mother had told her that the nobles valued their lands above aught else. But the look in his eyes when he had spoken of the unknown Rosalind...

If there was a Rosalind. What if it was all mad ravings?

Frustrated with her own whirling thoughts, Rowena drew the bench close to the bed and set about her task with renewed purpose. She grew increasingly aware of the intimacy of their situation. She was touching this man in a way she would never dream of doing if he were well, learning the smooth contours of his face in a way she did not even know her own. Gently she bathed the corded column of his throat, his powerful shoulders, wondering at the sheer masculinity of him, and feeling a more intense awareness of her own femininity.

When he groaned and tossed the coverlet from his chest, her gaze went to that wide expanse, which glistened with perspiration.

Her own breathing seemed more shallow, her chest tight. Although she knew it would help to cool him were she to bathe him there as well, Rowena dared not do so.

Thus she put all of her attention and energy into doing what she could—working on without ceasing, yet never growing less conscious of him as a man, even when her heavy lids sagged with exhaustion...

Rowena lifted her head from her arm, realizing she had fallen asleep. A low groan came from the bed beside her.

Instantly her gaze went to her patient's face. The light from the fire was dim but she could see the beads of perspiration on his upper lip. He groaned again, his head rolling on the pillow.

Hurriedly she dipped the cloth into the cool water and wiped it across his brow. The moment it touched him he sighed, raising his hand to rub his throat, though it was clear he had not regained consciousness.

Again she wet the cloth, this time applying it to his lean jaw.

Without warning, his eyes flew open and he grabbed her, pulling her against the burning heat of his chest. "Rosalind...must find her..."

Instantly Rowena leaned back, but in his fever her resistance only seemed to fuel his determination to hold her. His arms were like iron bands, pressing her to him, to the heat and strength of his body, the body she had not dared to touch.

From somewhere there came a response in her own body, a hardening of the peaks of her breasts that shocked her even as a shaft of inexplicable pleasure raced through her blood.

Then, just as suddenly as he had taken hold of her, she was released and he fell back, unconscious once more. Quickly she crossed her arms over her aching breasts, her gaze focusing on the smooth tanned skin of the stranger's chest as she wondered how touching it could have brought such a reaction from her.

She looked into his face. He was oblivious to her.

Of course he was. He had never thought of her at all. It was this unknown Rosalind who consumed him to the point that worry for her had fought its way up through the depths of his illness.

Rowena could only wonder in horror that she would react to this man as she had. All she could do to soothe herself was remember that when his health returned he would not recall this event. She would be wise to forget it as well.

She raked a hand through her hair, looking toward the shuttered window. How long until sunrise? No matter how long, or how ill he became, she was not going to touch that man again, not alone here in the darkness.

* * *

Rowena still had not done so when Hagar arrived, accompanied by Sean, not long after sunrise. Rowena found it hard to meet the older woman's gaze, and even harder to meet Sean's as she opened the door and moved back to the table, where she made a show of tidying up the things she had left out during the night.

Sean, who was garbed for fishing in a short tunic and heavy woolen hose, hesitated in the doorway as Hagar came forward, removing her cloak. He spoke carefully, and Rowena knew that he was thinking of their unpleasant exchange of the previous evening. "Good morrow, Rowena."

She nodded without looking at him, less irritated with him than herself, given her confused feelings about the stranger. In spite of this she spoke with bravado. "Good morrow. As you can see I am quite whole."

She felt him stiffen.

Hagar seemed to be unaware of their discomfort or else chose to ignore it. "So how went the night?"

Feeling her friend's attention upon her as he, too, listened for her reply, Rowena bent to put more wood upon the fire. "It was long. He has developed a fever."

The older woman went to the bed and reached out to place her worn hand upon the stranger's brow. "Ah, 'tis not good. You could have come for me."

Placing a pot of water on to heat, Rowena said, "Why would I wake you, good Hagar, when you needed your sleep? I did well enough on my own, and methinks he has cooled somewhat from the worst of it."

Never would she admit how difficult tending him had been, for she could not understand why herself. Now, in the light of day, she felt utterly foolish for reacting to the man as she had.

Hagar sighed. "Well, enough then."

Rowena was conscious of Sean continuing to study her. She looked up at him, forcing herself to meet his gaze. 'Twas her own predicament and no other's if she had gone a little mad in her reactions to this stranger. She spoke in what was a surprisingly normal tone. "Will the men not be waiting for you?"

He nodded jerkily, and she felt a stab of sympathy at his obvious dejection.

Affection for him made her add, "I would not take it amiss should you come by at the end of your day. If you are not too tired."

A hopeful glimmer lit his eyes. "Then you are not still angry with me?"

She shook her head. "I could not remain so. You are my brother."

A strange expression passed over his face, immediately replaced by relief. And then she had no more time to think of Sean, for Hagar said, "'Tis good you've decided to cease your squabbling, but we have other concerns to occupy us now. Methinks the man's fever may be increasing again."

Rowena barely noted Sean's departure as she moved forward to touch the sick man's heated brow. She felt a new wave of anxiety. Clearly the worst was not over.

While Rowena brewed more of her potions, the older woman set to tending their patient by unspoken consent. Thus it went over the next day and into the night.

No more did Rowena stay alone with the stranger as fever raged through his body.

If Hagar found it odd that Rowena would suddenly be eager for her assistance, she made no remark on it. Rowena could only be grateful, for there was no explanation she was willing to voice aloud.

Sir Christian Greatham, heir to his father's title and lands, opened his eyes and looked at the low, wood-beamed ceiling overhead with confusion. Where was he?

He sat up, taking in the fact that he was lying in what appeared to be a wide platform bed barely long enough to contain his full length. A woolen curtain separated it from the main chamber, but it had been drawn back. His gaze scanned the small but scrupulously tidy interior of a one-room cottage.

Where was he, indeed?

And how had he come to be here?

The throbbing in his head made him reach up. He was not surprised to discover that the pain seemed to originate with the lump he found, although he had no memory of how it had come to be there.

The last thing he recalled was riding his stallion along the edge of the cliffs. It had been full dark, and he had known the path was treacherous, but he had been determined to keep going, certain that he had nearly reached the end of his journey.

According to what he had learned when he stopped at a village near the English border, his destination could not be far ahead. The locals had shown open curiosity at his interest in finding Ashcroft, telling him that he would find little of interest there, naught but a tiny fishing village. From them he had also discovered why it was so little known, for it lay on the point of a narrow peninsula that was near impossible to reach from the inland side, due to the mountainous terrain and constantly swollen rivers. His informants clearly felt that the trouble of reaching Ashcroft, coupled with the lack of any noteworthy object at the end of such a journey, made the going nonsensical.

But Christian had a reason. A reason compelling enough to make him overlook any hardship.

Rosalind. The Dragon's daughter.

Once he reached Ashcroft he might discover if the fantastic tale told to him by a dying knight had any merit. That Rosalind might still be alive he could not fully credit, but he had to *know*.

Unfortunately, the delays he had encountered in finding the village where Sir Jack had said he would find her had left Christian incautious in his determination to reach it.

He had been told that the best route, the one that lay along the shore, was hardly better than the inland route. That it was barely traversable even in daylight. He had been driven by the knowledge that he had already been gone five weeks, three more than he had assured his sister he would be gone when he had left Bransbury. He had refused to tell even her where he was going because of his sworn word to the dying Jack. The more people who knew of Rosalind's possible existence, the more danger there was of her uncle, the present earl of Dragonwick, finding out before her safety could be guaranteed.

Again Christian rubbed his head. His last memory was of his horse rearing up, as a huge wave seemed to rise from out of nowhere. How he had come from that windswept shore to this bed was as much a mystery as where *here* might be.

Christian slid forward and swung his legs over the side of the bed. In spite of the increased pounding this caused in his head, he realized as he did so that he was completely nude.

At the same time he noted the sounds of someone stirring across the room. He followed the rustlings, and came up short as a woman rose from a pallet on the floor beside the fire.

The first thing he noticed was her hair, a fiery auburn that drew the eye as it hung about her in wildly tousled disarray. The second thing he noted was her long, lithe figure in a flowing gown of white. The third thing, and the one that gave him pause, was a pair of eyes so rich a green he could hardly credit their reality, for they were the color of newly grown moss. Darkly lashed, they had an almond shape that made them even more unusual.

So transfixed was he by those eyes that it was a moment before he realized the expression in them was decidedly apprehensive. He pulled the coverlet about his waist, aware that her slender body was poised as if ready to take flight. He spoke quickly, surprised at the dry and raspy sound of his own voice. "Pray do not fear me."

She raised her head, her eyes now filled with bravado. "I am not afraid, sir."

He tried to hold that gaze, but felt a wave of dizziness overtake him. It was with regret that he felt himself sink back on the bed. "That is quite wise of you, for I seem to be too weak to do you ill did I wish to."

Immediately her face softened in concern. "You have been very ill." In spite of her change of tone he noted that she remained where she stood.

He rubbed a hand over his face. "How long have I been here?"

"Four days."

Shock drew him upright. "Four days? But how...?"

His father needed him at Bransbury. Only Christian's determination to settle the debt to his former foster father could have taken him away, now that he realized his error in staying away for so very long. He must return!

She took a step closer. "One of the village lads found you unconscious on the beach. I...you were brought here so that I could care for you."

His mind teemed with questions, yet his confusion only served to make the weakness in his body more pronounced. "I recall nothing beyond riding along a rocky and narrow track wedged between a high cliff and a rolling sea."

She took another step closer. "Then you did not wash ashore from a ship."

He looked at her. "Nay, I was mounted, trying to find my way to a particular village. A place called Ashcroft."

"You have arrived at your destination. Well, near enough. My cottage lies in the wood nearby."

He took a deep breath. "This is Ashcroft?" She nodded and he felt hope growing inside him, for if he had found the village…

She spoke slowly, watching him with those amazing green eyes. There was an intensity in them that surprised him. "Why have you come here?"

He wished that he did not feel so very tired, so weak, so conscious of her mesmerizing loveliness. He sighed. "I am searching for someone. A young woman."

She bit her full lower lip. "Rosalind?"

He jerked, alert again. "Aye, but how would you know that? Do you know her?"

She shook her head quickly, seeming uneasy at his vehemence. "Nay, I know nothing of a Rosalind. I…you said her name when you were ill. You spoke of Dragons and dead babes. I thought you might be quite mad."

Disappointment added to Christian's utter exhaustion as he sighed. "I assure you that I am not mad." He raked a hand through his hair. "I want to…" He could not quite focus his mind on what it was he did want.

The next thing he knew he felt cool, gentle hands upon his brow. Her soft, husky voice murmured, "Do not worry over anything now. Lie still. There will be time enough for what you wish to do. All will be well."

He could not summon the energy to explain that he was needed at Bransbury…that he must…

It was full light when Christian once again opened his eyes, instantly recalling the events of the night. He sat up, glad for the strength that seemed to be returning to his body. Even as he thought this, his gaze searched for the young woman he had spoken to before.

She was there beside the fire, as she had been the previous night. This time she was garbed for the day in a woolen gown of deep forest-green.

There was guarded tension in that slender form, as there had been the previous time they'd spoken, but there was no fear in her captivating green eyes. She spoke evenly. "Good morrow, sir."

He could hear the huskiness in his own voice as he replied, "Good morrow, kind lady. Forgive me for not offering my thanks last night, for it appears I have much to be thankful for if you have taken me in and nursed me. Especially whilst knowing nothing of me. For my lack of chivalry, pray forgive me. I can only claim surprise at finding myself in these circumstances."

She inclined her head with an unconsciously regal grace. "Your thanks are well met."

He found himself watching her closely, realizing anew that she was likely the most beautiful woman he had ever seen, with those green eyes, well-formed features and auburn hair, now confined in a thick braid that hung to her hips. He heard the wonder in his voice as he asked, "Pray, do you mind my asking who you are?"

She seemed to stiffen, answering without looking at him. "My name is Rowena." She cast a fleeting glance in his direction, then added, "And you are?"

He noted her seeming agitation over giving her name, but could fathom no reason for it as he answered, "Sir Christian Greatham, of Bransbury."

Her gaze flew to his and she straightened fully, her fair brow creasing. "A knight!"

He frowned in turn. "Does that trouble you?"

She flicked her tongue over those full lips as if with nervousness, replying, "Nay, I have simply never met a noble. My mother did not... How does one behave with a knight?"

He shrugged, replying even as he noted the unfinished remark. "As one wishes."

She frowned thoughtfully, those eyes flicking toward him and away, and he could not help noting once more how beautiful they were with their surprisingly dark fringe of lashes. A man could become lost in those...

Abruptly he called himself to task. This woman's eyes were not what had brought him to Ashcroft. "Where are my clothes? My horse?"

She shook her head with regret. "I am sorry. The clothing had to be burned. There was nothing left of it, really. And the horse..." She again shook her head. "We saw no sign of a horse."

Christian raked a hand through his hair. God, what a fool he had been to continue on that night. The animal had been worth much in gold, but his value as a constant and loyal companion had been far greater. Christian's eyes widened as he realized that with the loss of his stallion, he had also lost all that had been in his saddlebags, including his dragon brooch. It was the symbol of his brotherhood with his friends Simon and Jarrod, and their determination to stand against the man who had murdered The Dragon. Hatred for the man who had perpetrated that crime rolled in Christian's belly for a brief moment before he overcame it.

If he had lost the brooch, he would not have it be for naught. He would discover if Rosalind were still alive. And if she was, Kelsey might pay for his crimes at long last.

Christian could not accomplish that clothed in a bed fur. He pulled the cover higher about his waist as he cast an assessing gaze over the young woman. "Are you alone here?"

She flushed. "Yes, but it was not I who... Hagar was the one who removed your..."

"You mistake me. I was not concerned with who might have removed my garments, only with attaining others. Who is this Hagar?"

"She is...a friend who lives in the village. An elder lady."

He sighed.

Rowena watched her patient with an embarrassment mixed with fascination that nearly overrode her caution and discomfort.

This man with the powerful form and gentle eyes was a knight! Just as her father had been.

She trained her full attention on the man before her. She had never grown accustomed to him ill. Conscious and fully aware, he was even more disquieting.

She tried not to let her gaze linger on the broad expanse of his naked chest and shoulders as she wondered if she was fooling herself to imagine that he would not recall any of what had occurred while she tended him. The fact that he seemed more concerned about his lost garments than with her should have put her at ease.

It did not. For she was even more eager than he to cover that smooth, tawny flesh.

Hagar was the only one who could aid her in this. Surely the older woman would be able to help her find garments to clothe her guest.

So thinking, Rowena said, "If you will await me I will go and fetch something for you. I...we...Hagar and I did not know when you might awaken, and gave no thought to what you might wear when, and if, you did."

Without waiting for a reply, Rowena took her warm woolen cape from the peg on the door and stepped into her leather shoes.

He spoke up. "Rowena, I would—"

But she did not stop in her flight from the cottage. "You rest. I will return anon," she stated, nodding in his direction.

She raced down the path through the forest to Hagar's cottage. She threw the door open without knocking. With an expression of surprise, the older woman looked up from where she was tending the fire as Rowena exclaimed, "He is awake."

"Praise be."

"He told me he is a noble. A knight. He is asking for his clothing. I have nothing to—"

Hagar stood immediately. "A knight, ye say? Of course ye have nothing for him to wear. We should have thought..." She bit her lip. "Sean is not of a size with him."

With a nod the older woman spun about and went to the chest that sat beneath the shuttered window. Quickly she opened it and withdrew garments from inside, laying them neatly on the hard-packed dirt floor, until she stopped, holding up a deep blue tunic. "I had saved this for Sean so that he might wear it when he grew to be a man." She touched the fabric gently. "It was his father's best, his marriage garb. Methinks Sean will never be so large, but I did plan to cut it down for him...." She glanced toward Rowena and away. "We will put it to good use this day instead. I also have my Duncan's hose, and a pair of shoes that have seen better days, but will have to do."

In no time at all she and Rowena were headed back down the forest path to the cottage. When they reached it Christian Greatham was standing in the middle of the floor with a frown on his undeniably handsome face, the bedcover wrapped around his lean middle.

Seeing him like that again, feeling his masculine presence, Rowena was doubly glad that the older woman had returned with her.

It was Hagar who spoke up. "There ye are, my lad. 'Tis surely good to see ye up and about."

He answered "Hagar? If I may call you Hagar?"

"Aye, that would be me name. And you are welcome to use it." She held up the clean garments as she moved toward him. "I've brought ye these. They may not suit ye so well, bein' a knight, but I think they will fit those shoulders."

Christian Greatham took the clothes with a formal bow. "You have my deepest thanks, gentle lady. I take it from Rowena that I must also thank you for helping to look after me when I was ill."

Rowena was unaccountably pleased at his deference to the older woman. She did not know how she had expected a knight to behave, but she had never imagined one would be so gracious to folk her mother had told her would be considered beneath him. Rowena said nothing, continuing to watch his interaction with Hagar.

The knight said, "Is there somewhere…"

Hagar motioned toward the bed. "Ye may pull the curtain. Rowena and I will await ye."

He bowed and moved off to close himself behind the bed curtain. In spite of the fact that the woolen curtain was heavy and opaque, Rowena turned her back and gathered up the pallet she'd been sleeping on.

Despite her efforts at distraction, the rustling noises behind the curtain brought forth vivid visions of that long hard body.

Once her bed was put away she moved to the fire to begin brewing an infusion of herbs that would further aid her guest in regaining his strength. Not that the knight needed any more assistance with that if his physical appearance was any indication.

But she did not wish to think upon that.

She continued to occupy herself until she heard Hagar say, "There ye be. Good, they do fit ye."

Rowena spun around, looking at him dressed and realizing that clothing did nothing to dampen the sheer masculine energy of this man, this knight named Christian Greatham.

"Do they not fit him well, Rowena?" the older woman said.

Rowena could not hold that blue gaze as he turned to her, though she noted that the vivid blue fabric, which hugged those wide shoulders as if made for them, only seemed to make his blue eyes appear all the more intense. She found herself looking down at the cup in her hands with uncharacteristic shyness. "Aye." She forced herself to face him, to say something. "They were the marriage garments of Hagar's late husband."

Christian turned to the older woman. "Dear lady, may I not attain some other garb less dear? I would not—"

Hagar hushed him quickly. "Do not worry yersel. My Duncan, he would be happy to see them put to good use, as I am." Rowena knew she was pleased at his having understood that the clothing was a gift of some consequence.

As before, he bowed. "I am honored."

Again Rowena felt inordinately pleased with this man—though she had no reason to be so, for he was no more than a stranger to her. A stranger whose life she might very well have helped to save, but a stranger nonetheless.

She told herself she was simply surprised, after the way her mother had led her to believe one of his station would behave.

Hagar turned to Rowena. "This lad needs something to fill his belly."

Rowena held out the cup. "I have brewed a drink that will help you continue to recover your strength. If you would take it I will serve you some of the rabbit stew from last eve."

The knight came forward to take it from her hand, saying, "My thanks."

Hagar asked, "What were ye doing hereabout, lad?

And what happened to ye that ye would be washed up on our uneasy shore?''

Rowena paused in the act of dishing up the stew and watched as he replied, ''As to the latter, I have no notion. I was riding my horse along the path, and it seemed a large wave might have hit us. But I am not certain. As for the former, I am searching for some-one.''

The older woman shrugged. ''Rowena told me of that. Ye are far from likely to find her here, sir knight. No strangers ever come to Ashcroft. The last being Rowena and her mother some fourteen years gone.''

Rowena found herself nearly pinned in place by that blue gaze. ''You came here fourteen years ago with your...mother?'' When she nodded, he said, ''Where is she?''

She frowned, uncomfortable beneath that close and curious scrutiny. ''She has been dead these three years.''

He raked a hand through his hair. ''Dead. Can you...do you know where you lived before coming here?''

''England. But I...'' She frowned, unable to meet his gaze as she suddenly realized that she did not wish to tell this man that she knew nothing of herself, her parentage. ''I—I do not wish to speak of it.'' She could hear the note of shame in her voice.

He took a step toward her. ''But I would know—''

Looking to Hagar with desperate eyes, Rowena said, ''Forgive me. I...must leave you in Hagar's gentle hands now. There are some things I need from the for-est.''

She did not remain to see the sympathy or understanding that came into the elder woman's gaze. Hagar would understand her distress, for Hagar and Sean were the only ones she had ever told of her ignoble parentage. Rowena grabbed up her cloak and left the cottage.

Chapter Three

The next afternoon Christian was still teeming with frustration as he waited for Rowena to return from another seemingly imperative errand in the forest. He felt a renewed wave of frustration each time he thought of what had happened when he attempted to question her about her life before coming to Ashcroft. He groaned, wiping a hand across his brow as he lay on the bed in the tidy little cottage.

His deep desire to return home could not be fulfilled until he had done what he'd come here to do. He must find the patience that had been so much a part of his nature all his life, but seemed to have deserted him of late.

He recalled the sad expression on Hagar's face as Rowena had left them the previous afternoon. At the time, he had been so filled with enthusiasm and hope that she, against all probabilities, might be Rosalind—even though the name appeared to bring no hint of recognition whatsoever. The fact had continued to trouble him as he'd questioned Hagar. "Why did Rowena leave so suddenly?"

She'd raked him with a glance. "Why do ye ask? What can it matter to ye?"

He'd realized that he would need to go carefully with these folk, who met few strangers, especially if Rowena were the one he was searching for. She would have been taught caution from an early age, from what Sir Jack had told him. Christian shrugged. "I would simply know of the one who saved my life. Perhaps I mean to reward her kindness in a way most fitting."

Hagar had looked at him closely, and he'd held her gaze without wavering, determined to make her see that he meant no harm. Finally she said, "Rowena will expect no reward and will likely take none. Though she's deserving of more than she'll ever receive. Her mother brought her here when she was four, just as she told ye. Mary, her mother, was mistrusted at the start, with her English ways and all. But even though she didna welcome prying about her own life, she was kind and helpful enough to others. And Rowena…" Hagar's fond gaze went to the door, through which the girl had just left. "She was a love from the outset. Our own cottage is just along the path through the wood, and my lad, who is of an age with her, wouldna stay away. He was hers from the start. As she grew, her care for me, Sean, all of the villagers was clear. It surprised none of us when she took to the ways of healing. Only eighteen winters she has seen, but her skill is far beyond those years, for it comes from true care for others."

Christian attempted to disguise his eagerness, as he realized that along with the age of the child, the mother's English background were surely too similar to be coincidence. "What can you tell me of the mother?"

Hagar shrugged with regret. "She died. 'Twas slow and painful, and there was naught Rowena or any of us could do to change it, though we tried."

"You know nothing of them before they came to Ashcroft?"

She clamped her lips together tightly, looking away. "I have told ye all ye need to know. Aught else is for the lass to say, or nay."

Christian was less than pleased. He wanted to explain that he had only Rowena's best interest at heart, that he felt she might be an heiress, but he had sworn to speak of the matter to no one. At the same time he chafed at this impasse, for he had heard enough to know that unlikely as it might be, he might have stumbled upon the very woman he was searching for.

It was Rowena herself he needed to question. Yet if she were Rosalind, her nursemaid mother would have taught her to be wary of revealing any information about herself. Her well-being, her very life, depended upon secrecy, for if Kelsey were ever to learn that the child lived he would surely make good on his previous effort to dispose of her. It seemed that even Hagar, who appeared to be quite close to the girl, knew very little of her before her arrival here. Though it did appear that she was hiding something, she clearly had no intention of saying more.

He had found no opportunity to speak privately with Rowena, due to Hagar's almost constant presence. In the short bits of time the older woman was gone from the cottage on some business of her own, the lovely

Rowena engaged herself in some important task, or simply left the cottage. Just as she had not more than an hour ago, when Hagar had gone to prepare a meal for her son.

Christian longed to challenge Rowena, but caution warned him not to create tension between himself and the girl.

Under no circumstances could he risk ruining a possible opportunity to see right done for The Dragon's daughter. Christian gave another groan of frustration and closed his eyes, telling himself that she could not run from him indefinitely. He must have an opportunity to begin to gain her trust before he could even hope to get her to confide in him.

Even if it meant more delay in fulfilling his long-neglected duty to his father.

So plagued was he by these thoughts that he felt little relief in knowing that in spite of the fact that he had been dreadfully ill, his strength was returning apace. That it had been Rowena's doing only made him all the more hopeful that she was the one he sought. For he would expect the uncommon in the daughter of a man such as The Dragon had been.

These thoughts continued to torment Christian as he looked toward the open door of the cottage only moments later. He frowned, uncertain as to what might have drawn his gaze there. It took only a glance to realize that the woman who leaned heavily against the sill was in dire circumstances.

The hands she clasped around the great mound of her belly were white-knuckled, and her face was twisted in a grimace of agony. Her pain had marred her face to the point where it was difficult to gauge her age with any degree of accuracy, but the wildly helpless and confused expression in her wide blue eyes told him that she must be very young.

He was on his feet and hurrying toward her before he even thought to move. She practically fell into his arms as she cried, "Is the healer here?"

He felt her surprisingly slight weight as he held her upright. "If you mean Rowena, she has gone to gather herbs from the forest."

Sudden and desperate sobs erupted, as the girl seemed to lose what little hold she'd had on herself. "But she mun not be gone. She was me only hope. The babe is coming and I've no one to help me."

He had suspected the part about the babe. As calmly as he could, Christian said, "I can fetch other help should Rowena not come back in time." He had no notion as to how long Rowena might be in returning. It could be any moment or hours, for all he knew. But the village was purported to be quite nearby. Hagar had said she lived only a short distance up the path through the forest.

With a desperate strength that shocked him, the pregnant woman grabbed Christian's hand, her eyes boring into his with inescapable entreaty. "You canna leave me. 'Tis too late. There is nay time. The babe comes."

Christian felt a shaft of panic, accompanied by disbelief. "Would this be your first babe?" When she gave a brief nod he added, "I have heard there's no way to measure the length of the first birthing with any certainty. Surely there is more time left than you imagine."

Those blue eyes held his and there was no mistaking the certainty in them. "I ken the truth. The babe has been many hours coming, but none would help me in my own village, as the babe's father is wed to another. I walked for many hours, even crossed a swollen river, ere a man on the road told me that there was a woman here who might..."

She doubled over, leaning her full weight against him once more as her whole body tensed and the breath left her lungs in a moan of misery.

Not knowing what else to do, Christian scooped her up in his arms and carried her to the bed. Once he got her there he realized she was clutching his tunic so tightly that he could not move away. Thus he was forced to remain leaning over her until the spasm that gripped her had passed and she released him.

Though what he should do after she finally did let go her tight hold on his woolen tunic, he did not know.

As a boy Christian had loved the animals around his father's lands. His mother had shared that love, encouraging him to assist her as she tended the horses, sheep and cattle about the demesne through illnesses and births. His beautiful and much beloved mother...

After she had died and his father had become so morose, Christian's love of animals had helped to sustain him. Later, at Dragonwick, his life as a squire was so ordered, his growing friendship with Simon and Jarrod so enthralling that there had been little time for such things. As a knight in the Holy Land he had been even further removed from animal husbandry. Yet he had not forgotten.

With animals, keeping up a strong, steady presence was often all he need do.

Something told him that this situation would require more participation on his part. And that was precisely why he was determined to find some way to get assistance.

Hopefully, he told himself that the girl might be wrong in her assessment that the babe was coming now. He could think of only one way to determine that.

Gently, he put his hand on her leg, as he looked at her exhausted face. "I will need to look...."

Eagerly she nodded, pulling at her gown to raise it. "Aye, you mun help the babe come."

Knowing that she had misunderstood his intent, Christian chose not to discuss the matter...yet. Carefully he took a glance...and sucked in a breath of shock and frustration. For the blood-streaked fuzz could be naught but the child's head.

Quickly he drew away, his mind reeling. She had been right—the babe was coming and it was happening now. There would be no one to see to it but him.

He felt her watching him, waiting for him to do something, to help her and her babe.

Taking a deep, silent breath, Christian met her eyes. "What is your name?"

"Nina."

He nodded. "I am Christian." Then, with what he hoped was more confidence than he was actually feeling, he said, "We'll see it done between us."

Her sigh of relief was short-lived as another spasm of pain tightened her face and made her close her eyes as she cried, "Please, now!"

Quickly he rolled up his sleeves.

Minutes or hours, Christian lost track of how much time passed before he lifted a shriveled and screaming man-child from his mother's body. In the end there had really been very little he could do but catch the infant as the young mother pushed him into the world.

But the rush of exhilaration and relief he felt at hearing the child's cry was great. He lifted the tiny boy, who would someday be a man, and as he looked into that wrinkled little face, thanked God for the gift of life with an even deeper reverence than he had each time he had helped a colt or a lamb come into the world.

Rowena stopped dead in the doorway of her cottage and stared.

She could not credit what she was seeing with her own eyes. There stood Christian Greatham with a damp and screaming infant in his two large hands. On the bed behind him lay the limp form of a young woman, her pale face lined with exhaustion. The expression on his own face as he met Rowena's gaze was at once triumphant and relieved. The same emotions were obvious in his voice as he said, "My God, Rowena. Look at him."

She shook her head in confusion as she moved to look down into the pink and wrinkled little face. "What has happened here?" She flicked a glance toward the mother, who still did not rouse herself.

There was barely leashed excitement in his voice as he said, "The babe was coming and there was no time to find you or anyone else. I had to..." He seemed overcome with his own sense of amazement.

"You delivered this babe?" She could hear her own incredulity, even as she ran practiced eyes over the infant, listened to the clear, healthy ring of its cry, took in the pink flush of its plump little body and maleness. "He seems fine enough."

The knight's face was filled with pride and wonder as he looked down at the tiny boy. "Aye, I believe he is."

Again she looked to the young woman. So white, so still. A tendril of alarm slithered through Rowena.

Deliberately calm, she said, "Look in the chest beside the door. You will find clean clothes to wrap him in."

Christian seemed to read her unease even as she moved toward the bed. "What..."

She did not look back, and her heart fell at the sight of the blood that was beginning to soak the bedcover. "Was there much bleeding during the birth?"

The man replied, with obvious surprise, "There was some bleeding, but not an untoward amount."

Rowena answered with forced calm. "Please, look after the babe. I must see to his mother."

Obviously Christian had now seen what she had, for he murmured in a tone of horror, "Dear heaven, is she..."

Rowena was already bending down to listen to her heart. "She is alive." Her own relief was great, but the amount of blood the young woman had lost told her that she must act quickly or it would not be true for long.

With haste born of desperation, Rowena examined

the young woman. Then she turned to the knight. "Did you remove anything?"

He stood there holding the infant, his face now dark with anxiety. "Nay, nothing. You came just as the babe…"

She nodded, then quickly scanned the bed once more. Although she had never encountered this complication, she had learned from a midwife in a nearby village that the afterbirth could cause hemorrhage and death if it failed to be expelled.

Rowena took one deep breath and was immediately encompassed by a feeling of intense focus and calm. It was a feeling that often came over her when a situation was most desperate. She did not know from whence this gift originated, but it had enabled her to do what she must time upon time.

The fact that it had not come in relation to tending Christian Greatham had troubled her greatly. Its return now when she needed peace most was all she required to face the task at hand with self-possession.

The young mother was so weak that Rowena could only rouse her with a tone of command. But Rowena did command, telling her that she must find the strength to help herself lest her child be orphaned, and the girl did manage to expel the afterbirth.

Only then did the bleeding ease. Rowena could take little relief in this, though she hurried to prepare a mixture that would help her patient rest as well as strengthen her.

The girl had lost so much blood.

Rowena was aware of the knight as he moved about the cottage, and wondered how he was faring with the babe. She was certain caring for a newborn child was not an accustomed task for him. But he left her to work over the mother, for which she was grateful.

It was not until she had changed the linens, given the young woman a potion to restore her blood, and watched her fall into an exhausted sleep that Rowena took a breath of relief. Slowly, on suddenly trembling limbs, she went to the bench next to the table and sank down upon it.

It was with a start that she felt a large warm hand on her shoulder. She looked up into Christian Greatham's concerned blue eyes. "I have put the babe in a basket near the fire." He paused, shaking his head. "That was the most amazing feat I have ever seen. You saved her life." The gentleness in his tone far overrode Rowena's awe that he would speak thus to her. It made her long for...what?

She spoke with deliberate restraint. "'Twas no great deed. It is what I have learned to do."

He frowned. "Nonetheless, Nina is alive because of you. I had no idea that she was not... All seemed to go well...."

Rowena shrugged, but avoided meeting his gaze as she recalled her own fearfulness on first realizing what had gone wrong. The thought of the young mother lying there in all that blood, and what the outcome might have been had the midwife not told Rowena about what could happen with the afterbirth, was overwhelming.

Despite her trembling, she said, "How did she come to be here?"

He shrugged. "I looked up and there she was. She said that a man on the road had sent her here. The folk in her village would not help her because the babe's father is wed to another.''

''A bastard.'' The words were a mere whisper of breath on Rowena's lips.

Christian obviously heard them, for he spoke with disbelief. ''Would you hold the babe's lack of legitimacy against him?''

She answered roughly, ''Never!'' She felt a new wave of shaking wash over her.

He seemed startled by her vehemence for a moment, but his voice was filled with concern as he said, ''You are trembling.''

She shook her head. ''I am—''

Before she could finish, she was being pulled up and into the warm, encompassing strength of his arms. Her face came to rest on the soft woolen fabric over his heart, and she felt the steady and even beat of it beneath her cheek.

Rowena grew very, very still. She did not know what to do, how to behave. For never, in all her wildest secret imaginings, had she thought that something like this would occur.

Yet in spite of her amazement she became aware of a feeling of yearning so intense that it further weakened her limbs and caused her to lean even more fully against this strange but fascinating man. He reacted by holding her even more tightly, stroking a gentle hand over her hair.

For a moment, Rowena closed her eyes. She had one memory only of ever being held this way—by her father, she believed, though she could not be sure. What she was certain of was that the feelings inside her in that memory were nothing akin to the odd but compelling ones that rose up inside her now. Feelings that made her heartbeat quicken and her body become aware in a way it never had been.

Only when he spoke, his voice a deep rumble beneath her ear, did she stir. "You are so very young. There must be someone else who could—"

The words brought Rowena back to the realization of what she was doing here, and to the fact that she could not allow this man to hold her this way. When she stepped back, he released her, and she met those blue eyes with heat as she said, "I do as I wish to do. I have been taken in, loved and accepted by those around me. I want to serve and care for them. Nothing means as much to me."

He reacted with surprise. "I did not mean to criticize. I but thought—"

"You know nothing of what you speak. You come from a different world. Here in Ashcroft, to care for the folk you love and respect is all important. These folk are my family."

She looked at him when he frowned in seeming consternation. "What of you, Christian Greatham? You have said nothing of your purpose in coming all this way to find your Rosalind."

He stiffened, his gaze searching hers for a long moment, before he said, "Fair enough. I have seen that you truly care for others. If you give your word to keep what I say to yourself, I will tell you what I can of her."

Even more puzzled than she had been, Rowena nodded. "You have my word."

He took a slow, deep breath. "Firstly, let me say that she is not *my* Rosalind."

She could not prevent herself from asking, "You mean you are not in love with her?"

He shook his head. "Oh, nay, not in love. I do not even know the woman." He seemed to study her more intently then, even as she felt an inexplicable sense of relief.

Rowena collected herself instantly, saying, "Then why are you searching for her?"

Christian spoke slowly and deliberately. "Finding her may be the single most important thing I do in my life."

She shook her head. "You speak without saying anything."

He looked away, laughing wryly. "Aye, I do." When he turned back to her there was resignation in his gaze. "It is simply that I endanger her life and her hopes for a future by speaking of her to the wrong person. She has been hidden away for her own protection, and may in fact not even be aware of her true identity."

Rowena threw up her hands in exasperation. "Still I understand naught of what you say."

He shrugged. "Perhaps I should begin at the beginning, with what I do know." He paused, and she remained silent, realizing that he was quite serious about this. "Fifteen years ago I was fostered into the home of a great nobleman, the earl of Kelsey. He was known to those who loved and admired him as The Dragon. He was a man of exceptional character and taught me much of what I know of being a man when my father was too lost in his grief over my mother's death to heed my own feelings of loss.''

''The Dragon,'' she murmured, not realizing that she had said the words aloud until he stopped to watch her. She smoothed her hair back from her brow with a weary hand. ''You spoke of dragons and dead babes when you were ill, and I thought you were...''

''Aye.'' He nodded. ''I can see why such rambling might mark me as mad, but I assure you I am not. You see, The Dragon was betrayed and murdered by his brother, who made it appear as if he had betrayed King Richard by plotting with his enemies. We—my two foster brothers, Simon Warleigh and Jarrod Maxwell, and I—were forced to give testimony that he had indeed met with these men, though we believed the meeting quite innocent, as he had declared.''

''How can you be so certain that your foster father spoke the truth?'' Rowena asked.

Christian seemed to hold himself more erect, as if the mere memory of this man was ennobling. ''Did you know of him, you would never ask that question. He held truth and honor above all else, and instructed for Simon, Jarrod and I to do the same, no matter what the outcome, though it helped to secure his downfall.''

Rowena felt that such blind faith might be foolish. Yet what Christian chose to believe was his own folly, so she said nothing for a long moment.

But she could not remain silent. Perhaps because, in spite of what her mother had said about her father and her own anger toward him, Rowena was desperate to know something of his world, of him. ''What has any of that to do with this Rosalind you search for?''

Christian rubbed a weary hand across his brow. "Rosalind was—is—the daughter of my former foster father. It was believed that she was killed in the battle for Dragonwick Castle. I myself saw the body, though it was covered at the time. We were told by Kelsey's men that she had fallen from the upper stair whilst trying to get to her father as he fought below."

"Then why do you search for her?"

"Because it has come to my attention that she may not have died that day. That she was hidden away by the nursemaid in order to protect her." His gaze now met Rowena's with a strange intensity.

She frowned. "You imagine she was brought here to Ashcroft?"

He did not break the force of that gaze. "That is what I was told only weeks ago by a dying man."

"But who was he and how would he know this?"

"He said that it was he who helped the child and the nursemaid to escape the castle. It was the nurse's red-haired child who Jack saw Kelsey push down the castle steps that day. Though the nurse was grieving her own babe's death, she was determined to save the little one who had also nursed at her breast. She begged his aid, as they had been lovers. Jack loved The Dragon as loyally as did I and my friends, and abhorred the fact that the earl's own half brother had wronged him so vilely. Jack felt that parting from his lover was not too high a price to pay in order to see the child safe. They never saw one another again, and it was only because he was dying that he told me what had happened. He knew someone had to know of Rosalind's existence if there was ever to be any hope of her returning to Dragonwick. Naturally, I had to come and discover if he had spoken true, and then to help her gain her rightful place if he had."

For some reason Rowena felt an agitation she could not explain. She rose and began to clear the table. "So you took him at his word, coming all this way with no more than that to go by. It could have been nothing more than a delusion brought on by wishful thinking. You said that this Jack felt as you did, that The Dragon had been wronged by his half brother. Perhaps in his illness he fabricated this notion in order to avenge his master before he died."

Christian stiffened, drawing himself up. "Aye, to a point, though I have told no one else of my quest. And not only because I gave my word to remain silent on the matter until I knew that she would not be placed in danger by my revealing the information. I...did not wish to give false hope to Simon or Jarrod. We have long waited for the day when we might see Kelsey brought low for all he has done."

Her brows rose. "So this quest you are on is a matter of vengeance. You have no thought for the woman herself."

He scowled. "Of course I want what is best for Rosalind. She deserves to have what is rightfully hers."

"Even if she does not wish to become involved in this vendetta? She may very well be happy wherever she is, especially if, as you suspect, she does not know."

He shook his head. "She must be made to see that she owes it to—"

Rowena interrupted him. "She owes nothing. Why

would anyone choose a life fraught with treachery and murder, to be placed in danger that is not of her making? It matters not, at any rate, for you have not found her. Whatever caused your dead friend to imagine that she might be in Ashcroft, he was mistaken. That is misfortune for her, for she would have found a good home here amongst the folk of Ashcroft. She could not have been expected to exchange her life for lands and titles.''

He frowned, but his reply was not what Rowena expected; he changed the subject so abruptly that she felt disoriented for a moment. ''I see that you love the people here as a family. But what of your real family, Rowena? Surely there is someone out there, even if both of your parents are dead. What of them?''

This unexpected question brought overwhelming feelings of shame and loneliness. Suddenly she could not hold the secret inside her. ''What of them, Sir Christian? I do not know. You see, my father was a knight, my mother a servant in his household. He never wed her, and his family did not want me after his death.''

Christian became very still. ''Your father was not wed to your mother? Who told you this?''

''My mother. Who would know better than she?''

He raked that thick dark hair straight back from his brow. ''But that is not possible—''

She stiffened. ''I assure you it is possible.'' She turned her back on him. ''I cannot stand about discussing matters you do not understand. I must fetch Hagar before Nina awakens. I will need her help.'' She hurried to the door.

He went after her, grabbing her wrist in a tight grip, desperate to get her to listen. "Rowena, please, I must speak with you—"

She winced, jerking away from him.

Christian held up his hands in supplication. "Forgive me, I had no intention of harming you. I but wanted to…"

Rowena did not linger to hear him out. She could not reveal the pain she felt at seeing him so shocked by her revelation. As she ran down the path, she asked herself why she should even care for the opinion of a knight about whom she knew so little.

She was but a moment's delay in Christian Greatham's life. Even if being held in his arms had made her feel truly safe for the first time in her memory.

Once he was fully recovered he would be on his way, possibly to continue his search for the young woman he hoped to use to avenge his former foster father. Whatever he chose to do, it did not involve her.

Chapter Four

In deference to the new mother and her child, Christian spent that night in the small shed beside Rowena's cottage. There had seemed to be a decided relief in her face when he suggested it.

He retired before Hagar—whom Rowena had brought back to the cottage with all haste—left for the night. Though the older woman had not pointedly ignored his presence, as Rowena had seemed to, she was too occupied with helping to look after mother and child for more than the briefest of exchanges with him. Yet during that conversation Hagar did make known to him her amazement and gratitude over his helping Nina.

Unaccountably, Christian found himself wishing Rowena would look upon him with such approval. He told himself it would make his task far easier if she did not display such unfathomable antagonism in the face of his efforts to discover more about her!

In spite of his whirling thoughts, the bed of hay he fashioned beneath the heavy furs was comfortable, and he slept late.

Yet as soon as he awoke it all came rushing back. He could not believe that none of what he had told Rowena had seemed to strike even the remotest note of familiarity with her. Could he be wrong in his belief that she was the one?

Christian did not think so. Her appearing here at the precise time that Jack had said Rosalind and the nurse had gone to Ashcroft was too much of a coincidence. He was especially certain because of Rowena's lack of knowledge about her past, other than having been told about being the bastard child of an English knight. The story should not have surprised him so, for of course she had to be told something about her past. It would have prevented her questioning too deeply.

Yet he thought again of how she had listened to all he had said without so much as blinking. It was, in fact, quite odd that she had not even considered it possible that she might be the one.

Could it be because she did not wish it?

Christian threw back the furs in frustration. Going into the cottage, he bade Rowena and Nina, "Good morrow."

Rowena barely glanced in his direction, seeming as agitated as the previous evening.

He was distracted from his contemplation of the stiff line of her slender back by Nina, who replied, "Good morrow, good sir." The young mother, who lay against the pillows in bed, glanced down at the child sleeping against her breast. She then looked up at Christian with a smile beaming with gratitude, though her cheeks were still quite pale. "I have no words to thank you for all you have—"

Christian held up a hand, forestalling her. "Your thanks are well met, though in all honesty 'twas nature and Rowena who accomplished the important tasks." He reached out his arms. "May I?"

Nina lifted the sleeping infant toward him.

He looked down into the tiny face, which seemed to have become so much more defined even over the course of a night. His heart swelled with gratitude that all had indeed gone well for this tiny being.

"Nonsense, you are to be commended for doing what you did. Many would have gone for help before even trying." Though Rowena's words were spoken stiffly, their content was approving.

While he could not deny a certain amount of pride as well as pleasure at her compliment, Christian gave a rueful laugh. "Had I felt that there was any choice, I would have done so. And quite gladly."

She looked from him to the child, those green eyes unreadable as they held his for a long moment before she turned away. He watched Rowena bustle about the cottage, the weight of the babe in his arms awakening a strange sort of yearning he could not explain.

A noise from without heralded Sean's arrival only minutes later. Through the open door Christian saw that he was riding in a small cart pulled by a donkey.

When Rowena swung around, saying, "Thank you for coming so quickly, my friend," Christian realized that she must have asked him to come while he himself was still sleeping.

The young man frowned as he entered the cottage, watching Christian as if he were a leper.

Immediately Rowena said, "I am nearly finished readying Nina and the child for the journey."

"What is this you say?" Christian questioned.

Rowena barely glanced at him as she said, "Nina insists on going home, where she can be near the babe's father. Sean has agreed to take her in his cart. They must go before the tide rises, for it will block the way to her village." She moved to hold out her arms for the infant, as if that action would prevent any argument.

It did not. Relinquishing the babe reluctantly, Christian scowled. "But she is too weak—"

It was Nina who interrupted. "They only do as I have asked. I want—need to be with my child's father. Surely now he will see that he must be with me." Her gaze was distant and determined.

Christian realized that she would not be swayed. He also saw the worry on Rowena's face. It was clear she would have insisted Nina stay longer if she thought there was any hope of her complying.

Seeming unaware of Christian at the moment, Rowena looked toward Sean. "You will see her safely to her home? Make certain the child's father is willing to care for them before you leave her?"

Sean bowed, his eyes lighting up when she smiled at him with gratitude. "Anything you ask of me, Rowena."

The response seemed overeager, to Christian's ears. Rowena always referred to the young man as a friend, but that did not mean he felt the same. Christian told himself that the tightening in his belly was due to the fact that a budding romance would only complicate his task. Now it was he who watched Sean carefully as the young man went about helping Rowena to prepare her charges for their journey.

The two friends spoke easily, as those of long acquaintance were wont to do. Their interaction gave nothing more away.

There was a lull as Sean awaited his next instructions from Rowena, who was dressing the child in tiny woolen garments. With a tense expression, he approached Christian, who was studying them from the bench against the wall, having taken the position when his own offer of aid was declined.

With determination, the dark-haired young man asked, "When were ye thinking to leave Ashcroft?"

Christian shrugged and replied to this unexpected question as casually as he could, considering the regret he felt at the idea. "Soon enough." He knew that he must indeed go ere much more time passed, if he was not able to gain any ground here.

Sean frowned. "Mither says ye are looking for someone. A woman named Rosalind."

Christian said, "I am."

"Ye have been told that she isna hereabouts."

He resisted casting a glance at Rowena. "Aye, I have been told. I cannot remain much longer. I have been away too long as it is, for I did tell my sister, Aislynn, that I would be home weeks ago. She and my father are..." He halted, not wanting to speak of his relationship with his family, nor wishing to reveal the guilt that rose at every thought of them.

In the silence that followed, Christian looked up and saw that Rowena had paused in the act of setting the swaddled babe into his mother's waiting arms. Their eyes met.

She watched him with an intensity that both shocked and inexplicably drew him as she said, ''You are leaving soon?''

''Aye.'' The word hung in the air between them. Was she, somehow, in some part of herself that she was not yet willing to acknowledge, beginning to understand that his presence here was of great import to her?

Time seemed to lengthen and stretch in an immeasurable way, until finally she turned away. He could read nothing in her tone as she said, '''Tis best to wait a bit longer after your recent illness. Just to make certain that you are fully recovered.''

Christian was left with no opportunity to consider her words. For when she moved toward the table and began to place small pouches into a larger one with studied concentration, Sean let out a barely audible groan. Christian turned to him, seeing his yearning eyes fixed on Rowena.

As if sensing Christian's attention, Sean turned to him with resentment. ''Why did ye look at her that way?'' Angry color rode his cheeks.

He was indeed in love with Rowena.

Christian did not know what to say, for the other man obviously saw him as a rival. This was as far from the actual situation as possible.

Yet Christian had no intention of revealing his true interest in Rowena.

Sean spoke again before Christian could even think of forming a reply. ''I will pray that yer family is not long awaiting yer return, English knight. Their peace will be mine."

Christian felt a momentary flash of guilt that when he left he might be taking away what Sean held most dear. He quickly brushed it aside. He felt sympathy for the young man, but could not allow that to make him hesitate in taking Rowena with him if she would come. If she was Rosalind, her place was at Dragonwick.

"Sean?" It was Rowena's voice.

He swung about without another word, and moved to her side.

"If you will take this to the cart?" She held up a woolen bag. "It contains clean clothes for the babe."

Stiffly he took the bag and went out without so much as glancing toward Christian again.

Christian then watched as Rowena turned and helped Nina to stand. The babe lay upon the bed as she gingerly wriggled to the edge. Rowena reached out to place a steadying hand beneath her arm as she took a deep breath and rose to her feet. Her weakness was clear, for she buckled almost instantly.

Without asking permission, Christian rose and went to lean over her. "You should not travel this day."

He could feel the tension in Rowena's slender body as she agreed. "He is right. You are not strong enough."

Nina's lips thinned obstinately. "I mun go home."

He gave a grunt of exasperation, bending down to sweep her into his arms. Neither she nor Rowena made any protest as he carried her to the cart.

As he set her on the narrow wooden seat beside a frowning Sean, Rowena appeared with the babe in a basket. Carefully she placed the sleeping child on the floor before them. "He will sleep for a time." Her gaze caught Nina's. "You must not forget to take the medicaments I put in the bag for you. They will help you to regain your strength more quickly."

The girl blinked back tears. "I willna forget." Her appreciative gaze included Christian, who had stepped back to allow them to talk. "I thank ye both. I…ye saved our lives and I kin niver…" She halted, wiping a tear on the sleeve of the clean gown Rowena had given her.

Christian nodded, unable to speak past the lump in his own throat as Rowena whispered, "Just look after the babe. And remember, if you ever need anything…"

The girl nodded and looked to Sean. "We mun away or we shall miss the tide."

Rowena stepped back beside Christian as Sean cast one more disapproving glance at them. Rowena seemed intent on wiping moisture from the corner of her own eyes.

Sean spoke roughly. "I'll call on ye when I return."

She shook her head. "There is no need to further disrupt your day. You must go about your own business."

As the cart pulled away, Christian realized that as obvious as it was that Sean loved her, it was equally obvious that Rowena was not in love with Sean. For there was never a hint of more than sisterly affection in her voice or expression in her interactions with the young man.

Christian told himself that his relief was due to the fact that things would be less complicated when she learned who she was. Sean would never be a suitable mate to the lady of Dragonwick. She would require a strong man, one who was capable of holding what was hers.

Surely he and Jarrod and Simon could help her to make that choice. Perhaps even Jarrod... He was not wed, had no ties to his father's lands and would fulfill all the duties of the man who must first wrest hold of Dragonwick, then hold it and restore it.

Aye, Rowena must indeed wed eventually, and the future lord of Dragonwick would be chosen carefully. That need not be for some time, at least. Christian would not be the one, in spite of Sean's fears that he had some romantic interest in her, for he had other responsibilities that must take precedence even had he been inclined to take an interest in The Dragon's daughter.

His father, whom he had remembered as a bitter and morose man, had aged, grown old and lonely without his son to aid him in holding his lands along the Welsh border. His joy in having Christian home was almost too much to bear, for it told just how greatly he had been missed. Because of that, Christian was determined to do what must be done in The Dragon's memory, then take his rightful place at Bransbury.

Lovely and fascinating as Rowena might be, his only intention toward her was to prove, or disprove, that she was Rosalind of Dragonwick.

Although Christian chafed at realizing it would be much more difficult to prove who she was if she herself did not know, he forced himself to remain hopeful. He might discover some other evidence that would point to the truth. In the event that he was able to find it, he would require the young woman's cooperation in restoring her to her rightful place.

That Rowena was as prickly a bit of womanhood as he had ever met did not bode well for his rushing the matter.

That she was wise and courageous beyond her years was also true. He had realized after she saved Nina's life that if she were The Dragon's daughter, he would have been proud of her.

If Christian had also felt an odd but compelling stirring as he had held her in his arms last eve, it was surely due to his own desperate hope that she was The Dragon's daughter. To see her restored to her rightful position would be to do her father the greatest good that could be done after all these years.

Rowena watched Sean, Nina and the babe leave with a sense of unease. She was feeling strangely vulnerable, and uncertain as to the reason.

She felt foolish now for her behavior the previous night. Clearly she must have misunderstood when she imagined that the knight had refused to accept her own lack of legitimacy. What he could have been thinking she was not sure and did not wish to examine at the moment. What she did know was that Sir Christian Greatham was utterly unlike what her mother had led her to believe a nobleman would be.

She felt a growing sense of wonder and surprise at Christian Greatham's gentleness and care for others. She had seen it first with Hagar, then with Nina and her babe.

That his anxiety for Nina matched her own had created a sort of bond between them that left her uncomfortable in an unexplainable way. His continued interest in the babe, the bastard son of a married man, touched her as nothing ever had. He had cared nothing for the child's lack of legitimacy. So why would he have difficulty with her own?

She found herself speaking without knowing that she was going to do so. "You are not as I imagined."

He gave a start. "You imagined me?"

Now she felt herself flush, answering too quickly, "Nay, not you in particular, but nobles in general.... I simply thought that you would behave as if you were above us—not only me, but someone like Nina and her child."

"I see." There was no emotion in his deep voice.

"Do you see?" She watched him closely. "Are most of your kind of a different nature than you?"

He shrugged, frowning as if her question was a surprise to him. "I would say not. Some are worse, many are better."

She felt a deep sense of doubt at the latter statement. Something told her that only an uncommonly decent man would answer thus.

It was this that made her say, "My mother told me that my father and his kind care for nothing more than their land and titles. She said that even those they love must come second. That is..." Rowena straightened her shoulders. "That is why he refused to marry her. She could bring him nothing of value."

Christian's frown deepened as she spoke. His eyes searched hers as he said, "And you believed her?"

"Why would I not? My father had rejected her—us." The admission was a painful one to make to this man.

He took a step toward her. "That is not the…" When she backed away from him, he visibly collected himself, taking a deep, steadying breath before he said, "Surely you have questioned this? Perhaps your mother took you away for some other reason."

"Why would I question her?" She felt an overwhelming sense of misery as well as protectiveness. "My mother was angry and bitter, but she loved me. She would not have hurt me for anything."

He raked a hand through his hair. "But—"

Rowena interrupted before he could go on. "I mean you no insult. I was only moved to speak out because you have been so kind and decent toward everyone during your time here." She turned away, brushing an unwelcome tear from the corner of her eye, not wanting him to see how upset she was.

He grabbed her wrist in a tight hold. "Rowena, if you would but listen—"

"Nay!" She shook her head without looking at him, jerking her hand away. "I will not listen." His implication that her mother could have lied to her was too disturbing to contemplate. For if it were true, it would mean that it was her mother and not her father who had wronged her. "You would ask me to question the woman who dried my tears when I fell down or woke from a nightmare." Rowena shook her head at this, for there had been many nightmares when she was small, ones from which she had woken terrified and confused at the visions of blood, the sounds of screams and the feeling of an enormous snake looming over her. She was frightened of snakes to this very day. Again she shook her head. "You would have me doubt her when she put me before herself in all she did."

Rowena could not think it. As she had told him, her mother had been angry and bitter toward her father, but she had loved Rowena. She would never have lied about such a thing. She could have no reason to do so.

Rowena spoke coolly. "You may mean well in your defense of my father, but you know nothing of us."

When she flicked a glance at him she saw that he seemed lost in thought, and was surprised when he said, "Forgive me for overstepping myself."

She took a deep, calming breath. "It is done." Rowena looked toward the woodland path that led away from the cottage. "I am needed elsewhere this day. I welcome you to the bread and cheese in the cottage when you grow hungry."

She was grateful when he followed her cue and said no more on the matter, answering without inflection, "I thank you for your hospitality."

She looked at him then and found those blue eyes studying her closely, as they did so often.

Unwilling to try to fathom that expression, Rowena turned away. She went directly into the cottage, gathered the things she would need into a woolen bag and took up her cloak. When she made to leave she stopped short with a frown. Christian had come to the doorway to watch her, his wide shoulders effectively blocking the way.

Pausing in the act of moving toward him, Rowena said, "I will see you ere night falls."

He shrugged, seemingly oblivious to her now. "As you will."

She waited.

He looked up at her then, clearly realizing that he was blocking her path. Nodding with apology, he turned sideways in order to allow her to pass. Although she felt strangely reluctant to come so close to him, Rowena could not bring herself to say so. She was feeling raw and exposed, too aware of her own mixed feelings about this enigmatic stranger.

It was as she was turning sideways to slip past him that their eyes met. Self-consciously, Rowena brushed her hair back from her suddenly heated cheeks.

Without warning he caught her wrist, and she winced. Christian raised it up and examined the bruise beginning to show there even as she noted its existence.

His voice was filled with regret as he said softly, "I did this last eve when I grabbed you, did I not?"

She nodded hesitantly. "I...yes, you must have."

He grimaced. "I am very sorry, Rowena. It was never my intention to cause you pain, of any kind."

She could no more look away from that earnest and compelling blue gaze than she could fly. His hand seemed to burn her where it rested on the delicate skin of her wrist. But when he broke eye contact to place his warm mouth against the spot, she gave a start at the streak of heat that flashed through her body.

She jerked her hand free. "I..." She had no words to give him. She was far too confused by the fact that that flash of awareness had settled like a burning flame in her belly.

She turned and fled, infinitely aware that Christian

was watching her and continued to do so until she disappeared into the cover of the trees.

Only then was she able to breathe more normally. It was as if being out of his presence had released her from the grip of some force. Yet now that it had passed she could not credit its effect.

She was being extremely foolish. Christian Greatham had no hold on her whatsoever.

As she had none on him. He had said this very day that he would be leaving soon. It was only surprise that he would behave thus that had made her react so.

Why would he kiss her wrist? She could only imagine that the nobles must have different customs than the common folk.

Yet as she traversed a little-used path carpeted with a layer of decaying leaves, she did not feel the familiar sense of peace that walking through the quiet forest usually brought her. She felt no joy in the occasional cry of a thrush or hawk fluttering amongst the canopy of oak and hemlock and pine.

She thought ahead to her visit with the elderly Agnes. The widow required regular doses of medicaments to aid the breathing problems that plagued her each year as winter approached, but could not manage the walk to Rowena's cottage. Rowena was quite aware that she was not expected. Her regular attendance was not due for two more days, but she was sure that she would be welcome.

And she knew she could not spend this day alone in Christian Greatham's company.

Chapter Five

The very next morning Christian watched Rowena warily from the doorway of the cottage. They had not spoken since she had run from him the previous afternoon.

Whatever had enticed him to kiss her wrist he did not know. He had thought at the time that it was simply regret at the upheaval he had wrought in her life, his regret that more was to follow.

His instantaneous and sensual reaction to that simple act had left him filled with self-doubt. In spite of the fact that he told himself any man would respond thus in the face of Rowena's beauty, his disquiet would not be laid to rest.

She had not returned until after he had sought his own rest in the shed. He had lain awake long after, his mind reeling not only with his own madness but also with all she had revealed in their conversation of the morning.

Now he understood her failure to realize that he might be speaking of her when he talked of Rosalind. Although it was doubtless done out of love, the woman she believed to be her mother had instilled in her a decided prejudice against the nobility. It would make persuading her that she could be Rosalind all the more difficult.

He looked at the slender line of her back as she busied herself with preparing the morning meal.

Christian knew that he must say something. It might help if he made her understand that he had not meant anything ill by kissing her. "Rowena, I..." He halted, not certain what he could say.

She watched him with those haunting and extraordinary eyes. With obvious reluctance she said, "Yes?"

"I am sorry that I kissed..." Unbelievably, he felt himself flushing as he admitted, "I can never remember apologizing to anyone so oft in my life. I have never had a need to do so...."

She stopped him with an upraised hand. "Please, do not explain. I realize that nobles behave differently from what I may be accustomed to. It is I who should apologize if I made you think I was unduly affected by it."

Christian was so amazed by this hurried speech that he was struck dumb. Here then, although it was not the truth, was a way out.

He felt a stab of discomfort, but quickly dismissed it. Since he had no reasonable explanation, there was no harm in Rowena thinking what she would. He could not have her know that for one brief moment he had felt...

He shrugged. "I...thank you for your good grace."

"You are most welcome." Her tone strengthened.

"But I must ask you to understand that there is something of more import to me."

He listened in silence.

"You are not to defend my fa—the nobles to me. I will accept you for who you are, having seen that you are a kind and gentle man. But no more than that. My mother's memory is dear to me."

Christian felt himself frowning. It was not his purpose to defend the nobility. He wished for her to understand that she might be one of them.

He nodded sharply. He simply had to find a way to explain that did not constitute a defense in her eyes.

They broke their fast in a slightly less tangible tension. Christian could not truly relax, however, for he could not help wondering how he was to go on from here. He could only pray that she would listen when the time came to explain all he knew of her past.

Rowena finished eating before him, saying, "You will pardon me, for I have work to do."

He nodded, there being nothing else he could say, even though he was certain she was making herself busy in order to avoid talking to him. "Go to it. I will clean away the meal, then take a walk, if you do not mind." He watched as she went and lifted the heavy lid of the chest at the foot of her bed and began to search inside.

His frustration did not distract him from the rise of interest he felt at the sight of the sheets of parchment she set aside as she dug deeply. Without pausing to think, he moved forward and saw that they were blank. His fingers flexed with sudden anticipation. "You have blank parchments."

She looked up at him with a frown of confusion, glancing back at the sheets. "Aye. I purchase them from the monastery where I buy my wines. I use them to label my dried ingredients."

His brows rose with surprise. "You can read and write?"

She shrugged stiffly. "Only well enough to label my goods. One of the monks taught me."

He studied her profile. Reading was a skill known by few of the nobles, even to the extent she mentioned, yet she spoke as if it were nothing. Again he realized what an unusual young woman she was. Watching her averted face, he knew that she would not be pleased to have him remark on it.

Instead he indicated the parchment. "Would you mind? I would dearly love to have one of the sheets."

A perplexed expression creased her brow, but she recovered quickly. "Most certainly." She reached down and plucked a sheet from the stack, holding it out to him.

Christian took it, and as he did his fingers brushed hers. Rowena started backward with a shudder, immediately turning to continue what she had been doing. "I...if you would be so good as to excuse me, I must finish here."

Christian stepped backward, somewhat appalled that she would be so averse to an innocent touch. She had shown no such aversion to him ere this. Perhaps she was more disturbed by what had occurred the previous day than she was willing to admit.

Roughly he told himself it mattered not. Except, of course, in relation to his quest in getting her to trust him enough to at least listen when he told her who he believed she was.

When she chose that moment to stand, holding a small leather bag in her hand as she said, ''I will be off now,'' he refrained from comment as to what errand could be taking her away this day. Then she was gone, never once truly looking at him.

He realized there was no understanding the unfathomable Rowena. More importantly, he had no duty to do so. His goal was to take her home to assume her rightful position at Dragonwick. Nothing more, nothing less.

Yet in spite of that logic, as Christian bent over the piece of parchment a short time later, a stick of sharpened charcoal in hand, she was still uppermost in his thoughts, and not solely because of her obstinacy. He also thought of her beauty, her courage and her strength. Driven by these thoughts, he found the rendering quickly began to take form. Yet as it took shape he had an increasingly vivid memory of how he had felt the day before when his lips touched the soft skin of her wrist—the passion and the even more shocking tenderness. These feelings drove his need to do the image justice, and resulted in some time passing before he felt that he had the details just the way he wished them to be.

Finally, though, Christian sat back to run a hand through his hair, shocked at the way he had given in to those thoughts. Self-consciously he rose and stretched. Even though he had fully recovered his strength, there did seem to be a lingering stiffness in his muscles from his days abed. It could not be due to the fact that more time had passed as he sat lost in reverie than he would have imagined possible.

Christian ran an assessing glance over the face portrayed on the parchment. Aye, he had captured Rowena more fully than he had thought to—that regally proud nose, the stubborn chin, the high cheekbones. She was hauntingly beautiful in profile, her almond-shaped eyes seemingly fixed on some inner thought.

In one corner, as in the drawing he had made of Jack, he had without being aware of it sketched the shape of the dragon brooch that was one of three Jarrod had had fashioned just after The Dragon's death. Christian felt a deep sense of regret that it had been lost with his saddlebag. For he, Simon and Jarrod had worn them proudly, not only as a symbol of their brotherhood, but also as a sign that the memory of their foster father, and the wrong done him, would always live in them.

A deep voice jolted Christian out of his reverie. ''What is this?'' He looked up to see that he had been so intent on his drawing that Sean had entered through the open door and approached the table without being heard. His gaze was fixed on the likeness of Rowena.

Christian shrugged, deliberately offhand. ''If you do not know then I have made a poor effort.''

Sean scowled. ''I know who it is, mon. Why have you done it?''

Christian cast a wry glance at him. ''Rowena gave me a piece of parchment. I felt like drawing on it.''

''Did Rowena tell ye that ye could draw her likeness?''

''I did not ask.''

''Where is she?''

Christian shrugged again, motioning toward the doorway. "Gone out on some business of her own."

The younger man watched Christian through narrowed eyes as he said, "Ye told me this morn ye mun leave ere long, that yer family will miss you. Surely, ye mun wish to ease them?"

Christian looked down at the drawing of Rowena. He shrugged. "I have lost my horse and my purse. I will have some trouble returning to England without them."

Sean squared his shoulders. "Although the horse could ha' been drowned and washed out to sea, it may only be wandering about. I could see me way to asking about the countryside for ye." His gaze swept over Christian. "I have no doubt it was an animal of some note."

Christian nodded. "The horse is an uncommon one, true enough." He held the other's gaze. "I would indeed be grateful if you could see him returned to me."

Sean bowed, not intimidated. "Would finding it see ye on yer way?"

Christian frowned. "Perhaps."

Sean glared at him. "I have ye and yer business here clear in my mind, English knight. I know that ye wish to bed my Rowena. I'll not have it."

His Rowena. If she were The Dragon's daughter, as Christian believed, Rowena would never be Sean's. But neither was she for Christian. He spoke slowly, carefully, feeling some sympathy for the other man's plight. "You have mistaken my intent here."

Even as he said it the very notion of bedding Rowena stirred his blood. But any man would feel thus.

Christian was in no position to acknowledge or indulge such an inclination.

Sean shook his head. "Ye have been told that the woman ye seek is no' here, yet ye willna go. Do not forget that I saw ye looking at Rowena, saw what is in yer mind."

Christian raised his head high. "You know nothing of my thoughts and would do well not to imagine that you do."

Again Sean ran unhappy green eyes over the drawing. "Then give me that."

This Christian was not willing to do, not even to ease this hothead's mind. "Nay, I never give my renderings away. They are a memento, if you like, of where I have been and what I have done."

The lips twisted disparagingly. "Do ye make a likeness of every woman ye meet, then?"

"Nay, only those of note." He did not add that he had rarely drawn any of the women he had known. When he had, it had not been based on romantic notions, as Sean obviously assumed.

Christian had begun drawing after his mother died, in an attempt to keep her likeness sharp in his mind. It had been at a time when his father would not have her name spoken, so deep was his grief, and Christian had desperately needed some connection with her. That he had recreated her likeness until he was actually able to do so with some skill had been incidental. Since then Christian had been moved to capture the likeness of many things, many people, the most recent being Jack, who had died with The Dragon's name on his lips.

Christian smiled at the other man, having nothing to

say that might ease his mind, for he could not tell him of his true interest in Rowena.

The younger man rose. "Keep your drawing, then. I need nothing from ye. But ken well that I have seen what ye have in mind no matter that ye deny it. As I told ye, Rowena is mine and I will warn her of yer purpose. Though she has shown ye some kindness, as she has countless others, it is me she will believe, for I have known her long and well. Once she begins to ask hersel why ye stay when ye have naught to keep ye, she will cast ye out. Ye'll find no easy mark with her, for she'll not be used as her mither was afore her."

So the gauntlet had been tossed.

Christian stood. "I see there is no convincing you."

"Nay. Ye shall be gone ere morning."

Christian shrugged, although he was aware of the fact that Rowena might indeed be moved by Sean's determination to play against her fear that her mother had been used and discarded. "Do your worst."

He was no less determined to take Rowena with him when he left. Christian would simply have to tell her what his real interest in her was in order to counter the other man's mistaken belief.

Surely he would be able to convince her to at least come with him to England. Once there she would take her rightful place, after he made her see who she was and just how desperately she was needed. Even more than she was needed here.

How he was to accomplish this he was not sure. He would simply have to believe that all would come unraveled one step at a time.

Sean's declaration had forced Christian to recall that

he could not afford the luxury of unlimited time. His return to England must come with all possible haste.

In spite of her warnings to speak no more of her mother, he must now find a way to tell Rowena all, and he must do so this very day. He must do it before Sean had an opportunity to voice his own unfounded suspicious.

Unfortunately, Christian had no notion of when Rowena would be returning to the cottage.

He was not certain if it was the lack of sleep during the previous night, or a slight lingering weakness from his illness, but he grew unusually tired. Thinking to do no more than rest his eyes, he lay down upon the bed, almost immediately falling into a deep but troubled slumber.

When he woke the interior of the cottage had darkened with the advance of evening. He yawned, stretching muscles that cried out for more activity than they had known of late.

A soft sound brought him more fully awake. Quickly he sat up, just in time to see Rowena moving from the table toward the open doorway.

Christian stopped her with a raised hand. "Pray, do not go, Rowena."

She swung around, her gaze apologetic. "I did not mean to waken you. Go back to sleep. I must go to see Hagar for a while."

He stood, realizing that he must act now before she saw Sean. "Nay, please wait. There is…there is something that I must tell you, something I have wanted to tell you for some while. Something of great import."

Now he had her full attention. "Of great import, you say?"

He nodded with determination, feeling more encouraged than he had thought to. "Aye, and the time for delay is long past." He indicated the bench along the wall. "Although you may not wish to listen, I beg you hear me out ere you grow too vexed."

Her smooth brow now creased by a scowl, Rowena sat down on the end farthest from him. Her tone was far from encouraging as she said, "What is it that you would tell me?"

Christian took a deep breath, realizing he had given away too much of his frustration with that last statement. He went on more evenly. "You know I did not simply happen upon Ashcroft, Rowena. I came here for a purpose."

She watched him. "Aye. You were searching for your Rosalind, but as you have been informed, there is no Rosalind in our village."

He nodded. "Yes, I came here looking for a Rosalind and I have been informed that there is no such woman here. But I believe that you are wrong in your assumption that she is not here." He held her troubled gaze. "I believe that you, Rowena, are Rosalind."

"Me?" Rowena could hear the incredulity in her voice. She shook her head at such madness, even as she noted the seriousness of Christian's expression. "How am I to make any sense of that declaration?"

He sat down beside her, taking her cold hand in his, and she was aware of how strange this situation and what he was saying was. At the same time the utter gravity in his blue gaze held her captive.

He went on slowly, seeming to choose each word with infinite care. "I believe, Rowena, that you may very well be Lady Rosalind Kelsey, the lost daughter of the former earl of Kelsey."

She jerked her hand from his, putting it to his forehead. "Is your fever returned?" His skin felt cool and dry. "Or have you simply gone mad?"

He grasped her hand again. "I am not ill. Nor am I mad. I am very sorry to have dealt you such a shock, and wish there were some other way I could think to say it, but I have tried time upon time over the past days with no success. I could think of nothing more than just to tell you outright."

Suddenly she realized that this was not some game or mistake on his part. The knight actually believed what he was saying.

That she, Rowena, was the lost daughter of the earl of Kelsey.

So this was what he had been attempting to get at with all those questions about her parentage. What a fool she had been to think he simply did not wish to believe her a bastard. But this madness was even worse.

Rowena jerked her hand away from his and twisted her fingers together in her lap. "I cannot allow you to go on like this."

He shook his head. "I agreed not to defend your father or other nobles. It is not my intention to do that, but to tell you what I believe concerning your identity."

She put her hand to her cheek. "Do you not see that for me to even allow you to go on is to say that there is a possibility that Mother could have lied to me? She would never have done so.''

He sighed, his tone earnest as he said, ''Unless she sought to protect you by doing so.''

Rowena shook her head as she looked up at him again. ''And how could such a lie protect me?''

''I have told you of Rosalind's father and how he died. The child was believed to have been killed in the same battle, pushed down the stair in the turmoil.''

She stood. ''I tell you this is madness. My mother would not have kept such a thing from me, would not have allowed me to believe something so painful for no reason—that I was a bastard child. Her anger toward my father, was so great that it could not have been feigned.''

Christian stood awkwardly, looking down at her with entreaty. ''Aye, I can see how it could be. You see, according to Sir Jack, who told me all of this, the nurse's own child was killed. As for her anger with your father, 'haps she felt The Dragon was responsible, that her little one would still be alive if he had not fought to defend the keep.''

'''Tis so far-fetched as to be impossible. You are desperate to find this woman, and see her in me because of that.''

He shook his head. ''You are of an age. You know nothing of your father, other than the tale that he did not want you. You came here from England with the woman you call your mother only months after the attack on Dragonwick keep. You have been taught to mistrust strangers.''

She covered her ears. ''It is not possible.''

Gently, he drew them away, his heart twisting at the pain in her gaze. But he knew that making her at least consider the possibility that she might be Rosalind was for her own good. "Rowena—" his eyes held hers "—have you never noted that your speech is quite unlike that of the locals?"

She frowned. "My mother always insisted that I speak as she did."

He lifted a dark brow. "But your mode of speech is like mine and other nobles. If your mother hated nobles so greatly, why would she insist upon this?"

"I...nay." Rowena backed away from him.

He let go of her and took a deep breath. "I can see that I have done badly here. I can further explain why I believe you may be the earl's daughter. You are under no obligation to agree. Only please listen to my reasoning, no matter how wrong you think it."

His request was made calmly, reasonably, but Rowena had heard enough. "You have not enough words to make me believe I am this..."

"Rosalind Kelsey, Lady of Dragonwick."

She shook her head. "'Tis impossible."

He held up a hand. "You are so very certain. How can I argue with that? Let us then assume that it is not you. But I ask that you allow me to tell you of her, at least. Of why I did think you might have been her, so that you do not leave this conversation thinking me completely mad, as you now do."

She frowned. "What matter to you what I think of you?"

Christian said, "Because even in a short time I have come to know that you are a woman of honor and good intent. I have come a very long way to find Rosalind and would not feel that I had done all I could if I failed to even tell you of her.''

Against her own will Rowena was moved by his words. She sighed. ''I will hear you, but do not take this as any agreement on my part.''

He nodded, seeming eager to go on. ''It gave me such hope when I heard that she might live. The present earl of Kelsey, the man who killed her father, had only just been forced to release Simon to his own keep. You see, Kelsey had given false evidence that a letter Simon had sent outlining our plans against him was referring to King John himself. The King's solution was to wed Simon to Kelsey's daughter and secure him a virtual prisoner in Dragonwick keep. Jack, whom I told you of, had come to realize that Simon was wrongfully accused and was injured in aiding him in his bid for freedom.'' There was a catch in Christian's voice as he continued. ''Jack died, but not before telling me what I have related to you. How could I doubt him after all that he risked and lost to help Simon?''

Christian took a deep breath. ''Being sworn to keep secret the fact that Rosalind might be alive, until I could assure her safety, I told no one, not even my own father, whence I was going. He waited thirteen long years for me to return from the Holy Land, where I and Simon and Jarrod had fought for the Knights Templars. And all because I was...'' He sighed, looking into her eyes. ''I would cause my father no more pain, would be the helpmate and son I should always have been to him, but I could not allow this one chance that Rosalind might be alive to go unexplored. My friends and I who fostered under her father have long thought on the day that we might avenge The Dragon.''

Rowena heard the pain in his voice when he spoke of not only The Dragon but also his father, yet she could not think of Christian's difficulties now, nor the fact that he had been to distant lands and seen things that she could hardly even dream of. That he had made a connection between her and these dramatic events and people was far too overwhelming.

He went on, clearly agitated. ''I have set aside all to come here, to find Rosalind. Though you cannot heed it, I find the similarities between you uncanny, so much so that I cannot understand how you can fail to at least give the notion some consideration.''

What was she to say to him? She had seen for herself what lengths this man was willing to go to find Rosalind of Dragonwick.

She did feel some sympathy, but she could not simply go along to placate him. ''You must understand that the child must be dead, that the man, Jack, had to have been mistaken in what he told you.''

''Then why did he know of Ashcroft? Why are you here, you who are of an age with the woman I seek? Who have no clear understanding of your past?''

She shook her head even more firmly. ''I know not except perhaps that 'tis all a strange coincidence.''

He watched her, measuring her. ''You cannot truly believe that.''

She returned that look. ''I can believe nothing else. Never in all our years together did my mother utter even one word of a place called Dragonwick, or any other name you mentioned. You tell me that the nurse and this Jack were lovers. How could she simply walk away from him and never speak his name or aught of him again?''

"Because she was willing to do so to protect you. She must have loved her own daughter. Perhaps she could not bear the thought of losing you as well. Perhaps she was willing to do anything to prevent that.''

Rowena raised her hand to rub her forehead, which was beginning to ache with the strain of thinking.

He pressed on. "Surely you cannot deny that the coincidences are too great.''

They did seem so, but... Her mother would never...

Or would she? Could she have kept so much to herself for so long in order to protect Rowena? Instinct told her that her mother's love had indeed been that great. For even if this impossible tale were true, she had been her mother. Nothing could change that in Rowena's heart.

"But what she said of my father... How could she allow me to believe that I was...that he never wanted me...''

Christian's gaze was sympathetic, but no less determined. "As I said, perhaps she did feel that it was his fault that her child had died, that she was forced to hide you away.''

"Even if I was prepared to believe any of this, to think that all I have ever thought was a lie, what would it mean to me? What effect could it have on my life?''

He spoke matter-of-factly. "Why, you would come with me to England and we—Simon, Jarrod and I— would do everything we could to see you take your rightful place as the lady of Dragonwick.''

She put her hands to her cheeks. "Leave Ashcroft? I could never do that. I am needed here. Never could I contribute to the pain others might face in seeing me installed in such a position. This Lord Kelsey will not give up his place willingly."

Christian did not argue the point, though he frowned darkly. "You are needed there. The people suffer great hardship under Kelsey's rule. There are many who would gladly do whatever must be done to see you in your rightful station."

She swayed, her chest feeling too tight to take a proper breath. He caught her, holding her upright with his strong arms, and she was instantly aware of his sheer maleness, the warmth of his body just inches from her own.

It was impossible to look at Christian, for she suddenly realized one painful thing. Now she knew why he had watched her so very closely. Why it had seemed as if he might have some interest in her.

There had been nothing personal, only his resolve to find this other girl. His determination needn't convince her that she was someone she was not, even if she felt inexplicably drawn to him, as always.

Embarrassment and confusion made her face heat as she murmured, "I cannot...I must not even consider..."

She closed her eyes as a tear slid out from beneath her lids in spite of her efforts to prevent it. "In some part of myself there is a wish to believe this wild tale, to imagine I had a father who loved me. Yet I dare not do so, for my own good. I am a bastard, sir knight, unwanted by my father or his family."

"Do not allow your pain to blind you to the truth."

She looked up at him, unable to hide her agony. "My mother would never have had me suffer the shame of believing such a lie for so long without cause."

"Not without cause. As I said, it would have been to protect you."

Her head fell forward against his chest. "It is not to be borne."

She felt those strong arms close about her, pulling her against the solid wall of his chest. He was so very certain, and her mother had been gone for so long.

Looking up at him, Rowena murmured, "I know not what to think. You make me see things differently, make me long for…"

She did not know what she longed for. She only knew that she felt safe in his arms as she had not felt in years. That the hard length of his body was warm, and so very masculine.

Suddenly, as his eyes met hers, she felt a difference in him, something that made her catch her breath as she had when he'd looked into her eyes the day Nina had left the cottage.

His gaze moved to her mouth and she, inexplicably, felt it soften—open.

Whatever was happening? She did not know. She knew only that when she began to breathe again it was much more quickly, and that there was an expression in his eyes that was strange and stirring in a way she did not understand.

Then, before she could even begin to try to comprehend, Christian bent his head, his lips meeting hers. A shaft of heat streaked through her, weakening her limbs and making her sag against him. His arms tightened, holding her firmly, surely, inescapably.

And Rowena had no wish to escape.

She lifted up her own arms to clasp them around his neck, offering her lips more fully.

Chapter Six

"Rowena!"

A gasp of shock intruded upon the haze of her response. Dazedly Rowena looked over Christian's shoulder. And met Sean's horrified and angry gaze.

"How could you?" There was pain and betrayal in the accusation as he backed out the open door.

Shocked at the fact that her friend was reacting so strongly as well as shamed at having given in to the kiss with such abandon, Rowena reached out a trembling hand toward him. But Sean was not to be the rock to which she might cling in her confusion. He turned and ran from the cottage.

"Rowena?" It was Christian's voice and the word was a question, but she could not comprehend what he was asking. Perhaps because she was so far from understanding what had just taken place.

She met his blue eyes with misery, and he took a deep breath, dropping his hands from her back as he said, "Forgive me. I did not mean for this to happen, should not have touched you. That is not why I am here, not what I want from you."

She swallowed hard. Had she not known this? Yet somehow there was hurt inside her, a feeling of loneliness that left her chest aching.

He asked again, "Rowena?" Now she had the feeling that he wanted her to choose, between all he represented and all that was familiar to her—her life, Ashcroft, Sean, the folk who came to her for healing.

Slowly she shook her head, and saw the disappointment in his handsome face.

Unwilling to think of the regret she felt at having displeased Christian, she pulled away and raced after Sean. She only knew that she must go to him, to what was known, though she did not understand why her friend was so hurt.

She found him at the top of the cliff overlooking the sea. He stared off into the distance, a stark silhouette against the darkening sky.

"Sean?"

He spun around to face her, his eyes damp.

Tears!

Shaken by them, she whispered, "Sean, obviously I have hurt you, and badly. I do not understand why you would be so affected by—"

His rage was an accusation. "Ye do not understand? How could ye not, Rowena? How could ye let the mon touch ye?"

She shook her head, feeling like a fool even as she wondered how she had indeed allowed that to happen. But she was still confused at the depth of Sean's anger. "I do not know. He was comforting me and he…I… It meant nothing." She took a step closer, studying his stormy countenance. "What I do not understand is why you are so angry with me. Certainly it was wrong to let him kiss me, but…''

His eyes flashed resentment and pain. ''Ye know, do ye not, that he only wishes to seduce ye? I saw what he was about and meant to warn ye before it was too late, though ye did not heed me when I told ye ye should not be alone with him. And now ye have fallen in with—''

Chagrined at this reminder of his early warnings that she was not to trust the knight, she interrupted, ''I have not fallen in with him. I told you that it was a mistake.''

''He willna stay, and it will be for ye as it was for yer mither.''

She was stung by this remark, but realized that Sean did not know of the man's true interest in her. Refusing to let him see how badly this hurt, Rowena shook her head as she replied with deliberate calm, ''He does not wish to seduce me, Sean, no matter what you might think.''

He frowned at her and she added, ''You know that Sir Christian came here looking for a woman named Rosalind?''

Sean swept the air with an impatient hand. ''And what has that to do with anything?''

She took a deep breath, finding it difficult to voice the words aloud. ''He believes that I am she.''

He took a step backward, his face registering his shock. Yet he recovered almost instantly, and spoke with even greater outrage. ''That is a lie he told ye to—''

With more impatience than she intended, Rowena

cut him off. "It is not. I believe that he is sincere in this belief."

Something in her face must have penetrated his rage, for he said, "How could he think such a thing?"

Quickly she told him all Christian had said to her about Rosalind and the strange parallels to Rowena's own life.

When at last she finished Sean sputtered, "He is mad." Though his words were still angry, there was an undeniable doubt in his eyes.

Rowena took a deep breath and let it out slowly. For how could she pretend to herself that she did not feel a certain amount of doubt herself, no matter how impossible it all seemed? "At the least, very badly mistaken."

Sean scowled at her, his face hardening again. "Ye may allow him to convince ye, but I do not trust him. This could all be his way of tricking ye into falling in with his plan to bed ye."

She blushed. "Have done with that. I have told you, Christian Greatham does not wish to seduce me. He has told me as much."

"Then he has a strange way of showing it." Sean turned on her once more, clearly outraged anew as he cried, "Do not forget that I saw ye in his arms. Ye were letting him kiss ye, touch ye, Rowena."

She was not sure why she had allowed it, and heard the desperation in her voice as she tried to explain it away. "I was...he spoke of my finding out about my father and I...you know how I have wished to know of him." Her eyes met Sean's. "You have seen how hard not knowing has been for me all these years."

She halted at the continued fury on his face. Pride rose up inside her, though she felt no lessening of her own uncertainty. She was determined for Sean to let the matter go, as it was her own concern. She raised her head high as she said, "Why does his kissing me matter so greatly to you? I answer to myself and no other."

He startled her then, throwing his arms wide, clearly exasperated beyond reason, shouting, "Why does it matter so greatly to me? How could ye not know the answer to that? How could ye be so blind to my love, my desire for ye?"

She felt the world tilt around her, and she seemed to hear her own voice come from far away. "Love? Desire? But you are as a brother to me."

Her shock did not blind her to the pain that flashed in his eyes. "Aye, that I ken, but I thought ye must have some notion of my feelings."

She shook her head, unable to accept this, with all else that had risen up out of nowhere to change her thoughts about herself, her life. "It cannot be. We love one another, yes, but not in that way."

"I have loved ye that way for as long as I can recall. I have thought that we would marry, have a family—" His voice broke.

Again she shook her head. "What of all our talk of Berta?"

He glared in defiance, looking much as he had when they were eight and he'd told her he was going to take his father's boat out alone if she wouldn't go with him. "That was meant to make ye see that I have become a man. To look at me differently."

She closed her eyes. "How have I been so blind?"

He spoke in a harsh voice. "I thought that it was only a matter of giving ye time…. But ye did not see me. Instead ye looked to that…let him…"

The next thing she knew she had been pulled tight against him and Sean's lips came down on hers.

His mouth was awkward and punishing, yet she remained passive beneath that assault because of her love for him. Even after he softened the kiss, tried in his own inexperienced way to elicit a response, she felt nothing.

As she realized this, understood that her reaction to Christian's kiss could not have been more different, she told herself that her response to the knight was in no way significant. He was a man who knew how to kiss a woman, how to draw her out.

As unexpectedly as he had taken Rowena into his arms, Sean set her free. He turned his back to her, wiping his hand across his mouth as if in disgust.

Rowena watched him, forcing herself to see the pain she had brought him as he stared out over the open sea, at the sky no less stormy than his well-loved face. She did love him, with all her heart. But not in the way he wanted.

"I am sorry, Sean. So very sorry."

He stared down at her, his lips twisting as he searched her eyes. "Ye can keep yer pity, Rowena."

He turned and hurried away along the cliffs. This time she made no move to follow, realizing that she would only make things worse by doing so.

Somehow she knew that she could never love him in the way he demanded. The very thought of it left her utterly unmoved, other than with empathy and sadness.

If only Rowena could love Sean the way he wanted her to. Things would be so much easier.

But even though she had no real experience in these things, she knew that one could not make love happen. It was something that just was, or was not. Even her pain over Sean's tormented tears could not bring it about.

Suddenly she wondered if Christian had ever cried for the love of a woman. She couldn't imagine it. He seemed too sure of himself, his control over himself and his emotions too much a part of him. He'd so easily set her aside after he'd kissed her. When she had been so...

She groaned aloud, uncertain as to why this disturbed her.

All Rowena wanted was for things to be the way they had been before the knight had arrived. Sean would never have spoken of his feelings for her if he had not been so angry and jealous over what he thought was going on between her and Christian. Perhaps he would have outgrown it without ever having done so. She would have danced at his wedding to Berta someday, but now that he had declared himself, things could never be the same.

Rowena trudged along the clifftop, her arms around herself as she stared out at the gray clouds. As she did, her certainty that it was some other girl the knight sought began to weaken even further.

Why would a dying man point him to Ashcroft for no reason? Why were there so many uncanny coincidences between Rowena and this girl? But it was not possible. Rowena could not believe she could be Rosalind.

She had nothing but disdain for the nobles and their love of lands and titles.

Even if the impossible should somehow prove possible, she could never accept a place amongst the nobility. Was not Christian asking her to behave in a way she despised, by asking her to expect others to put themselves in harm's way in order to have her—or rather, Rosalind—restored to her position of lady of Dragonwick? It was wrong, even if, as he said, they would do so gladly.

Realizing the path of her thoughts, Rowena shook her head violently. Nay, the tale Christian Greatham had told her could not be true.

She was not the child of the earl of Kelsey. To even allow herself to imagine that she could be was nothing short of self-delusion. It was only her desperation to know something of her father, of her past, that made her doubt the truth for even a moment.

Rowena had much to lose by allowing herself to believe such nonsense. She had found a place here in Ashcroft, was loved and needed. She would not throw all that away for anything. Even if there was the remotest possibility that she was the daughter of the man Christian had called The Dragon.

Still, if and indeed she was sure she could not be this daughter, who then was she?

For as long as she could recall, Rowena had longed to know just that.

Here in Ashcroft there was no way of finding out

who her father was. There was no way to even imagine what he could have been like, for there was no one like him.

As a child, she had imagined him to be somewhat like the village smith, who always spoke to her kindly when they met. But it did not take long for her to realize, even from the little her mother had said, that her father could not have been like the good-natured smith. His life and the world he lived in were so far removed that it might as well be the moon for all that she could accurately picture him or his surroundings.

She and Sean had discussed it many times, neither of them knowing enough to be able to comprehend the life of a knight. Yet her friend's very presence, his desire to help her, had been a comfort in the lonely times.

With the thought of Sean came the memory of his stormy eyes, his tormented expression. How was she ever to live without his support?

Suddenly a thought entered her mind, a thought so unprecedented and unexpected she could not forestall it.

What would happen if she went away for a time? Surely Sean would have an opportunity to think on his feelings, to realize that he did not care for her in the way he currently imagined. Perhaps they could have a fresh beginning.

She, who had always wondered about her father's world, could see for herself where she had begun. 'Haps it would help her to accept what her father had done, to forgive, and go on with her life.

The question was, would Christian Greatham agree

to such a scheme? Would he be willing to return her here once she had learned what she would?

There was no way of knowing without approaching him.

Did she have the courage to do so? Perhaps she did, for the events of the past hours had shaken her to the core of her being, made her realize that there was much she did not know, and that she was capable of doing something to change that fact.

Rowena found herself turning back to her cottage.

Yet almost instantly she hesitated. The kiss…

How was she to face Christian?

She shook her head. It had meant nothing. She had been in need of comfort; he had tried to comfort her and it had gone awry.

For his part, he had made it quite clear that he had not meant for things to happen as they had. That he had no intention of doing anything of the sort again.

Rowena recalled Sean's accusation about the knight trying to seduce her. If she was honest, she realized, there was at least a possibility that in some part of his mind Christian might have imagined that kissing her, developing a closeness with her, might aid in convincing her to accompany him to England.

Well, it was not necessary. If she could be assured that he would not attempt to prevent her from returning home, she might indeed go with him.

With a firm tread she walked on.

She found Christian where she had left him. As she entered the cottage, he glanced around from where he was putting wood upon the fire.

Slowly he turned, his expression watchful, and Rowena swallowed hard. Now that the moment to tell him what she was thinking had come, it was more difficult than she had imagined.

Instead she found herself asking, "Can you tell me more of what happened to Rosalind, to The Dragon?"

Christian nodded immediately. "I will tell you what I recall." He waited until she reseated herself before beginning. "The story started a very long time ago. More than fourteen years, in fact. I was fostered to the earl then. Rosalind was his only child, and he doted upon her and his niece, Isabelle. His wife had died giving birth to little Rosalind.

"The earl's half brother, a very selfish and greedy man, was jealous, not only of The Dragon's lands and titles, but of the respect he garnered amongst all those who knew him. Realizing that Prince John, who was acting in King Richard's place, was of a very similar ilk, the younger Kelsey convinced John that The Dragon had plotted against the king. He gained John's sanction to take the castle in order to secure it for the crown. In the fighting he murdered the earl and, we thought at the time, four-year-old Rosalind."

Rowena could not help the slight unease that rolled over her. In spite of her insistence that this could not be her, she whispered, "Murdered. You believe her death was deliberate?"

Christian watched Rowena as she wrapped her arms about herself protectively. He wanted to comfort her, but he had already seen what havoc that could bring.

Finally, with the impulse under control, he said, "Aye. The man we are speaking of is capable of great ill. He cares for nothing so much as his own gain, even to the point of cold-bloodedly murdering a child. It is the very depth of his evil that convinces me that Sir Jack and the nurse would have gone to whatever lengths they must to protect a child from him.''

Christian knew all of this must come as an enormous shock, yet he was frustrated with Rowena's failure to see that she had a duty to at least find out if she could be Rosalind, which he believed she was. Yet as this went through his mind, he realized that he had not actually given that much thought to how the young woman would react when he found her. He had been bent on finding her and doing everything he could to see Kelsey denounced.

Perhaps Rowena's denials were in fact a good sign. Did it not bode well that she was not the kind who would leap at the chance to be a great heiress? Wasn't the fact that she was reluctant to believe even more proof that she was of sound and honorable character? As he would expect the daughter of The Dragon to be.

He spoke softly. ''Rowena.''

She looked at him with troubled green eyes, eyes that had the power to tug at his heart. He heard the emotion in his voice as he said, ''I want to tell you that I understand how shocked you must be.''

A wry smile curved her lovely mouth. ''Nay, I think you do not understand.''

He shrugged. '''Haps you are right. 'Haps it is impossible for anyone to understand what it would be like to learn—''

She interrupted him roughly. ''To learn, if it is all to be believed, that what little you had been told about yourself and your life is a lie.''

He sighed. "As I have said, it was no longer possible for you to live in the home of your birth with any safety, nor anywhere that Kelsey might learn of you. As The Dragon's daughter you would have been heir to your mother's extensive dower lands, if naught else. Your uncle, who is now the earl, would not have been above seeing you dead to gain them. As he had, in fact, believed he had done when he attacked the keep. The lies would have been a necessity, to devise new identities for you and the nurse. As a child you could not be expected to hide the truth, and at four you were young enough to forget."

She held his gaze with those green eyes and he saw the anger beneath her pain. "Do you have any notion what it is like to believe you are a bastard, that there is no one anywhere who would welcome you because of it?"

He took a deep breath. "I do not. But one of those I hold most dear in life was born without benefit of marriage, and it has never mattered to me for even one moment." He knew that what he said could hold little comfort, for it did not change her life, but he did want Rowena to know that her parentage mattered not in the least to him. For even if she was not The Dragon's daughter, was indeed the illegitimate child of a knight her mother had known, Christian would not look upon her differently.

She watched him closely. "What manner of man was this Dragon, to instill such a loyalty that you would go to these lengths to search out a daughter who might not even exist?"

He felt himself smiling in spite of the pain that still

lay in his heart whenever he thought of his former foster father. "A better man than any other I have known. He was not one to go about dropping kind words like rain. There was simply an honesty about him, a strength of character that is rare indeed, and when you did get a compliment from him it was wholehearted and deeply meant. I once saw him bested on the practice field by a man who had come to seek a position as man-at-arms. Most men in The Dragon's position would feel they had to save face after being knocked to the ground by a green lad who'd only practiced with a wooden sword. The trembling farm boy stood there in complete fright, but The Dragon leaped from the ground, embraced the fellow and offered him a place in his castle guard. He said he would be happy knowing that there was a better fighter than he guarding his family." Christian shook his head. "He was a man to instill honor, decency and fairness in others, because he lived by them.

"In the end it was his willingness to think the best of others that was his undoing for he knew that his brother was not as honorable." Christian's mouth twisted with disdain. "All knew it. The Dragon simply did not imagine that hatred and dishonor could run so deep in his half brother, for it could never do so in his own heart."

"I see." She sighed heavily. "Would that such a man were my father." She squared her slender shoulders. "Yet I cannot allow myself to believe such a thing simply because I would have a father. A name."

Christian scowled. "I believe he is your father."

She took a deep breath, her gaze searching his face. "You truly do believe this?"

"Aye."

She looked away. "While I was gone I came to think...that I might be able to..."

"Yes?" The word was spoken carefully, but Christian could not deny the ray of hope that flickered inside him.

She shrugged. "What matter that I tell you, for 'tis all madness. You would never agree to my terms. You love the man you call Dragon too well to be willing to accept that I might not wish to see him avenged."

He continued just as carefully. "Pray, tell me what you are speaking of."

She swung around. "I...Sean and I have had words...."

"He is in love with you."

She stared at Christian. "How blind must I have been that I did not see what a stranger could?"

He shrugged. "You did not wish to see. You do not have such feelings for him."

She scowled. "That is not what I wished to speak to you about. Yet it does have some bearing on the notion of going with you to England."

"You will come with me?"

She held up a slim hand. "Hear me out. For I believe you will never agree to my terms and I will not go otherwise."

"Name them."

She did not answer directly. "I do see that the evidence is great, though it all seems so incredible. And a part of me does wish to go. I would give much to learn of my father's world. Yet none of what you say feels even the least bit familiar."

Again he spoke carefully. "That is not surprising, since you recall so very little of your life before coming here."

She seemed resigned to this fact as she answered, "I cannot argue that."

He watched her, unable to disguise his rising hope.

She grimaced as she added, "As I said, there is a condition."

"Again I say name it."

She faced him without wavering, her eyes now filled with determination. "I ask that you pledge to return me here to Ashcroft when I bid you, in spite of your feelings on the matter. And that you will do nothing to try to coerce me into staying."

"But—"

Firmly she said, "I will not go unless you give me your word." Her gaze filled with entreaty. "You must realize it is the only way I may feel I have some part in determining my own life once we leave here. I will be powerless in your world, without friends or a home of my own."

"We shall be that to you, Simon, Jarrod and I, as well as our families."

"Please."

Christian took a deep breath and let it out slowly. How could he deny her? Even if he were inclined to stand on his honor and declare that he would never attempt to coerce her—even without making a formal pledge—he could not say so. The pain and uncertainty in her gaze would not allow him to belittle her fears.

Falling down upon one knee, as he would when swearing an oath of fealty, he said, "So I do swear." He then rose.

For a moment she looked at him with shock and amazement. "Do you mean you would agree so easily?"

He frowned. "I have done so."

He could see that, far from lessening her uncertainty, what had just occurred seemed to have added to it. "I have agreed to accompany you?"

He nodded. "You have."

"Rowena."

She looked around, knowing Sean's voice well, though she felt a trace of reluctance because of the continued anger evident in it.

"Ye are going with him?"

"Aye." She glanced down at the small bundle of belongings that rested on the edge of her bed. It had taken very little time to gather the few things she meant to take with her. She did not wish to ask Christian to carry them in the event that they grew too heavy for her.

Christian had gone to Hagar's to discover if there had been any word of his horse, or another. He had informed her that both he and Rowena would be leaving Ashcroft as soon as possible.

Rowena could only assume that Hagar must have told her son the news of their departure.

Sean came toward her, his gaze pleading, and she knew she had guessed correctly. "Please do not do this," he said hoarsely.

"I must." She avoided looking into his eyes. "I will learn what I can of my father."

"He is using ye."

She knew he was speaking of Christian. "I am using him."

"Rowena!" The torment in his tone and expression were too painful to witness.

She told herself that she was doing the right thing. By the time she returned, Sean would be over this madness. He was so young and only needed time to think. "You and I will benefit from a time apart."

His voice was rough. "I will never mention my feelings for ye again if ye will but stay. We can go on as we always have."

She met his gaze sadly. "That is not possible. Too much has been said between us. When I come back, enough time will have passed that we can have something different."

"Then let me be the one to go away for a time."

She shook her head, speaking gently. "I have given my word. I will keep it. As I said, I will learn what I can of my father. You of all others know how much that means to me."

His expression was incredulous. "You do not actually believe that you are this Rosalind."

She grimaced. "How can I? But I must find out. I must know."

Hagar's voice came from behind them. "Sean."

They both swung around at the same time. The older woman was watching Rowena. "Sean did not tell you that a horse has been found?"

Rowena shook her head.

She could see the regret as well as the resolution in the older woman's face. "You will leave at first light." Here, then, was someone who understood her need to go. "You must go with God."

"Thank you, Hagar. I love you."

"As I do ye, lass."

Sean spat out the words. "Ye do not approve of this!"

"'Tis not my place to approve or not to approve. 'Tis my place but to love and to keep the secret that Sir Christian has been here and taken Rowena off with him—as he has bade me. As will ye and all others in the village, me lad."

"Mither."

"Ye mun let her go, Sean. If the knight speaks true about who she is, we ha' no right to keep Rowena. Her destiny lies away."

Rowena rose and went to enfold the older woman in her arms. "It matters not what proves to be the truth. I shall return to you and my life here."

Hagar held her tightly, making no reply.

Sean groaned and hit his fist against the wall. He moved forward, then stopped to grab up something from the table before running out the door.

Chapter Seven

The sky was just light enough to see the treacherous path before her as Rowena followed Sir Christian Greatham away from her home the next morning. Slowly he led the way down the cliffs to the beach below, glancing back often to see how she was faring. He did not speak, and for that she was grateful.

Rowena avoided meeting his gaze. She did not wish to talk. She forced herself to face forward, not to look back as she left the only life she could remember.

It had been a good life, and when she returned she hoped she might come back with some knowledge of herself that would help her to go on with more peace than she had heretofore known. There was no doubt in her mind that she would be coming back. Even if by some improbable stroke of fate it was revealed that she was indeed Rosalind Kelsey, she had no intention of forsaking all she knew and trusted.

Rowena cast an uncertain glance over Christian's broad back. Since she had agreed to accompany him, the knight had limited his conversation to the details of their journey, though he told her precious little of those. Rowena was content with this, as she had never traveled farther than the nearby villages and did not know what to ask.

One day had not given Rowena much time to say goodbye, nor to think about what a drastic step she was taking. Perhaps that was fortunate, for she had not been able to completely set aside her fears.

There had been one unpleasant moment when Christian had asked her what had happened to the drawing he had left on the table. Instantly recalling that Sean had taken something when he had run from the cottage, Rowena had nonetheless informed the knight that she had not seen it.

It was the truth. She had not, and had only a suspicion that Sean had taken it.

Though he had cast more than one speculative glance in her direction, Christian had said nothing more. What could he say? He would not accuse her of taking the drawing, and he had no way of knowing if Sean had been there to see her.

They had not spoken again until late last eve, when he had come to her with a scowl on his handsome face. "Rowena, you do not perhaps happen to have any coin, do you? Though we will eventually reach Avington without it, our journey would be made much more simple for having some."

She had nodded quickly. "I had forgotten that all your belongings were lost."

She moved to the chest beside her bed and began to withdraw its contents. Only when she reached the bottom did she at last remove a fair-size velvet bag. She stood, holding it out to him.

Christian had moved forward with obvious amazement. "Where did you get this?"

She shrugged. "My mother showed it to me when I was fourteen. She said my father had given it to her when he sent her away. I use only what I need, as did my mother."

He poured out a handful of gleaming coins, some of them gold. "This is a veritable fortune."

She looked at him. "I take it you see this as even further proof that I am Rosalind." He watched her and she said, "My father need not have been the earl of Kelsey to have given this to my mother."

Christian had shrugged then. "I will see that I keep a reckoning of every penny, and return it to you."

She had no doubt of his honesty. It was her own strange attraction to him that made her move away from him.

When her foot suddenly slipped now on the rocky path, Christian reached back to clasp her arm in a steady grip. "I am fine," she murmured, drawing away from him, though she felt like a fool. She would do well to concentrate on whence she was going.

With a bow, he reached for the bundle she carried. "Give it to me."

She raised her chin defiantly, but he continued to hold out his hand. Realizing that she had little chance of winning, she handed it over in silence.

He nodded with approval. "Now, have a care. It is extremely slick."

She cast him a scathing glance. "Do not worry. I know these paths."

He frowned but went on without further comment.

When they, at last came to a more open and easily traversible portion of the beach, Rowena looked up to see that a man stood not far ahead of them. He held the reins of a great black stallion in his hands, his face wary as he watched the animal. Nearby lay what looked to be a saddle. As he noted their approach, the stranger's expression seemed to ease and he lifted a hand in greeting.

Christian's stride lengthened and he reached the man and horse before her, taking the reins in his hand and running an affectionate hand across the powerful neck. Rowena watched as that great beast leaned down to nuzzle the knight's shoulder.

Deliberately she studied the ground as she took the last steps toward them, feeling somehow uncomfortable with Christian's tenderness toward the horse. For some reason it caused a tightness in her own throat to see how grateful Christian was to see the stallion returned to him.

She looked to the other man, a squarely built fellow with a thatch of auburn hair. He seemed more than happy to have released the horse, and watched the exchange between man and beast with obvious amazement. He said, "Once I had managed to get the saddle off him, m'lord, I couldna get it back on."

"My saddle?" Christian seemed to note it for the first time, releasing the beast, which followed him with amazing docility as he went to kneel on the ground beside it. He opened a leather pouch that hung from it. With a grin that made her heart turn over for the boyish joy in it, he pulled out a heavy velvet cloak of deepest midnight blue, then reached in again, and removed another much smaller object.

"Do you see, Rowena? It is here, the brooch Jarrod had made for me right after The Dragon was killed."

She moved closer, her gaze taking in the heavy brooch, which bore the symbol of a dragon. It was a very distinctive piece, and Christian's pleasure could not have been more obvious. "It must mean a great deal to you."

"More than you know." He turned to the other man. "Would you give me your name, sir?"

"Dougal of Langton, m'lord."

Christian reached into Rowena's velvet purse, which he wore on the belt Hagar had given him. "Please take this as a token of my thanks. You have done me a great service this day by returning not only my horse, but my belongings."

Dougal took the gold coins with wide eyes. "I thank ye, m'lord, but 'tis too great a sum. I couldna keep the things when I learned that the horse was being sought by its owner."

"Your honesty and humbleness are to be commended. But no sum is too large for your kindness in returning Gideon and the brooch to me. I assure you that their value far exceeds that amount."

The fellow ducked his head, appearing pleased at this praise. "I wouldna have asked it, but ye are most welcome. Now I mun get back to my work."

Christian bowed, and Dougal bobbed his head to both him and Rowena before taking his leave.

Immediately, Christian donned the cloak, clasping the dragon brooch over his breast. He placed Rowena's bag inside one of his, then began to saddle the stallion, which held perfectly still under his familiar hands.

Rowena stood silent, waiting, not sure what she should do. Yet as she continued to watch the proceedings, it was suddenly clear to her that she would be expected to mount that great animal with Christian Greatham. Looking at the saddle, she could not imagine how this was to be borne.

How could she possibly place herself in such intimate contact with a man as powerful and unknown to her as the stallion he rode? A man whose kiss had brought about an awakening inside her that she would much prefer to forget?

But what could be done about it?

Nothing!

She should have thought, should have known this was coming. She could not walk to England. Much as she might have preferred it to being in such close contact with Christian, he was in haste to return to his own family, and would never agree.

Thus it was that when he turned to her, the animal prepared for the journey, she said not a word concerning her misgivings. Clearly thinking of nothing beyond being on their way, he said, "I will mount and pull you up after me."

He was in the saddle in one swift motion, reaching out to take her hand even as he nodded toward the stirrup. "Rest your foot upon mine and I will draw you up." When she hesitated for a brief instant, he spoke reassuringly. "Do not worry. He will not harm you."

This statement, however kindly meant, did not speak

to her real difficulty. But Rowena would rather perish beneath those sharp hooves than admit the truth.

Raising her head high, she took the offered hand, placed her foot over Christian's and felt herself sailing through the air and into the saddle. She had no time to think of anything else then, for the moment she was seated behind him, Christian started off. He urged the eager stallion forward, its long strides devouring the sand beneath them at an alarming rate.

Never in her life had Rowena imagined traveling at such speed, and she found herself clutching the back of the knight's cloak. Yet as they moved on and she began to grow more accustomed to the motion and height, she became more aware of the man who sat before her.

From behind, Christian's body was no less masculine and distracting. His broad shoulders flexed with each command to the responsive stallion.

Rowena found herself becoming flushed, though the day was quite cool. It was with fixed determination that she set her mind to examining the vegetation along the path. Yet she knew the hours ahead of her would be long indeed.

Christian did not stop until the last of the light had died in the sky. He could have kept on riding, would dearly love to do so, but he did not wish to jeopardize Gideon, carrying two as he was. Even though the stallion would not be overstressed by the addition of Rowena's slight weight, her presence on his rump might throw off his stride enough that he might stumble in a hole in the darkness.

Christian drew the horse to a halt on the banks of a stream he had stopped at on his way to Ashcroft. He turned to address Rowena, who had said very little during the past hours. "We are stopping here. I will get down, then help you to dismount."

Her soft, "Oh," sounded more like a groan than an answer, and he realized that she must be tired. He had been so occupied with getting on his way, with his thoughts of how Jarrod and Simon would react to his bringing Rowena to Avington, with his worry over what his family would be thinking at his long absence, that he had not considered Rowena.

Well, that was not entirely true. In some ways he had been too aware of her, of the gentle warmth of her behind him. Mayhap he had chosen to concentrate so intently upon other matters because of that.

Yet now he realized he should have been slightly more attentive to her well-being. Quickly he swung out of the saddle and held up his hand, trying to gauge her expression in the darkness as she hesitated.

Slowly she placed her hand in his, then remained motionless on the stallion's back.

Puzzled, Christian said, "Do you not wish to get down now?"

She shifted slightly and a soft gasp escaped her. Her voice was a barely audible whisper. "I...my legs...they tingle so."

Instantly he realized that he had indeed pushed her too hard. Rowena had never ridden a horse before.

He reached up and took her into his arms, knowing that there was no way to avoid the pain she would experience, but wincing as she uttered a second hoarse cry. As carefully as was humanly possible, Christian held her against him, until the worst of the pain seemed to ease and her body relaxed somewhat. Only then did he slowly lower her legs until her feet rested upon the ground, though he continued to hold her tightly against him, supporting her weight.

When she raised tormented eyes, illuminated by the bright crescent moon that had now peeked above the tops of the trees surrounding the clearing, he said, "Forgive me. I should have thought, should have considered your inexperience...."

She shook her head. "Please, do not take all the responsibility. I should have said something...."

Guilt tightened his chest at her refusal to blame him. He spoke gently. "Can you stand if you hold on to me?"

She nodded and gingerly wrapped her arms about his waist.

Christian was appalled at the jolt of heat that passed through him. He was determined to ignore it. Rowena was in agony.

Without another word he raised one hand to pull one of the furs free from the saddle. Being careful not to jar her, he spread it on the ground, then lifted her. In spite of his determination to control his reaction to her, he felt a further stirring in his lower body as he became aware of her sweet curves against him.

With sweat beading his upper lip, he settled her upon the fur with great care.

Then he quickly went about building a fire. As he did he continued to castigate himself, not only for the response he did not seem capable of controlling in spite of his self-assurances to the contrary, but also for allowing her to come to such a state.

Daylight did not bring a great lessening of Rowena's misery. The tender skin of her inner thighs was so abraded that she could not bear to have them rub together. She had put a brave face on things last eve, telling a clearly concerned Christian that she would be fine after a good night's sleep.

He had nodded and gone about setting up their camp. When he had come to check on her once more, Rowena had feigned sleep, too exhausted to make conversation.

With daylight came the realization that she still did not wish to tell Christian how bad it was, and that she had slept very little. How could she do so, knowing as she did that he wished to continue their journey? Conversely, how could she remount that horse?

The moment Christian rose from his own bed across the still-smoldering fire, he came to kneel beside her. His blue eyes searched hers, and finally he said, "It is bad."

Though she wished otherwise, Rowena could not deny it. "Aye. I am so very sorry."

He made a sweeping motion with his hand. "Do not worry on that score for now. We must accept what is." He held her gaze. "I think you must allow me to see how bad it is."

Rowena stiffened. "Nay, I—"

He halted her. "I must know if you require a physician."

Quickly she exclaimed, "I do not!"

His lips twisted wryly. "Forgive me if I insist on

knowing this for myself. Being responsible for your well-being and safety after convincing you to come with me, I cannot simply ignore this problem.''

She gave a reluctant sigh. ''I know what needs to be done to help myself. But I cannot fetch the ingredients that are required.''

Eagerly he stood, his voice tinged with relief. ''Of course! For a moment I had forgotten your aptitude at healing. You of all people know what should be done. I can fetch whatever is needed.''

Doubtfully she asked, ''Do you think you could bring back the ingredients I require? It will mean gathering some in the wood.''

His gaze was determined. ''If you tell me what they look like I will do my utmost. If I collect the wrong ones I will keep going back until the correct ones are found.''

She sighed, leaning back on her makeshift pillow of boughs, deciding that she might as well tell him all. ''Then let us try, for to be completely honest I will not be able to ride for some days lest I treat myself.''

Christian took a deep breath, then nodded grimly.

She lost no more time. ''The wild marjoram you will find in the wood, and rose petals may be had if you can locate a nearby farm, as well as some type of fat.''

He nodded. ''How much will be required?''

She shrugged. ''Enough to mash into a paste that will cover the abrasions from knee to thigh.''

He grimaced. ''Is it really so very bad?''

She gave a sharp nod.

Christian's expression grew even more determined. ''I will return anon.''

Rowena watched him go off on his horse, then eased farther back against the fragrant boughs with a groan of misery. It took no small effort to disguise the degree of her pain from Christian. Yet she was determined to continue to do so, for he was clearly beset by guilt.

It seemed a very long while until he returned with the plants she had requested. But as the sun was not yet very high in the sky, it had likely been a fairly short span of time.

He had, thankfully, found exactly what she required. And in more than sufficient amounts.

Immediately he said, "Pray, what needs doing next?"

Eager for the release she knew the medicine would bring, Rowena told him what to do. The tasks were accomplished with surprising efficiency, Christian being responsive to her every direction.

When the paste in the wooden bowl had cooled, Rowena held out her hands. To her chagrin she saw that they were unsteady from the pain she had been suffering since the previous day.

The moment he saw the way the bowl quivered in her grasp, Christian frowned. "You cannot tend to yourself."

She pulled it close against her, wincing as the sudden movement sent a jolt of agony through her lower limbs. "I will do it well enough."

He shook his head. "You must see that is not reasonable."

She refused to look at him, afraid he would detect the horror she felt at the idea of his touching her so intimately. "You cannot—"

With unwavering perseverance, he took the bowl from her trembling hands. "I intend naught but to help you, Rowena. I will be gentle."

She had no doubt that was all he intended. It was her own thoughts and feelings that were in doubt. In spite of her pain, the very notion of Christian putting his hand on her...

Nonsense. He simply wanted her well so they could be on their way.

Surely she could control her body's unfathomable responses to this man, given the circumstances. She found herself chattering nervously. "I am sure you have seen many women's legs."

His voice was rueful as he replied, "Not as many as you might think."

Her gaze ran over his face as she searched for any sign that he was mocking her. But she saw only self-derision in his wryly twisted lips and arched dark brows. Surprise made her say, "How could that be?"

He seemed to be studying the contents of the bowl with great concentration. "Mayhap I am less appealing to the female sex than you might imagine."

Rowena did not think so. Reticent and particular, but not unappealing.

For reasons she could not even begin to fathom, Christian's revelation pleased her.

He pushed her gently but insistently back onto the fur, and she did not fight him. He drew her gown up her legs with slow and obvious care, but Rowena was fully conscious of the fact that Sean was the only other male ever to see her legs, and he had not done so since they were twelve.

When her thighs were finally bared to those blue eyes, she felt a flush of heat that shamed her. Quickly she reached to tuck her gown about her bottom in an effort to preserve her modesty and give herself a moment to calm the beating of her heart.

When she raised her gaze to look at his face she felt even more mortified. There was only horror in those blue depths as he stared at the raised red abrasions that ran from knee to thigh.

His gaze came back to her face, his voice hoarse as he said, "Forgive me."

She shook her head. "There is nothing to forgive."

Slowly Christian dipped his fingers into the bowl. His gaze met hers again and he whispered, "I will try not to hurt you."

She gritted her teeth and said, "Pray go on. Lest you have no heart for it?"

A muscle flexed in his lean jaw. "I have the heart for it well enough." Then, with a deep breath, he reached out and with infinite care began to slather the mixture over the wounds.

The contact of that cooling medicament on the painful flesh was so indescribably sweet that Rowena could not withhold the sigh of relief that emerged from her lips. Her head fell back and she went limp. Unfortunately, that reaction began to change as Christian's gentle but firm fingers traced their way farther up the inner parts of her legs. She began to note that in spite of the coolness of the paste, his fingers were warm, and where they touched her skin she felt a strange and pleasurable tingling.

Her gaze flew to his face, and she saw that he

seemed intent on nothing more than applying the salve. Rowena closed her eyes, shamed anew at her reaction. Yet as Christian went on, the sensations continued, and the trembling in her body became more pronounced. A honeyed warmth pooled in her lower belly and her heartbeat quickened to a thrum.

She soon realized that the pain, which had seemed nearly unbearable, had become a distant irritation at the back of her mind. Rowena turned her face to the fragrant boughs and breathed through slightly parted lips as her limbs grew weaker and weaker and the delight in her belly spread downward.

And even as she reveled in these sensations she could only be grateful that the knight had no idea what she was thinking or feeling. But when his gentle fingers brushed against the upper regions of her inner thighs, Rowena could not seem to restrain a restless movement of her hips.

Immediately, Christian's touch ceased. "Have I hurt you?" he asked in a barely recognizable voice.

Rowena opened her eyes, praying with all her might that he would not be able to read the truth. But even as she said "Nay," she noted the way he wiped at a line of perspiration above his mouth with the back of his hand. The same hand he had been using to apply the cream to her legs.

Her gaze skittered away from his and back. "I...the pain is much improved. Mayhap you have put on enough."

He swallowed hard, looking down into the bowl with rapt concentration. "Fair enough, then. There will be more than sufficient should you need further applications.''

She forced a smile, though he was not looking at her. ''That is good. I...think it would be well if I were to rest now.''

Hurriedly he stood. ''Aye. I will...tend to my horse.''

With that he moved off, taking the bowl with him. She watched as he reached out to take the reins of the animal from the tree limb to which he had tied it, then halted, looking down at the bowl in his hands as if he did not know how it had gotten there.

Rowena could not fathom this apparent agitation. Unless...? Was it possible? Could he, too, feel...?

He moved back to her, holding out the bowl at arm's length. ''I am going to water Gideon. I will leave this with you.''

As she took it, being careful not to come into contact with those all too distracting fingers, he said, ''Use as much as you will. I would happily gather more of whatever is required if that will help us be on our way.''

Although she knew it was ridiculous, Rowena felt a rush of disappointment. She lowered her head. ''I should not have come. This is all for naught. It is a waste of your effort and mine.''

His powerful body stiffened from head to toe. ''You are not saying that you wish to return to Ashcroft already?''

She raised her chin. ''Surely even you can see that it has become more complicated than either of us expected.''

He looked out into the surrounding forest, his face set.

She frowned. ''When I said I would accompany you I had no notion of the difficulty I would cause. After all this effort to deliver me to Avington you will surely be disappointed when I ask you to take me home.''

''If that day comes you must allow me to be responsible for my own disappointment.'' Without another word he strode away, taking the horse toward the stream. In spite of the fact that she did not doubt the sincerity of his regret at her infirmity, she could not help realizing anew that its greatest import as far as he was concerned was that it hindered their journey.

Rowena told herself that her distress was completely unwarranted. What other reason could there be for his agitation?

Christian did not put any more of the cream on Rowena's legs. Even though they stayed beside the stream for what remained of that day and the next, he did not so much as offer to touch her again.

Yet every time he recalled how deeply and erotically he had been moved by applying that salve, a service that had begun so very innocently, he was hard-pressed to control his own reactions. But it was the feeling, however mad and impossible, that Rowena had responded to his ministrations in an intimate way that completely unsettled him.

The way she had shifted her hips, the flush on her delicate cheekbones...

Nay, it was not credible. He simply saw what he wished to see because he had been driven to the point of near madness by what he was doing—by the thought that her legs, though marred by her injury, were long and perfectly formed, that they could wrap about a man's waist...

'Twas far worse even than the visions he had suffered after kissing her. Those he had been able keep under control, except at night when alone in the darkness. Then he was hard-pressed to believe his self-assurances that he had only been trying to comfort her.

He groaned in frustration as he splashed cold water from the stream over his face and torso. It was their third morning in this camp and he had risen from his bed as soon as there was sufficient light to mark his path. He was fully conscious of the sleeping Rowena as he left camp, his unwilling gaze lingering on the gentle outline of her body beneath the fur.

He was more than anxious to be on their way to Avington. There he would have not only the familiarity of his life, but the presence of his friends to remind him of what he was trying to do here. He intended to prove that Rowena was The Dragon's daughter, not to become involved with her.

He was bound by duty and honor to go home and help his aging father.

Knowing that nothing could be gained by lingering over his morning ablutions, Christian rose and went back to the camp. When he arrived he was surprised to find Rowena not only awake, but standing. As he watched, she bent and began to roll up her bed.

He went toward her quickly. "What are you doing?"

She did not meet his gaze as she continued. "Preparing to leave this place."

"But you are not..."

Her eyes met his then and there was stubborn determination in those mossy-green depths. "I am well enough to travel. If I were not, I would not keep it from you, for to do so would only cause further delays."

He frowned. How could he argue?

She finished rolling the fur and pointed toward Gideon. "However, I shall not ride astride."

He nodded. "I will take you up before me in the saddle." Though the images this thought created were far from calming.

He could not help but hear the horror in her tone, nor could he ignore the fact that she took a step backward. "Nay, I will sit behind."

"But you will not be able to stay mounted unless you ride astride."

She faced him squarely. "I will hold on."

There was nothing more to say. She was adamant, and he was not of a bent to argue. Yet even though he was relieved that he would not be required to travel with the distraction of Rowena draped across his lap, he felt unaccountably annoyed that she was so excessively reluctant to be held by him.

Did Rowena know how very close he had come to losing control as he had spread salve on her poor raw legs? No matter that he had reminded himself time and time again that she was hurt and in pain, he had responded to the sight of their slender length like an untried lad. Their velvety softness had awakened cravings he was hard-pressed to control.

He had done so by reminding himself that only the

veriest knave would act upon his desire with her in such a state.

He swung about without another word, readying his own belongings with undue concentration. When their fast had been broken and their few supplies gathered a surprisingly short time later, he spoke in as even a tone as he could. "Are you ready, then?"

She looked up from brushing crumbs of the bread Christian had brought from a nearby farm from the skirt of her gown. "I am." She stood and came toward where he was holding the reins of the stallion.

Christian could see no hint of concern in those lovely eyes.

So be it. He could be as unmoved as she. He nodded and swung up into the saddle. When he held out his hand, she took it without hesitation and swung up behind him, saying, "Please give me a moment before you start."

"Of course." He held the stallion very very still as she settled herself against his back, wrapping one arm about his waist. Not marking this intimate contact other than to lift an ironic brow, he waited.

Finally she said, "I am ready."

Christian nudged the stallion forward with a gentle pressure on his ribs. Only when he noted that Rowena indeed seemed to have a fairly stable seat did he urge him to a slightly faster pace.

But not too much faster.

Christian was only slightly frustrated at their speed, for at least they were moving forward. Anything was an improvement over the last two days with nothing to occupy him but his own disturbing thoughts. Even the sweet torment of her arm about him, the gentle weight of her slender form against his back, was preferable to that.

Chapter Eight

The next days passed in a blur for Rowena. The abrasions on her legs were better, as she had said, but other portions of her anatomy were just as unaccustomed to riding. She fell upon her bedroll each night, barely able to consume what food the knight presented to her beforehand.

If she had the energy to be grateful, Rowena would have been so. She wanted to think of nothing, not about her own uncertainty about agreeing to accompany Christian to England, nor about her unwanted and unexplainable attraction to him.

She knew that Christian Greatham did not feel the same toward her. He wanted nothing more from her than that she prove to be Rosalind of Dragonwick.

Yet by the fourth day of travel, Rowena's determination to set aside the attraction that had surfaced with such intensity was wearing thin. With each hour that passed she thought more and more about things other than her sore posterior, her aching arms and lower back.

She had become increasingly aware of the hardness

of Christian's belly beneath her hands whenever she had to hold on tightly, of the solid and masculine strength of his back. She sometimes found herself breathing deeply of the warmth, fresh air and sweat of him, catching herself to keep from sighing aloud, the scent seeming to make her feel languid and agitated at one and the same time.

She wanted to lie against him, to experience the feel of his hard body against hers as she had when he had kissed her.

Although Christian had been nothing but kind to her during the past days, his eyes troubled as he asked her how she was faring each time they halted, she knew that he was not enjoying the ride, either. It was apparent in the rigid line of his back and the stiffening in his body each time her tired arms slipped lower on his waist.

Could he be regretting his decision to bring her? Had some doubt about her being The Dragon's daughter entered his mind?

The tension in him was more than obvious as he briefly glanced around on the fourth afternoon and said, "We are coming to a village. Please pull your hood up."

She was surprised not only by the request but by the fact that he meant to go through a town. One of the few pieces of information he had volunteered was that he was deliberately skirting such places, as they had no military escort.

Rowena drew her hood up close about her face even as she said, "Why do you go there if you expect trouble?"

He shrugged. "I mean to buy supplies, and 'twould be some distance to come back from where I wish to make camp. And pray have no fear, I do not expect trouble. I simply prefer to be cautious when traveling with a woman with a face such as yours."

Surprise made her blunt. "What mean you, a face such as mine?"

He glanced back again, his gaze moving over her features, then away. His voice was without inflection as he stated, "You are easily the most beautiful woman I have ever laid eyes upon, Rowena. There are those who would not be above attacking one lone knight to possess you."

So amazed was she by this pronouncement, no matter how calmly it had been said, that she was left utterly mute. Christian thought she was beautiful?

"Pray do as I say and do not show your face more than you need to," he pressed.

"Aye," Rowena murmured, pulling her hood more closely about her face, wishing she could summon even a trace of irritation at his autocratic manner. But the warmth of knowing he found her beautiful prevented it, even though she knew the words really meant nothing. He had told her with his own mouth that he was not interested in her, right after he'd kissed her.

Still, as they halted some time later, she found herself watching him surreptitiously.

Christian went about the work of readying their camp for the night with quiet efficiency. Just as, she realized, he must have done on each of the previous evenings, when she'd been too sore and exhausted to take notice.

Guilt made her flush and move forward when he began to spread her bedroll upon the ground. "Please, I—I will do that for myself."

Seeming to be roused from some distracting thoughts of his own, he straightened and met her gaze distractedly. "It is nothing."

She frowned up at him. "It is something. I am not accustomed to having others dance attendance upon me. I will not trouble you to do so."

First scowling, then arching his dark brows, he bowed and handed her the bedroll, before going to take the makings of the evening meal from his pack. She had the uncomfortable impression that she had somehow offended him.

Yet she could not fathom why. She was only trying to prevent him from continuing to extend himself on her behalf. Holding her head high, Rowena made her bed. Yet as she did so she couldn't help wondering if her desire to look after herself was because she had always done so. Or could it be due to her discomfort with Christian in particular caring for her? Especially when an offhand comment that he found her beautiful could move her so.

When she began to gather wood for the fire he said nothing. He simply used it to get a cheery blaze going.

When they had finished the bread and cheese he removed from his packs, she sighed, running her hands through the gritty hair at her forehead.

Biting her lip, she looked across the fire at Christian. "I..." She raised her head, feeling foolish at this hesitancy. "I would like to wash."

He seemed somewhat vexed for a moment, before

nodding. "Of course, I should have considered it myself."

His reply made Rowena shrug. "You are not responsible for me."

The firelight flickered over those strong lean features as he watched her without answering. Feeling very self-conscious, she asked, "Where did you water the horse?"

He stood. "Come."

She stood in turn. "One moment." Quickly she went to her bag and removed soap and the only other garment she had brought. It was a shift of fine white wool, identical to the one she wore.

She then followed as he led her a short distance to a pond. The dimming light made it difficult to determine its source, but the water did not smell stagnant.

Rowena glanced back toward the camp. Though it was not far, the few trees and the pond's slightly lower elevation might afford her some measure of privacy.

She looked up at Christian, her gaze trained on his hard chin. "You have my thanks. I will return anon."

"You will have a care?"

She nodded. "I can swim. If aught was to happen you will be within hearing."

He took a quick breath and nodded, before striding away.

Only when she had given the knight more than sufficient time to return to their fire did Rowena begin to disrobe. But it was not until she had slipped into the water, wading in far enough to cover her shoulders, that she began to feel the least bit secure.

With that feeling of security came a great enthusiasm

for ridding herself of the grime of the road. Her hair she left for last, working diligently to cleanse it. Though it took several applications of soap to make a lather in the tangled mass, she finally succeeded, closing her eyes as she leaned back to rinse.

She was standing with her head tilted back when she felt something slithery and very definitely alive brush against her leg. A shrill shriek of shock and fear issued from her throat before she could even think to stop it.

There was no doubt the creature was a snake. Snakes were the only animals that frightened her. They had for as long as she could recall, even invading her nightmares as a child.

Still shrieking, and breathing as if she had run a thousand miles, Rowena started toward the bank. The water, clogged with vegetation, hindered her frantic efforts to escape from what she now saw as a serpent's lair. It seemed to cling, to drag at her limbs and hair.

She had not yet reached the shore when Christian came crashing into the pond toward her. "Dear God, what is it?"

Driven by her terror and panic to get out of the water, Rowena splashed toward him, sobbing, "Sn-sn..."

Only when his hands closed on her shoulders did she come to her senses enough to see the fear in his eyes, as he said again, "What is it?"

She shuddered, wrapping her arms about him, clinging to his strength and protection. "Sn-sn-snake."

The relief that came over his face was mixed with a growing amusement. "A snake? Is that all?"

Stung by his reaction, Rowena was for a moment too shocked to speak. Then, with an anger she had not even felt arising, her open hand connected with that lean cheek.

The ensuing stinging in her hand was what finally brought her to her senses.

With horror she watched as Christian's eyes widened in amazement, even as she felt her own grow round. She covered her mouth with her hand, crying, "I...forgive me! I should not have—"

"Nay, you should not." He rubbed his cheek.

She frowned with both chagrin and irritation. "You should not have laughed at me. I am afraid of snakes." The very thought of the creature touching her made her shudder from head to foot once more and she crossed her arms over her breasts to comfort...

Her breasts!

Her eyes widened even further. Dear heaven, she had forgotten that she was completely naked.

And it seemed that Christian realized the fact at the same moment as she. He colored noticeably, his gaze raking her before it flew back to hers.

Their eyes held.

Christian shook his head. "I am sorry."

Sorry for what, he was not sure. That he had teased her? That he had seen her like this?

Nay, he was not sorry for that. Never that.

His gaze slid back down over her, taking in her smooth white neck and shoulders, the breasts that spilled over her crossed arms. She was as lovely as a woodland nymph, her body lithe and glistening in the dying light.

He felt the muscles in his belly clench. His fingers

itched to trace those curves and planes, to move lower, where his view was obscured by the closeness of their bodies.

She spoke so quietly then that he thought for a moment he had imagined the words. "Do you truly think I am beautiful?" But when he looked back into her face he could see she expected a reply.

He could only tell the truth. "More so than I ever imagined anyone could be."

Suddenly and quite inexplicably Rowena was no longer afraid, could not even recall why she had been. She felt her gaze softening, and her heart began to pound with a very different emotion as her gaze flickered to his lips and back to his eyes.

Christian's blue eyes darkened. His hand slipped lower on her back, slowly tracing its way to her waist, where he halted, his fingers seeming to curve around that indentation possessively.

A tingling warmth sliced through her body and she shivered.

When his gaze dipped to her lips, Rowena felt them part, her breathing quickening. She dampened them with the tip of her tongue, and Christian groaned softly, deeply, sensuously.

The sound made her shiver again, this time more forcefully, the gooseflesh rising on her skin, though she was not in the least bit cold. Could simply looking at her mouth make him react that way? It was an amazing and strangely powerful thought. Never in her life had she felt more alive, more aware of herself as a woman than she did in this moment.

She studied his mouth—so sweetly formed, inviting,

yet stubbornly masculine at the same time. Without thinking she reached up to trace it with a finger.

When Christian had kissed her before it had been out of confusion and anger and, yes, desire. This time it was because there was nothing else he could do.

His mouth found her soft one with unerring accuracy.

The fact that Rowena tilted her head back, appearing to welcome him without reservation, only encouraged him to cast aside the last of his restraint. His other arm closed around her back, drawing her closer to him.

Rowena reveled in the feel of his strong arms about her, but was thwarted in her desire to be closer by the fact that her own arms were crossed in front of her. Determinedly, she pushed away until she could free them, then reached up to pull him back down to her eager lips when he looked at her in confusion. She threaded her fingers in the thick hair at his nape, savored the intimate maleness of the back of his neck.

Christian could feel the press of her breasts against his chest, and cursed the fabric of his tunic, which prevented the touch of flesh against flesh. He reached one hand to the hem of his garment and became aware of the water all about them.

He groaned. They were still standing at the edge of the pond.

Drawing back from her, he leaned his forehead against hers, taking deep ragged breaths as he tried to calm himself. She continued to kiss his cheeks, his jaw and chin, agonizingly erotic kisses that nearly drove him mad with need.

Calling upon all his strength, he held her away, his

voice hoarse as he told her, "Not here, Rowena. Not in the pond."

Her gaze focused on his. Christian could see the desire there—desire she did not try to hide.

Rowena had not known that desire would be like this—this aching, undeniable need. She could no more command it than she could any force of nature. "Where then?"

Fresh needles of hot and aching urgency spiked through him. He swallowed hard.

His gaze holding hers, he raised her in his arms to carry her back to the camp. To the softness of his bed of furs.

Rowena turned her face toward the curve of his neck, her lips gentle but oh so pleasurable as she pressed eager kisses against that tender skin. He looked down at her, his gaze finding a small crescent-shaped birthmark on the curve of her shoulder blade. He bent and touched it with his lips, his tongue, and she shivered, her arms grasping his neck more tightly.

It was all Christian could do to walk on legs that suddenly seemed too weak with desire to work properly. He laid her on his bed next to the warmth of the fire. The rosy glow gilded that perfect skin and made fire dance in the heavy tangle of her damp hair.

Rowena reached out to him, beckoning Christian into the slender circle of her arms, more alluring in her openness to him than she could even imagine. He came into them with a feeling akin to reverence.

Dipping his head, he kissed her lips slowly, lingeringly, before moving down to take the rigid tip of one breast in his mouth.

She gasped, her hips arching.

He ran a hand down her body, spreading his fingers over her lower belly and feeling it flutter beneath his touch. But when he slipped his fingers lower still, dipping them into her damp sweetness, she gasped and cried out as she made to pull away. "What are you—"

Softly, he whispered against her temple, "Let me please you." For some reason giving her pleasure meant more to him than anything he could recall.

Trembling, she eased back into his arms. Christian had to close his eyes to control the rise of his hot need.

Gently he plied her softness, and her breath came more quickly, her arms held him more tightly. And then she cried out again, this time with joyous release.

Christian held her until her body grew still in his arms. Though his passion lay like a coiled snake inside him, he was more concerned with her, holding her quivering form close against him. He pressed another gentle kiss to that crescent-shaped birthmark, and she shivered.

Realizing that she must be chilled, Christian murmured against the curtain of her hair, "When we reach Avington we shall have a proper bed, as befits The Dragon's daughter." He could hear the husky yearning in his tone.

Her words were barely audible as she said, "I may not be she, Christian."

He continued to hold her tightly, his desire for her infusing his voice with certainty. "I know that you are. I have wanted you from the moment I saw you, knew you for who you were even then." He punctuated the words with fierce kisses on her neck and shoulders. "This is only the beginning, my sweet. Our pleasure will grow over time. Once you take your rightful place I shall come to you at Dragonwick whenever I can. We will—"

He became aware that her body had gone completely rigid.

This reaction, following so quickly upon the ripples of desire that had just gripped her, caught him by surprise. It took a moment for him to realize that she was pulling away from him.

"Take your hands from me."

Christian could hear the dazed tone of his voice as he gasped, "What say you?"

"I said take your hands from me. I will not be used as your pawn."

He shook his head, his body going cold as he saw the anger in her expression. "What are you talking about?"

"Sean had the right of it from the beginning. You are not above seduction in order to get what you desire."

He reached toward her and she shrunk away from him. Christian lowered his hands. "That is not true. Do you really believe I would…that this happened because I think it will make you want to stay in England?"

"What am I to think? Clearly your lying with me will not be allowed to interfere with what is of import to you."

He took a deep breath. "I did not—"

She lifted her chin, her gaze challenging. "Are you

saying that I misunderstood? Are you offering me a proposal of marriage?''

He felt his face drain of color. ''I...nay, I cannot do so.''

Rowena pulled the edges of the fur about her with surprising dignity, considering the circumstances, and he could not help a grudging admiration. It only made him want her afresh.

But marriage?

He could not offer that. His destiny lay at Bransbury. Never would he have the time or the fortitude to do what he must for his father, while at the same time wresting hold of the chaos that reigned at Dragonwick.

Yet he would not have Rowena think he had only been using her. He stretched out a hand. ''You do not understand.''

She glared at him. ''I understand better than you might think.''

Christian stopped himself. He realized that to attempt to explain would be a mistake. He had to go home to his family, and even discussing it was fruitless. Better to let her be angry. Perhaps if she were angry enough, her outrage and resentment would act as a wall to this unreasonable desire. For despite his knowing that it was nothing short of madness, he wanted her still, even more desperately now that he knew what response she was capable of.

Rowena looked up at the high wall of the castle with some trepidation. They had passed such places from a distance. As they drew closer now, Rowena was shocked at the sheer immensity of it.

Into her mind flashed that old, but not forgotten memory of looking up at such a high stone wall. Clearly this was not her first glimpse of a castle.

She said nothing of this to Christian, who rode in heavy silence before her. She had said not one word to him since the previous night, and he had seemed content with her demeanor, except for when she had deliberately climbed astride this morn. Knowing this was the last day of their journey, she had decided that she could well afford to risk injury. Anything to keep from having more contact with the blackguard than necessary.

How it galled and humiliated her each and every time she recalled just how far he was willing to go to win her over to his cause. Yet if the truth were known—and she prayed that it would never be—she was most outraged and horrified by the fact that she had been such an easy victim. That a part of her still desired this man was more painful than words could ever articulate. But he had awakened a depth of passion inside her that nothing could have prepared her for.

Even to touch his cloak, to hold it in her hand to steady herself as they traveled, made her skin burn. But that was nothing compared to the unrelenting ache in her heart that had begun the moment she realized what Christian Greatham was doing.

He thought that by taking her as he had, he would mark her so completely that she would never go back to Ashcroft.

Well, he was wrong. She had made no commitment to remain in England, and would not do so. She would not have her feelings used by this man in his quest to avenge an earl long dead, no matter how justified it might appear to him.

All her mother had told her about nobles and their desire to protect their lands above everything came rushing to the forefront of Rowena's mind.

Why had she agreed to accompany Christian? What could ever come of her having done so? She knew so little of him, or the people he was taking her to.

Again she looked at the high stone walls.

Christian slowed the stallion. "Rowena?"

Not wanting him to know how agitated she was, she raised her chin. Then she answered with as much aplomb as she could manage, feeling pleased at the evenness of her tone. "Why do you hesitate?"

She felt the motion of his wide back as he shrugged, and she wished she could see his face. "I just… Simon and Isabelle are very good people. Pray do not allow your anger toward me to prejudice you against them."

Rowena spoke haughtily. "You give yourself too much importance, sir." She felt him stiffen, but ignored it. "I do not know these people or if they will welcome me, but I assure you that I will treat them with civility."

He frowned. "They will accept you."

She continued to hold her head high. "You cannot know what their reaction to me will be. You told me yourself that you mentioned to no one why you had gone to Scotland. They may not share your certainty that I am Rosalind."

"That is true," he replied reasonably. "Yet they will hear me out without rejecting you out of hand."

Rowena could only marvel at his certainty, as well

as wonder about the nature of such friendships. She sighed heavily, momentarily forgetting her resentment of him. "Can you be so very sure of that?"

He nodded and started forward again, his attention on the castle ahead. "I can."

Now that she had raised the question, Rowena could not quite capture his assurance concerning the matter.

How, indeed, would his friends react to her?

The stone edifice seemed to loom above them and a strange sense of unreality overtook her. It grew increasingly more pronounced as they passed through an arched gate, entering into a greensward with many outbuildings and more people milling about than she had ever seen in one place.

She was so overcome when Christian halted his stallion at the foot of a set of wide stone steps, outside a high wide inner structure also made of stone, that she allowed him to help her down without guarding herself from his touch. Nor did she take much note when he stepped away from her instantly and led her up the steps and through an enormous oak door.

She followed him, her eyes raw from not blinking, as he led the way down the center aisle of a wide room with a high, wood-beamed ceiling. On either side of them were castle folk setting up tables. Clearly the evening meal was not far off.

Christian spoke to an older woman, who was garbed in a clean woolen gown with a clean white apron pinned to the front, as she came through a smaller door at the far end of the chamber. "Beatrice, where is Lord Simon?"

The woman's brown eyes shone as she curtsied.

"Lord Christian, welcome back to Avington. The lord and his lady are in their solar."

Christian cast Rowena a quick glance before starting toward a narrow stair that opened on the opposite wall. "Come."

Rowena hesitated.

He swung around, his gaze finding her again. When he spoke once more she realized even through the fog that enveloped her that his tone had softened. "*Please* come."

She nodded, moving past him. After only the briefest of hesitations, Christian followed her up the stairs.

It seemed to take no time at all to reach another wide door at the end of a long corridor there. Christian knocked firmly.

"Come!" answered a deep male voice.

Christian opened it and she hung back with reluctance, watching him stride forward. Angry as she was with him, he was at least known to her.

From the doorway she saw that the chamber was large, but not overly so. She had a quick impression of tapestry-covered walls, high windows and heavy furnishings. A cheery fire burned in the hearth, and a man and a woman sat on either side of a chessboard.

She was able to glean no more than an impression of fine garments and regal bearings before the man stood. "Christian! Dear God, where have you been?"

Christian strode across the lush carpet with a smile of gladness. "Scotland."

The man came forward to accept his ready embrace. "Scotland?" He pushed back quickly. "We have been dying for news of you. Do you have any idea what a ruckus you have caused, going off like that without telling anyone? Your sister wrote and—''

''Aislynn wrote?''

''Aye. She said that you had pledged to be gone no more than a fortnight. She wondered if you might perhaps be here at Avington. Or if Jarrod or I might know something of your whereabouts.''

''Jarrod? Is he here?''

''Nay, he has gone off to Bransbury to search for you.''

Christian ran a weary hand over his face. ''Dear God, I have made a mess of it, haven't I?''

The dark man, who could be none other than the oft-mentioned Simon, said, ''That you have. And I expect your explanation to be a very good one.''

Christian turned to where Rowena hesitated in the doorway. ''It is, I assure you.''

Rowena saw that the other man was now watching her, too. There was a perplexed expression on his lean, handsome face.

Rowena turned to the woman, who seemed to study her closely from a pair of unusual black-lashed, violet eyes—eyes as remarkable as her other arrestingly beautiful features. A cap of scarlet velvet covered her hair and seemed a perfect foil for her ivory skin.

They all waited in silence as Christian beckoned her forward. ''Rowena, would you please come in? I would like to introduce you to my dear friend and his wife, Lord Simon and Lady Isabelle of Avington.''

Rowena could feel the lovely woman's gaze upon her. She forced her feet, which felt so heavy that she could barely move them, to take her toward them.

Christian continued. "Forgive my rudeness, Isabelle. For the concern I have caused you I am deeply sorry. I can only tell you that in a moment you will understand why I would behave so thoughtlessly."

Rowena saw that the lady was not looking at Christian, but at her, as she replied, "Your apology is well met. It is indeed a very great relief to see you hearty and whole, but my curiosity has been piqued. We have never known you to be accompanied by a lovely young woman."

Rowena felt herself flush.

Christian cast her a quick and unreadable glance, even as he sketched a bow to the lady Isabelle. "Allow me to present Rowena."

As Lady Isabelle nodded, Rowena could not help noting that Christian seemed different with this woman, more formal and courtly. He had never treated *her* thus.

Not that she would wish for it, she told herself quickly. She had no desire to be treated as a noblewoman. For, as her mother had told her, noblewomen were pawns in the game of passing lands back and forth between powerful houses. They were not respected for who they were in their own right.

As if his patience would only extend so far, Lord Simon prodded, "And who might Rowena be to you, Christian?"

Christian laughed huskily, and Rowena could see the brightness of his blue eyes as they met the other man's with sadness as well as an unmistakable trace of barely leashed excitement. "You recall the knight, Sir Jack?"

The other man nodded, though a puzzled frown creased his brow as he said, "How could I forget him?'' He reached to place a protective and possessive arm about his lady's slender shoulders. ''Isabelle and I owe him a great debt for his aiding us in our efforts to gain our freedom from Kelsey—a debt that can never be repaid.''

Rowena saw the sudden sheen of tears the woman blinked from her eyes as a husky-voiced Christian continued. ''Sir Jack revealed something to me the night he died, a secret with such profound consequences that I could not disregard it even though I could not be certain it was true.''

''What could he possibly—'' the other man began.

''He told me that The Dragon's daughter was still alive.''

''But, dear God, how…?'' Lord Simon sat heavily in his chair. ''It cannot be….'' He looked at Christian. ''Why did you not tell us ere this?''

''I had sworn that I would not do so until I could be certain of her safety.''

''What has changed concerning that?''

Christian watched him. ''There could be no safer place on earth than with myself, you or Jarrod, Simon.''

The other man nodded his dark head. ''That is indeed true. Were she to be found, there could be no safer place. For any one of us would lay down our life for the daughter of The Dragon.''

Christian reached to take Rowena's trembling hand in his. In her uncertainty over what reaction the other two might have to what he was about to reveal to them, she did not pull away as he spoke with barely leashed excitement. ''I have found her.''

The man was not the only one to draw in a sharp breath of shock.

In spite of her trepidation, Rowena held her head high, for her pride was all she had to hold on to.

"Dear heaven," Lady Isabelle whispered. "You mean…" Her wide and amazed gaze found Rowena.

Christian nodded. "I believe Rowena is indeed Rosalind of Dragonwick."

Those lavender eyes locked on Rowena's. The expression in them could only be taken for happiness. Rowena found herself holding her breath as the noblewoman moved toward her, her next words emerging in a voice filled with hope. "My sister!"

Rowena heard the words and felt a sense of unreality that was beyond anything she had hence known in a season of many unbelievable revelations. The very thought that she could be this elegant and perfect woman's sister…'twas too much to bear.

The world seemed to tilt, then to spin, and helplessly Rowena reached forward, desperate for some anchor to right herself. "Sister…I…" The spinning world grew dark, and then there was only blackness.

Chapter Nine

Isabelle's statement sent Christian's mind reeling. Yet the sight of Rowena crumpling before his very eyes jarred him into motion, and he caught her in his arms.

Isabelle's soft voice intruded upon his shock. "She has fainted. Quickly, bring her into the bedchamber."

Christian followed his friend's wife as she led him to their enormous bed, which had already been turned down in preparation for their retiring. Gently he laid Rowena's still form upon the clean white linens.

Isabelle sighed and put her hands over her own pale cheeks. "I should not have told her in that way. I have shocked her too greatly. I was simply so..."

Simon moved to put a protective arm about her. "Nay, do not carry on so, dear one. I am certain you did surprise our guest, but it is likely that exhaustion from her journey has also affected her."

Gently Isabelle touched Rowena's face and Rowena stirred, sighing, but did not fully rouse. She said, "Simon is correct. She is exhausted. Let us go to the other room."

Relieved, Christian sighed as well. He felt not only

sympathy, but a deeper sense of tenderness that he could not fully understand.

Once in the outer chamber he looked to the others. "I am sure Simon is correct." He caught and held Isabelle's eyes. "Though I admit that I am somewhat shocked by the news myself. How could you and The Dragon's daughter be…"

Simon arched black brows as if to ask his wife how she would deal with this.

She shrugged. "I shall tell it. I do not mind so very much. I realize I am glad to have it known no matter how painful. For it means that others will know that my upbringing with Kelsey may have scarred me but—" her voice broke for a moment, yet she recovered quickly "—his blood has not tainted me."

Christian could not help seeing that, in spite of everything, a part of Isabelle still loved Kelsey. After all, he had reared her, no matter that he had been a cruel and unloving parent.

Isabelle went on. "When last I saw my father at court, directly after he had bidden King John to put Simon to death for the supposed wrongs he had done him, Kelsey was so angry at my support of Simon that he revealed that I was not his true daughter. He said that my mother had been with child when she had wed him, and she had named The Dragon as the father. Thus the man I loved and revered so greatly was not the uncle I thought him, but something much greater." There was a catch of pride and happiness in her voice.

Even as he felt awed and moved by her tale, Christian could not help but be aware of the difference between her and Rowena. Rowena, who had known none of the privileges of her rank, was shamed at the thought of being a bastard. Isabelle, who had known naught but privilege and wealth, was secretly and genuinely pleased to learn that she had been conceived thus, if it meant The Dragon was her father.

Would that Rowena could be brought to feel so.

He was not left to consider this for more than a moment, for Simon said, "Tell us of the young woman and how you came to find her."

Without hesitation Christian did so, beginning with the night Sir Jack had died, and ending with their arrival at Avington. The only things he left out were the intimate exchanges that had taken place between him and Rowena.

Simon's voice drew him from his thoughts. "It is all quite incredible, Christian." He sighed. "No one would wish for this to be true more than me, or Isabelle, as you can see."

She nodded, her lavender eyes filled with longing. "It would mean that I do have some family."

"But," continued Simon, "there is definitely a problem here. Rowena remembers nothing. She may not be The Dragon's daughter."

Christian scowled, even as he met his friend's gaze. "Rowena is. I am certain of it. As certain as I have ever been of anything in my entire life."

Simon held his gaze. "You said yourself she is not sure she is the one."

"He is right." Rowena's voice came from the open doorway of the bedchamber.

Christian's scowl deepened as he looked at her, saw the way she leaned weakly against the jamb. Quickly she righted herself when she saw him watching, coming forward with her head high. "Forgive me for fainting that way. It has never happened before."

Simon motioned to the chair he had been sitting in when they arrived. "Pray sit. You are still unwell."

Though Christian could tell she did not wish to admit to any weakness, Rowena sank down upon the chair. She lost no time in meeting Simon's gaze. "I agree with you, my lord. I have no proof that I am the woman Christian sought. Although he was able to convince me that there could be more than coincidence in our circumstances, I am far from certain."

Christian spoke with more irritation than he meant to. "Why must you continue to fight me?" He was instantly sorry when he saw the way Rowena stiffened.

Into the uncomfortable silence that followed, Isabelle said, "I for one find the fact that Rowena is so willing to voice her own uncertainty a good sign." Her lavender eyes ran over Rowena with obvious approval. "Many young women in her position would leap at such an opportunity. And there is no denying that she has my un—my father's red hair."

Rowena sighed. "I realize that learning I am the one would mean a great deal to all of you." She looked to Isabelle. "Christian has told me what a fine man your father was and I wanted to believe… But now that I am here it all seems so impossible. Many people have red hair, especially where I come from. Neither any of you, nor I, can allow wishful thinking to make us see what is not there."

Simon replied with calm reason, though he studied Christian closely. "It is quite unlike you to be so hot-headed, Christian. I agree with Rowena. Much as I would love to see that bastard brought low by taking back what is rightfully Rosalind's, we must go carefully here. None more than Isabelle and I know what power Kelsey wields with King John, even to this day.''

Christian chafed under this reminder, even while he realized that he had been far more apt to rush headlong in his thoughts and actions since finding Rowena. Yet did not the circumstances warrant it?

Rowena distracted him by saying in a troubled voice, ''Christian has told me little of your difficulties with the English crown.''

He listened as Simon explained in concise terms how he and Isabelle had been forced to marry by royal command after Kelsey had falsely informed the king that they were plotting against the crown. ''In that and in other matters Christian has ever been the one to think matters through to their best purpose. Were it not for his bringing two very powerful men to court to speak on my behalf, when Kelsey denounced me to the king for the second time, Isabelle would now be a widow, our coming child doomed to his cruel and emotionless teachings.'' He put his hand on his wife's slender shoulder.

Isabelle reached out to cover his hand with hers. ''I would not have allowed it, love. I would have found some way of escape.''

Rowena could see that their love for one another was strong and it raised in her a longing for...for what? She found her attention becoming fixed on Christian.

Giving herself a mental shake, she said, "I would never place others at further risk on my behalf."

Christian scowled deeply.

It was Simon who answered her. "We will not invite trouble where none is offered. But if you are The Dragon's daughter, I for one am willing to do what must be done to set this matter right. I simply urge that we be as certain as we can be before acting, although I do believe that what Christian has told us is compelling in spite of your lack of memory. Rosalind was not even four when she...when we thought she was killed. If you are she, we will do what we must to see you in your rightful position. If Kelsey somehow manages to discredit you, you will always have a place here with Isabelle and me."

Rowena turned to Christian, knowing her gaze was accusing. "You have not told them."

He cast her a look of exasperation. "There has not yet been time." He turned to Simon and Isabelle. "Rowena's mother—the nurse, as I believe her to be—has schooled Rowena very thoroughly in the notion that nobles care for little beyond their lands and titles. That they are willing to die for such things without regard to their families. She has no wish to live amongst us, but came only to learn what she could of her father."

"That notion is utterly false," Simon stated with some heat.

It was Isabelle who nodded and spoke with calm and patience. "I know full well how difficult it can be to overcome the teachings of a misguided parent. We shall simply allow Rowena to get to know us."

Rowena shrugged, facing them directly. "Forgive

me, my lord, but if I have heard correctly, you and Lady Isabelle's difficulties could have been avoided if you had not been bent on revenge against this Lord Kelsey.''

Simon, Earl of Avington, frowned darkly. ''That is—''

Isabelle interrupted him gently to address Rowena. ''Simon had nothing to gain from his efforts against Lord Kelsey. He but sought to right a wrong. I for one cannot say that I regret his action. If he had simply forgotten his duty to The Dragon we would never have met.'' Those lavender eyes became speculative. ''Rowena, do you not believe that not only honor but fate must sometimes be served, no matter what we mortals might intend in our lives?''

Rowena shook her head quickly. ''Nay, I will not believe in fate. For if it exists it has doomed me to the regret of never knowing the love of my father, and doomed my mother to the pain of her loneliness. I will not be bound to the past. I simply wish to learn what I can and go forward with my own life as I choose.''

She saw the sadness in Lady Isabelle's eyes, but knew she would not withdraw a word she had said.

She carefully avoided meeting Christian's gaze.

Isabelle replied carefully, ''Then we will do our utmost to accept your wishes.'' She moved to Rowena's side. ''In the meantime, I would offer you a bed and rest. For I think it is what you need now, most of all.''

Blinking back tears at this kindness, Rowena followed her to the door that led back out into the corridor. She felt Christian's eyes upon her as she left, but made no move to acknowledge him.

For what was there to say?

If he had made some other reply, perhaps, when she'd challenged him as to his intentions toward her... But he had not. She did not really want anything from him. What she wanted most was to go home, as she had told them.

Her life, all she knew, was in Ashcroft. Simply being here, meeting Isabelle and Simon, made her all the more certain of just where she belonged.

She was a simple woman, accustomed to a simple life. Never would she feel comfortable living in such a place as this keep, surrounded by luxury, with all these folk to wait upon her.

Only the possibility of discovering who her father was kept her from begging to return home this very night.

Rowena looked at the pile of gowns upon the bed with a frown. She met Isabelle's gaze even as she began to shake her head. "I could not possibly—"

Isabelle interrupted her. "You could and will. I have too many gowns. You have only the one you are wearing."

"But I would not accept char—"

"I mean to offer none. My...father saw to it that I was more than adequately dressed in my life at Dragonwick. I shall never be able to justify having another gown made in my lifetime unless I find some use for some of those I already possess."

Rowena's longing gaze slid over the pile of rich fabrics, lingering on a velvet of so deep a green that she had not known it existed outside the most shadowy depths of a forest.

Again she looked to Isabelle, who stood watching her with obvious forbearance.

As if seeing that Rowena was wavering, she added, "Do you not see that you must have clean garments?" She waved a hand toward the pile on the bed. "These are what I have to offer, lest you would have me call my women to fashion new ones for you."

Rowena ran a hand over the rough wool of her own gown. It was not clean and had not been for some days. But she had never realized how poor the quality of cloth was until now, having never even seen fabrics of the kind laid out before her.

Was she being churlish to resist so? She sighed. "I...you are far too generous. Thank you, Lady Isabelle."

"Isabelle," the other woman replied.

"Isabelle."

The raven-haired beauty smiled and nodded. "I will leave you to dress, then. I am certain the gowns will need no alteration." She cast assessing eyes over Rowena as she ended confidently, "We are of a size."

Rowena could not help knowing that she took this as some indication that they might indeed be sisters. She realized that both of them were tall for women, but refused to put any undue significance on the fact. She said only, "We are."

Isabelle smiled with quiet pleasure. "Martha will come to assist you."

"Oh, nay, please, I would not have anyone bother—"

"'Tis no bother to anyone, Rowena. The servants here are happy in their duties. You will not be able to do up some of the lacings yourself."

There was nothing to do but nod in acquiescence as the other woman moved toward the door with obvious relief. "I will see you in the hall shortly."

Again Rowena nodded.

Isabelle paused in the doorway. "I am so very pleased that you have come."

Even as Isabelle exited the chamber, Rowena could not help feeling that her welcome here at Avington, the clothing, Isabelle and Simon's kindness, were all being accepted under false pretences. How would they all, including Christian, feel if they came to believe she was not Rosalind?

Would their attitudes change? How could they not?

Rowena could not allow herself to let down her guard, to actually believe she was Rosalind, that she had had a father who had doted upon her, loved her. She could not bear the way she would feel to see the inevitable change in their attitudes toward her.

In her attitude about herself. She would be doubly devastated to go back to being the unwanted bastard child who had been so easily cast away.

Martha arrived to help her lace up a pale yellow gown, the simplest of those Isabelle had given her, but of a finer wool than Rowena had ever imagined. When she was finished, having arranged Rowena's hair into an intricate braid threaded through with matching yellow ribbons, she informed her that Isabelle welcomed her company if she would attend her in the hall.

Feeling self-conscious, Rowena went to join the

other woman, who smiled widely, telling her, "You are indeed lovely."

"I...thank you, I...Isabelle."

The other woman nodded and motioned for her to follow as she said, "There is much to be done."

And much there was.

Rowena went along, listening and learning as Isabelle discussed the running of the keep with the cooks, the laundresses, the seneschal and untold others. When the cook spoke to Isabelle of her husband's bloating and lethargy, it was Rowena who said, "Give him green rue. It may be eaten or consumed in a drink."

The cook bowed with gratitude and Rowena nodded in return.

When they had moved on, Isabelle said, "You have my thanks, and I would be grateful if you would impart some of your healing lore to us here."

"I would be happy to do so," she replied. "I am grateful for the gift God has given me and would share what knowledge I possess."

"I love my duties as lady to Avington," Isabelle confided to Rowena. Ruefully she admitted, "My father felt I was unable to do aught but tend my own appearance."

It was clear that being lady of this keep brought her only joy. Yet Rowena could not help thinking that Isabelle's situation would be uncommon amongst her kind. She had the great fortune to love and be much loved by the man who had wed her, quite unlike others of her station.

Yet her position was dependent on the toil of so many. Rowena sighed.

"You seem troubled." Isabelle's voice intruded upon her thoughts.

Watching her closely, Rowena asked, "Does it never trouble you that all these folk have put their own lives second to tending to yours and your possessions?"

The moment the words were spoken Rowena wished them back. She had not meant to offend one who had treated her so very kindly, however much that kindness was based on her belief that Rowena might be her sister. She shook her head. "Pray forgive me. I should not have…"

Isabelle smiled gently, her gaze searching Rowena's face. "Once I might have agreed with you on that. I was of little use to anyone, including myself. But when I had the opportunity to take up the duties of my position, everything became clear. What I do here—manage the running of this keep and the housing of its folk—is of grave import. When the lands do well the folk of Avington have plenty. When they do not, Simon will provide from the stores here. If the folk are threatened they may come to the keep and depend upon these strong walls to protect them."

"But they might not require protection, except when some enemy tries to take the very things you say protect them."

Isabelle shrugged. "Is it really thus where you come from? Have there never been those who would take what others have? No invading armies?"

Rowena sighed. "I…suppose there must have been. I have heard tales of the Norsemen raiding farther up the coast from Ashcroft."

"Do those folk not band together under a strong leader whom they trust?"

She shook her head. "I believe he is picked from amongst the clans that exist in Scotland. He does not take his place simply by an accident of birth."

"Are not those who are chosen often the sons of great leaders?"

"I believe so."

"Because great men beget great men." She put a hand to her belly. "I only pray that my son will be as good a man as his father."

Rowena had already come to respect the other woman. She could not find it in her to dismiss her way of thinking out of hand.

If for no other reason than the return of courtesy where so much had been given.

She bowed. "You have given me much to think on."

Isabelle bowed in return. "I thank you for listening. Now, if you would excuse me, I wish to lie down for a short time before the evening meal. Simon insists." Her smile was fond.

Rowena nodded. "Pray do. The babe must tire you."

When Isabelle had gone, Rowena sighed. Although she was not convinced that the way of the nobles was indeed best, she did indeed respect Isabelle.

Yet that did not mean she must give up her own way of seeing things. She need not agree to take part in what to her seemed wrong.

While waiting for the evening meal to begin, Christian listened as Simon said, "There are some folk at Avington who came from Dragonwick after Kelsey took control. We must question all those who had association at the castle and might remember the young lady Rosalind. Even though they do not recognize her, changed as she would be by the years between, they might recall something that would arouse a memory in Rowena herself.''

Christian nodded, although a deep frown etched his forehead. "I have told you what she does remember of her childhood. Unless something is said that breaks loose a piece of memory that she is not consciously aware of, it will do little good. As you have noted, she was very young at the time of her leaving Dragonwick. Nonetheless, questioning your folk is as good a notion as any.''

"I will set my men to finding out who might be of help.''

Christian rubbed the back of his neck. "They must have no hint of why they are being questioned.''

Simon shrugged. "I will not inform the men of our purpose. Thus they will not reveal anything even inadvertently.''

Christian nodded. "I will join your men, of course.''

Isabelle spoke up gently, from her place beside Simon. "There is no need for that, Christian. We would greatly love the pleasure of your company after these many weeks.''

He shook his head, albeit with equal gentleness. "I cannot sit here at the keep waiting for word. I would much prefer to be doing something.''

He saw Isabelle and Simon exchange a glance. She bowed her regal head as she replied, "As you will.'' It was a gesture he had seen Rowena make, and only added to his certainty that he had found the right woman.

Yet none of his revelations had merit unless Rowena changed her mind. Frustration tightened his throat as he realized they could be doing all this for naught. For even if they did find some definitive proof, Rowena did not mean to stay.

He drew himself up. He could only tell himself that once she realized what her mother had told her of nobles was false, she would change her mind about returning to Scotland. Suddenly Christian felt a feathery tingling of awareness even as he heard Isabelle say, "Here is Rowena, at last."

He braced himself, as he always did, for the sight of her. Because unwanted as it might be, he knew that tug of desire would come, as it always did.

His gaze came to rest upon her, standing at the bottom of the stair leading into the hall, and he realized there could be no preparation for the sight that met his eyes.

Rowena was garbed in a flowing gown of deep forest-green velvet. The fabric seemed to cling to each curve of her form with unabashed sensuality, molding hips, narrow waist and full breasts that would have captured eyes less eager than his.

Christian's attention moved upward across the deep scooped bodice, over a long white throat in which he could see the beating of her pulse.

He feasted on each feature of her face, that stubborn chin that now seemed soft and surprisingly vulnerable. He noted the flush that rode high on her cheekbones, and looked up into a pair of eyes that had darkened to match the green velvet ribbons threaded through her intricately upswept hair.

"Is she not lovely?" Isabelle murmured in an approving and almost maternal voice.

Had anyone ever been more lovely?

Isabelle spoke again. "She is shy. You must bring her forward."

It was not Christian who rose to greet her and lead her to table, but Simon. Christian could not move. He felt as if he had been mortared into place.

Rowena offered but a moment's hesitation before taking her host's outstretched arm.

Clearly she had heard Isabelle's remark, for she said, "You are too kind, Lady...Isabelle. 'Tis the finery that has made me so." She cast a quick and appreciative glance at the skirt of the green velvet gown. "Anyone would be beautiful in such a garment."

"That is not entirely true. Do you not agree, Christian, that the gown is so well displayed because of its wearer?" Simon added gallantly.

He swallowed. There was nothing he could say but the truth. "I have never seen anything more lovely." He was suddenly beset with images of her looking even more compelling, her eyes dark with passion, her lips swollen from his kisses.

Rowena's gaze met his for a long and oddly vulnerable moment before it skittered away, and he could only be grateful that she could not read his thoughts.

She directed a soft half smile at Simon, then dropped her gaze, the thick fringe of her lashes dark against her ivory cheeks. "I thank you all. Now, please say no more, for you have indeed made me shy."

Simon helped her into her seat. "Then no more shall be said."

Christian felt his lips tighten almost painfully as he held back all that he would have told her—all he could never tell her. He did not know how he would ever sleep again without thoughts of her tormenting his dreams. He could never admit how his very flesh seemed to come to tingling life whenever she was near, how he longed to see her smile at him as she had Simon.

On the heels of that thought came the realization that his physical attraction toward Rowena could not explain the depth of his reaction to her. For it went beyond that. He felt a sense of wonder and awe in her nobility of bearing and character. The garments she wore only emphasized what he had already seen.

She would be a fine and noble lady to Dragonwick if only she would accept the role.

Surely that was the reason he was reacting so strongly to seeing her this way. He had neither the inclination nor the stamina to take on Dragonwick— nor the proud Rowena.

Christian spent the following day with several of Simon's men. They managed to locate a surprising number of folk who had been at Dragonwick. None of them had lived in, or frequented, the castle.

He did learn something that disturbed him greatly from a man and woman who had recently left all they knew at Dragonwick to live with family members. The farm of the man's sister was quite small, but the couple was clearly grateful to be there.

This he reported to Simon, Isabelle and Rowena at the evening meal. The man, Luke, had said, "Pray tell the lord that we are very glad to be here and that things are bad at Dragonwick, very bad. The people are hungry, the lands barren. The lord has locked himself up in the keep and makes no effort to tend to the estates."

Simon frowned. "Kelsey?"

Isabelle was shaking her head. "My f— Lord Kelsey has ridden out every day of his life. Although it is only by way of keeping command of every aspect of life at Dragonwick he spent his every hour overseeing it."

Christian shrugged. "Not of late, apparently."

Isabelle's face grew troubled.

Christian went on, feeling Rowena's attention upon him. "Luke said that never a day has passed that The Dragon has not been missed, and that others who are not afraid to speak of it feel the same."

In spite of his disappointment at not finding anyone who could help to identify Rosalind, Christian was gratified to see the loyalty that was still apparent toward their former lord. He said, "Once Rosalind has been brought forward there will be much support for her amongst the common folk."

He could only wonder what Rowena made of any of it. Meeting her gaze, he saw the horror in those green depths.

With studied calm she rose and said, "Forgive me, I mean no insult to any of you, but I have made myself known on this subject. I want no war on my behalf. Now if you will excuse me…"

She walked away, her spine erect, leaving Christian to wonder if there had ever been a wench more stubborn, or desirable, than Rowena.

Chapter Ten

Only two days after walking out on their conversation about Dragonwick, Rowena stood in the open doorway of the keep watching with amazement the events that were taking place in the courtyard. Yet as Christian greeted his newly arrived family, she also experienced curiosity and unwanted longing. She had little fear of her feelings being noted. The attention of all present was fixed on the two new arrivals.

Word that Lord Greatham and the lady Aislynn had begged entry had sent them rushing from Isabelle's solar, where Rowena, Isabelle and Simon had been partaking of some mulled wine in the cool afternoon. Christian had been noticeably absent, as he had been at each meal for two days.

Not that Rowena would allow herself to care. She had occupied herself with teaching the castle women what she could about healing. The fact that they were so eager and grateful for her knowledge helped ease her unwanted yearning for the dratted man, somewhat.

It was the nights that were hardest. It was then that she was beset with thoughts of how his touch had moved her, of how her body yearned to relive that experience, no matter how she longed to put him and passion in the past.

Roughly she called herself to task, focusing on what was happening in the courtyard. As did Rowena, Isabelle and Simon stood back on the steps to allow the three some measure of privacy in their reunion.

The girl, small and pale, leaned down to say something to Christian, and fell into his arms.

Instantly Isabelle hurried down the steps. "Bring her into the keep."

There were several moments that could have been chaos if not for Isabelle's steady nature. And soon Aislynn was in bed, tucked beneath a heavy coverlet, her exhaustion evident in the circles beneath her eyes.

Isabelle had only just turned and said, "We must leave her to rest," when Aislynn opened her eyes and raised up groggily.

Rowena listened as the others all spoke at once.

"Aislynn, are you well?"

"Do you hurt anywhere?"

"Is there anything you need?"

Holding up a hand for silence, Christian moved to the edge of the bed. "Aislynn, Father told us that you have been wounded. You should not have traveled so soon."

The girl raised a trembling hand to smooth tendrils the color of moonlight back from her brow, her delicate features and diminutive size making her appear ethereal and fragile. "I am fine, only tired. The wound does not pain me overmuch."

Watching her, Rowena thought she saw something

haunted in the eyes that were the same color as her brother's. The young woman sat up slowly. "I would meet everyone."

Christian did the honors. "Aislynn, this is Simon Warleigh and his bride, Lady Isabelle." When Aislynn's gaze slid onward, he added, "This is Rowena."

Aislynn nodded and Rowena felt the way her eyes lingered on her. "I am pleased to meet you all at last."

Lord Greatham stepped forward, drawing all eyes to him as he addressed his daughter gently. "That is quite enough for now. You must rest."

She smiled at him and sighed. "As I said, I am fine and feel quite silly about worrying you all." She turned to Christian. "I am most interested in hearing why you had us worry so."

He looked to Rowena and she moved toward him. At the same time Isabelle gave her a nod of support. Christian said, "I am very sorry, Aislynn, but I was sworn to silence by a dying man. I could tell no one." He hesitated. "I had been informed that The Dragon's daughter was alive and that I had to journey to Scotland to find her."

"Alive?" Aislynn's incredulity was clear. "But she was killed in Kelsey's attack on Dragonwick Castle, along with her father."

Christian caught and held Rowena's gaze, and she felt her heart thump with anxiety as to what Christian's sister would make of all this. "Mayhap not," he replied.

"Mayhap?" She looked to Rowena. "Are you The Dragon's daughter?"

Rowena could only return her measuring gaze. "I know not. Your brother believes I am."

Aislynn sagged back in amazement, and now Isabelle's tone, however quiet, brooked no dissension. "There will be time for this later."

Aislynn stammered, "B-but—"

This time her father said, "Nay, no more now. It will all wait until you are rested." Yet even as he spoke Rowena could feel his amazed blue eyes upon her.

She was beginning to feel as if she were some just-discovered creature, both fascinating and unbelievable at the same time. The thought was not pleasing. Raising her head, she caught his gaze as she passed by him, holding it.

He did naught but give her a polite nod as he allowed both her and Isabelle to precede him out the door. Once in the corridor he seemed to have lost interest in her. The face he turned to Christian was naked with joy and relief. "Christian, you are well?"

His son nodded. "I am. I can see that I have worried you and Aislynn greatly. I can only beg your forgiveness."

Rowena saw the moisture that glistened in the older man's eyes, which he quickly wiped away as he raked a tired hand over his face. She could not help being moved by this sign of paternal love. It made her long anew to know who her own father had been.

Had he been the kind of man who would cry at the return of his son or daughter?

She would likely never know for certain.

Christian was very pleased to see his father and sister, for he had worried greatly about what they must be thinking. He was shocked to see them here. His father never left Bransbury, and Christian's guilt over bringing him away from the lands was great. The injury he had sustained after an accident on his horse some years previous made it difficult for him to spend long hours in the saddle. It had also left him with a slow, halting gate that tore Christian's heart when he recalled the physically powerful man his father had been when Christian had left England for the Holy Land.

In spite of his concern and guilt, he found himself noting Rowena's dejection and wondering at it. Wondering if she was unhappy here. If she would be wishing...

He raised a hand to stop her as she moved away. "Rowena."

She spun around, her almond-shaped eyes wide, uncertain.

He went toward her, reaching for his belt. "I have something for you." He held out the velvet bag she had given him in Ashcroft.

After a long hesitation, Rowena took it, being careful not to touch him. Christian tried not to think about that or the fact that he had gotten the gold to replace hers from Simon days ago.

Surely he had been too busy with questioning the locals to give it to her. He had not waited until he need not face her alone.

He turned his attention to his father. "You said it was by Sir Fredrick's hand that Aislynn was shot, when she and Jarrod were returning from Ashcroft, where they had gone to look for me?"

"Aye, it was Sir Fredrick. He had followed them after having come upon them at a market."

"Your sister has been to Ashcroft?" Rowena asked eagerly.

"So my father says. But she and Jarrod did not stay long. When Aislynn told Hagar that she was my sister, Hagar told them that we had gone. They were forced to stop at Kewstoke, which is held by Jarrod's brother, when Aislynn was wounded. Jarrod is still there, as it seems his brother is ill. In spite of her recent injury Aislynn insisted upon coming here to find me."

His father gave a stiff nod, which Christian took as anger to match his own. "Sir Fredrick must be completely mad. I look forward to the day when I can make him pay."

"Who is this Fredrick?" Rowena asked.

"Kelsey's right hand. He cares for nothing but his master. Those two have wrought much ill in all our lives and will continue to do so as long as they are allowed."

Rowena stepped back. "I will leave you now. My lord Greatham." She dipped her head toward his father.

His father bowed. "Lady Rowena. I am so pleased my son was able to bring you home. In spite of the fact that we were so very worried for him."

She seemed to stiffen as he said the word *home.* "I...thank you for your kindness, my lord."

With that she turned and made her way down the hall to her own chamber. As soon as the door had closed behind her, Christian took a deep breath and said, "Father, I am truly sorry for the concern I have caused. I know it must have been great to bring you from Bransbury.''

His father put a hand to his shoulder. ''Yes, but leaving it is not so great a worry as it would have been in the past.''

''What say you?''

''Llewellyn has decided to treat with me.''

''How is that...?''

''His daughter Leri has married Gwyn ap Cyrnain.''

''Aislynn's intended. What the—''

His father held up a forestalling hand. ''Nay, have no care for Aislynn. She is well content with the way it has gone. Leri is carrying Gwyn's child.''

Christian took a deep breath. If Aislynn was not unhappy, then...

His father added, ''Of course, I cannot stay away indefinitely. The region is too unstable, but I would have gone when I learned that Aislynn was hurt at any rate. She has been a good child....''

Christian's stomach tightened at his father's pain. Aye, unlike him, Aislynn had been good and dutiful. And it was this realization that moved Christian to hold his father's gaze as he said, ''I will be a better son than I have been thus far. You have my word on it.''

His father clasped his shoulder. ''You are a good son.'' The moisture in his blue eyes told how moved he was.

It was his father's grateful tears that made Christian all the more determined to do his duty. No matter how his yearning thoughts strayed to a proud young woman with a kind heart and sad green eyes.

* * *

Jarrod Maxwell arrived at Avington only days after Aislynn and her father. With his raven hair and eyes he was the most exotic man Rowena had ever seen, yet she felt not one tug of awareness of him as a man.

That awareness was reserved for one who gave it no value. That he had returned her purse with more gold than it had previously held only served to remind her of his sense of honor. He did indeed keep his word.

Deliberately she kept her eyes from finding Christian as Jarrod stormed across the floor of the great hall. His cloak billowed out behind him and the dragon brooch at his shoulder flashed in the light of the candles as he approached the high table.

When all who had gathered for the meal began to talk at once he did not immediately reply. Instead he cast what seemed a resentful glance toward Aislynn.

Rowena allowed the conversation to go on about her, unheeding as she watched Aislynn's face. For her part Christian's sister seemed defiant and angry.

Clearly there was something going on between Christian's sister and the mysterious dark knight, though no one else appeared to note this as they all talked of Jarrod's recent inheritance, and Aislynn and her father leaving his brother Eustace's lands at Kewstoke without warning. Perhaps Rowena was so very sensitive to such things because of her own confusing and unwanted feelings for Christian.

She was pulled out of her reverie as she realized they were now speaking of her. Jarrod Maxwell's expression was as amazed as all the others' had been as he sank down on a bench, his gaze on Rowena's face. "Can this be true?"

Again she was forced to reply with reluctance. "I know not. But as Christian is so certain, I have come here to see if the truth can be found."

She felt Christian watching her with his usual disapproval. She raised her chin high.

Rowena turned her attention back to Aislynn, saw the way the fair woman's burning eyes seemed to collide with the dark knight's, and realized she knew very little of Christian's sister. The young woman had spent most of the past days in bed, and Rowena had taken her recent illness as explanation. Truth to tell Rowena had been grateful to avoid having to explain her situation to one more person who would try to convince her that she must take her place at Dragonwick.

As if reading her thoughts, Isabelle spoke up. "Let us talk no more of Rowena's plight for now. Can we not enjoy the pleasure of one another's company for a few brief moments? For we have not all been under one roof before."

There were nods of assent. Yet Rowena saw that Aislynn seemed to have little thought for anything other than Jarrod for she continued to cast unhappy glances in his direction as he talked with his friends.

Rowena could not fault the other girl, for she had been hard-pressed to hide her own hurt from those around her. She would very likely continue to be so no matter how she might wish it were otherwise. None of them seemed to note her own silence as the meal went on.

When Isabelle finally rose, suggesting that the ladies go out to the garden, allowing the four men to go to an antechamber to talk, Rowena was happy to comply.

She did not wish to hear of any plans they might have concerning her. Thinking about her feelings for Christian, being so near him, only served to confuse and torment her.

Yet she found her gaze lingering on those broad shoulders as she left the room with Isabelle and the clearly unhappy Aislynn.

They had not been in the garden long when Jarrod Maxwell came striding down the path behind them. He halted before Aislynn, his dark eyes fierce on hers, though his words were polite enough. "I would have a moment of your time, Lady Aislynn."

She cast him a haughty look. "I would not leave my hostess so rudely."

Isabelle smiled knowingly, making Rowena think she, too, must have seen the tension between the two. "Pray do not concern yourself, dear Aislynn. I do not mind in the least, for clearly Sir Jarrod has something of grave import to discuss with you." She looked at Rowena. "You do not mind, do you, Rowena?"

Surprised at being asked for her opinion, she said, "Nay, do as you will."

Aislynn glared up at him. "I prefer not—"

The words were cut off as the knight took her arm in a tight grip and fairly dragged her away.

Isabelle was smiling as she settled herself on a stone bench.

Rowena looked at her. "Are you not concerned about her? He seems very angry…"

"No more than she is." Isabelle continued to smile in satisfaction. She passed a gentle hand over her belly. "Simon and I, we have had our moments."

Rowena did not know what to make of this. She could not imagine herself becoming so openly angry with Christian. It would only reveal how very much she hurt.

Better to keep her pain inside her where it was safe. That was what she had done all her life. It was the only way she had been able to deal with her feelings about her parentage.

Not that she and Christian were in the same position as Simon and Isabelle, or even Jarrod and Aislynn. Christian's interest in her was due to his all-consuming need to avenge his foster father. Her kisses, caresses were nothing to him.

She found herself thinking again of Jarrod's demeanor toward Aislynn. "How can she enjoy being dragged about?"

Isabelle's eyes took on a secret womanly gleam. "Often what gives one the most irritation is also what heats the blood. She chose Jarrod. He is the impulsive one." She went on with a possessive look in her lavender eyes. "My Simon is the determined one, the steadfast one."

For some reason Rowena felt a trace of defensiveness on Christian's behalf. He might not have been all that she would wish for as far as she was concerned, but he was a very decent man, a most uncommon man. She spoke without thinking. "Christian is quite determined and steadfast if his efforts to find and bring me to England are to be considered. He is also kind and fair and respectful of others, even those who are not of his class. He even delivered the child of a young woman who had gotten herself involved with a man who was wed to another.''

Isabelle watched her thoughtfully. "Most amazing. And he a nobleman!''

Rowena frowned, realizing that she had managed to contradict her previous statements about nobles. ''I...he is still arrogant and willing to do whatever he must to secure lands and titles.''

Rowena turned away. "I will speak no more on it. Christian Greatham has no need of my defense.'' She found herself blinking back tears as she made a great show of examining a rose bush.

"Are you well, Rowena?'' Isabelle asked gently. "Forgive me if I have upset you.''

She shrugged. "I but pricked myself on a thorn.''

"You must have a care. They can get beneath your skin and are near impossible to remove.''

"Aye.'' Just as her attraction for Christian seemed to be.

Rowena was still in the garden with Isabelle when sounds of an uproar reached them from beyond the garden wall. The two exchanged a shocked gaze and hurried toward the arched gateway.

The sight that met Rowena's eyes made her suck in a breath. For there in the courtyard, mounted on his stallion, was Jarrod, holding an obviously shaken but strangely beaming Aislynn across his lap.

It was clear that they must have been out of the keep, as the legs of Jarrod's white stallion were spattered with grass and muck.

Christian and Simon raced up to meet them, having somehow managed to reach the courtyard ahead of her and Isabelle. Jarrod's arm tightened around Aislynn as he said something to the two men.

His voice was not audible to Rowena as she continued forward at Isabelle's side, but Simon's stunned cry, "Attacked by Sir Fredrick!" was.

She watched as Christian reached to his side for a sword that was not there. He shouted, "We will go after him."

It was Aislynn who lifted her head from Jarrod's shoulder to say, "Nay, Christian, rest easy." Her adoring gaze lingered on the profile of the man who held her. "Jarrod has let him go."

Christian raked an unsteady hand through his dark hair. "Let him go? Are you mad, Jarrod?"

The man in question frowned. "Nay, not mad, simply unwilling to begin my life with the woman I love in bloodshed."

"Love!" Isabelle cried, hurrying forward. "I saw it."

Rowena followed more slowly, hearing Christian say, "You and Aislynn?"

His sister lifted her chin. "Aye, and we will be married immediately."

Jarrod held her to him tightly even as his gaze found his friend's. "If your father will allow it."

She clung to him. "Nay, even if he will not. For I will be your wife."

Jarrod looked to Christian. "I would not have her defy her family. If you would not have me…" His black gaze was both yearning and resigned.

Christian shook his head. "Not have you, my friend? Who would I want more for my own sister than you who have been brother and friend to me? I am sure my father will feel the same.''

Lord Greatham, who had come upon them unnoted in the turmoil, said, ''I would be honored to call you son.'' He moved to stand at Jarrod's stirrups, holding out his arms.

Aislynn slipped into them with a cry of joy. ''Thank you, Father.''

Rowena watched this scene with an aching heart. Not only did she feel a sense of yearning that made her gaze linger upon Christian, she also found herself wondering what it would be like to be held in a father's arms, to feel precious and beloved.

And if not a father, then a man—a man who looked at her as Jarrod did Aislynn.

There was no point in wishing for what was not to be.

Jarrod and Aislynn were married quickly and quietly by the priest at Avington.

They had eyes for none but each other.

Throughout the ceremony Rowena found herself, time and again, watching Christian, who wore a velvet tunic of so dark a green that it was nearly black. He seemed remote and powerful, and so undeniably handsome that she ached with yearning just to look at him. For his part he appeared utterly unaware of her, moving forward to congratulate his sister and friend.

She told herself she would not have it any other way. She knew how he felt about her and would not have him guess at how deeply conscious she was of his every movement, his every word, his every smile.

She ran a self-conscious hand over the skirt of the burgundy velvet gown she had donned for the ceremony. The ribbons in her hair were the same color as the underdress, which showed at the neckline and in the long slashes on her sleeves. She told herself that she had not garbed herself so finely on Christian's behalf, but rather in honor of the occasion.

Although Jarrod returned not only Christian's but the others' embraces with great enthusiasm, he did not loosen his hold on the hand of the tiny woman at his side. His love for her was there in each wondering glance, each eager touch as they all moved to the great hall, where Isabelle had ordered a feast to be served.

Feeling an outsider in these events, Rowena lingered to one side as the others took their places at table. It was Christian, to her amazement, who seemed to note her disquiet.

Christian was conscious of Rowena with every fiber of his being, as he always was. Garbed in burgundy and gold, she was so very lovely that he dared not even look at her, after one brief glance as she entered the chapel and his heart began to beat like a battle drum. Yet he could not keep his gaze from straying to her, from seeing the way the burgundy velvet was a perfect accent to her ivory skin, nor the way her red tresses shone more beautifully than the gold ribbons that graced them. Nor could he keep his heartbeat from quickening when he noted the tantalizing curves of her full breasts where they pressed above the low neckline of her gown.

He knew when she held back as they entered the

great hall. He felt her reticence almost as if it were his own, and his desire was overshadowed by a need to ease her uncertainty. He wanted to reach out to her, to assure her that she was welcome.

He also knew how difficult it would be to stop there. His desire for her, as it had been from the first time he'd seen her, lay ready to spark out of control.

Surreptitiously he glanced back and saw the bleakness on her face. Against his own resolutions and good sense, he walked away from the happily chatting group around the newly wedded couple and held out his hand. "Come."

Her gaze met his, her green eyes widening with uncertainty.

He smiled encouragingly, watching her expression change to gratitude and another more troubling emotion, which called out to something fierce and unquenchable inside him. Although he knew her reaction was due to his being kind in the face of her loneliness, rather than any real feelings toward him, it was devastating to his self-control. He felt a tightness in his throat, in his lower belly, and wondered if he had gone very mad to put himself through this torment.

Yet he could not turn from her now, hurt her as such an act surely would. His disquiet did not ease as he placed her hand on his arm.

Even through the heavy velvet of his sleeve it was as if the contact burned.

Slowly, doing his utmost to ignore his reactions, he led her forward and seated her at table. To his dismay he realized that the only other place available was the one next to her.

He seated himself gingerly. Bringing her to table was one thing, making polite conversation with this overwhelming awareness between them was quite another.

None of the others seemed to note the heavy silence between him and Rowena. Even if they had he was not prepared to break it.

Perhaps it was his desire to focus on anything beyond the woman who sat so still beside him that precipitated Christian being first to notice the man who had come to stand at the edge of the dais. A tall thin fellow who seemed somehow familiar, he stood uncertainly, his cap in his hands.

Simon seemed to become aware of his presence in almost the same moment, for he motioned him forward. "Come, Walter. You wish to speak with me?"

Conversation at the table stilled as all eyes looked to the newcomer.

The man nodded, obviously self-conscious to have interrupted them. "I am sorry, my lord. I thought that you would wish to know that I have learned of one who may have known the lady Rosalind as a child."

Christian now realized that this was one of the men they had questioned about Rosalind. He felt the fine hairs on the back his neck rise, and leaned forward eagerly. Beside him, Rowena did the same.

"Tell us." Simon urged him.

Obviously realizing their interest, Walter spoke with more confidence. "My daughter, Laurel, she has just come with her husband and children to pay a visit. I was telling her that you have been 'round, asking if any of us had known the child, or seen her about the keep. I did not, nor did any of my family. We were common farmers. But Laurel tells me that when she was a girl she made a friend of one of the lesser knights' daughters. She says that this girl, this Jannelle, did know the child, though Laurel has not seen her for years.'' He shrugged. ''There was but one time after The Dragon was killed and we left Dragonwick. During that chance meeting at a fair Jannelle told Laurel she was to be wed and that she was going to live at a place called Brillington.''

Christian's father spoke up. ''I know those lands.''

Simon held up a hand, his warning gaze touching each of them at the head table. ''We will discuss this in a more private place.''

Instantly Christian was aware of how dangerous it might be to discuss this matter before those assembled in the hall. Although there were none here who would be likely to hold any alliance to Kelsey, even an inadvertent mention that they were making inquiries about Rosalind after recently bringing a strange young woman to the keep might arouse interest.

Isabelle said, ''The ladies and I shall continue our feast. We expect a full recounting of the details.''

Simon nodded.

He rose and Christian did the same, as did his father. Jarrod followed, but only after a long, lingering kiss from his wife.

As he left the hall Christian could not imagine that such a love was in his own future. When he married it would be to the woman who could best give of herself to Bransbury.

But the emptiness that accompanied that thought was so painful he could not allow himself the luxury of contemplating it now. He must attend to the business at hand.

The moment they entered the antechamber, Christian looked to his father. "You say you know of Brillington."

"I do."

"Is it far? Will we be able to take Rowena there or fetch the woman here quickly?"

His father shrugged. "'Tis no great distance, no more than four or five days. But I would suggest we find out if the lady Jannelle does indeed still live there ere we risk taking Rowena from the protection of this keep. Even though none know of her identity, her accompanying any enemy of Kelsey's would mark her a target. Sir Fredrick seems to have taken far too much note of what we do of late."

Jarrod expelled a heavy breath. "I should have killed Fredrick when I had the opportunity."

Christian shrugged. "Do not flog yourself, Jarrod. Even if Fredrick were dead, Kelsey has fostered hate and madness in many. Another would only rise up to take the knight's place."

Simon nodded. "We must keep Rowena here."

"Then I shall go to Brillington," Christian said.

His father held up a hand. "Nay, I am the one to make the journey. Lord Brillington, whom I know, may be far more apt to allow me to bring his wife here."

Christian frowned. "But your leg."

His father stiffened with pride. "I am more than able to perform such a small task. I have managed to keep order on my own lands while you were about your own affairs."

Christian stiffened with regret. He would only begin to rectify his mistake when he took over his duties at Bransbury.

He bowed to his father.

His father bowed in return. He then looked at Simon. "If you would not mind provisioning me I would leave upon the morrow."

Simon replied, "Whatever you require, my lord. Be it men or supplies."

Christian said, "It may aid in convincing the lady's husband to allow her to come if there is ample guard to assure her safe journey."

His father looked at him with approval. "Aye."

Simon nodded. "It shall be done."

"There is just one more thing," Jarrod stated. All eyes turned to him as he added, "Whilst all this is going on, Aislynn and I can go on to Bransbury."

Christian grimaced. "That is not your responsibility, Jarrod. I am the one who should go to Bransbury."

Simon frowned. "You may certainly do so, Christian, but what of Rowena? You have said that you gave your word to take her home if she chooses to go."

A heavy silence fell as Christian realized that he could not argue this. It was not his promise that kept him mute. It was the thought that she might indeed decide to leave while he was gone.

He would never see her again.

It was his father who said, "Though Llewellyn has agreed to make peace, it would be best if someone of authority was there in the event that something untoward occurs."

As they went on with their planning, Christian said

nothing. He could not. His guilt increased apace as he told himself he was just being a fool. The day would come when either Rowena would accept her responsibility and remain here, or she would indeed return to Ashcroft.

Either way she would be beyond his reach. The ache that thought brought could not be indulged, no matter how he wished otherwise.

Christian looked up from his contemplation of the drawing he had made of Rowena at Ashcroft as the door behind him opened slowly. Aislynn had brought the sketch back from Scotland, where she had taken it from Sean. Christian's father had returned the drawing to him.

Lord Greatham had come each night he had been at Avington to talk with Christian. Perhaps it was he.

Christian's gaze widened considerably as he saw Rowena slip into the room, closing the portal quickly behind her. Confusion creased his brow, but he said nothing as she came forward. His gaze flicked over her, seeing that she was garbed as she had been for the meal, in the burgundy gown.

He stood, realizing that he had been staring. He looked down at the drawing. What might she think at finding him studying her likeness this way? "Rowena, what…" He attempted to put the drawing behind his back, then sighed, realizing what a completely foolish gesture it was.

She came to stand beside him, her gaze widening as she saw what he held in his hand. "What is this?"

He looked down at the rendering, saying nothing.

She reached out and took it from him. "Where did this come from?"

"I did it the day I begged a sheet of parchment from you at your cottage."

"So this is what Sean took that day."

He scowled. "You knew?"

She faced him defiantly. "I knew that he had taken something from the table. I did not know what it was." She drew a deep breath. "I had not seen it."

He nodded, but she did not see him. She was looking at the drawing.

She turned to him, her voice barely a whisper as she said, "Is this the way you see me?"

The wonder in her eyes, the confused feelings he'd been having throughout this day, made him vulnerable. He could only tell the truth. "Aye."

She closed her eyes, swaying, and he reached out to her, catching her close against him. "Rowena, are you well?"

She opened those heavily lashed green eyes and put a finger to his lips. "Shh."

His heart thudded as he searched for reason. "Rowena, why have you come here?"

She shook her head. "I...must we talk? I suddenly find I have no words...."

Christian had no more will to resist his desire for this woman.

His arms tightened around her. And she bent to him like a string to a bow.

Chapter Eleven

Rowena had not imagined that this would ever happen. She had come here meaning to tell Christian that she had no more wish to remain at Avington.

The sense of longing brought on by the wedding, her acceptance of kindness and support from all those here under false hopes, pressed down upon her like a weight that could not be ignored. Especially after she had seen this very day that Christian had only to offer her the slightest bit of courtesy and warmth for her feelings to be sent into utter chaos.

Finding him studying the drawing of her, seeing the way he had portrayed her, had changed everything. There was no way she could fail to see the wonder with which he viewed the woman in the drawing.

Her.

All the misery of the past days evaporated like so much haze.

She sighed, allowing herself to rest against him, to revel in his strength. In all her life there had never been a moment such as this, when she felt so very safe and cared for and wanted.

She raised her head, knowing that her lids were heavy as their eyes met. "Kiss me, Christian. Kiss me."

He groaned, bending his head to do as she had bid him.

Christian wanted her, wanted her so badly that he ached with a fierce and burning need that weakened his knees. His blood rushed through his veins with such force, firing his loins so intensely, that he could not recall why he could not have her.

What a fool he had been to resist this wanting—this need that was as life-sustaining as breath.

His hands traced her back, her slender waist, the flare of her hips. He chafed in frustration at how the heavy velvet hampered his efforts to mold those lovely curves, even as he slanted his mouth to deepen their kisses.

He felt her arms close about his neck as she gave back measure for measure to his questing mouth. Joy rose up in accompaniment to his desire.

Heady as it was, he needed more, and pushed her gently away. "Let me..."

She resisted for only a moment, easing back as his hands found the laces of her gown. With more skill and speed than he would have imagined himself capable of, he pulled them free and tossed them on the floor.

She gazed up at him with heavy lids, her green eyes the color of damp moss, as the gown sagged loosely from her shoulders. Slowly, her eyes never leaving his as he did so, Christian drew it down to fall about her feet. Quickly he sent the undergown of gold after it.

His avid gaze moved to the fullness of her breasts beneath the gossamer fabric of her shift. The tips seemed to swell and harden beneath his regard.

His manhood rose at the very sight, and he had to close his eyes and breathe deeply in an effort to control himself.

Even as she heard him breathe deeply some inner imp made bold by her desire and his obvious passion prompted her to whisper, "Are you so shy then, my lord?"

"Shy?" He opened hungry eyes to meet hers. He pulled her close once more, molding her to the length of him, making no effort to shield her from his ready longing. "I am near unmanned by the sight of you. I but attempt to hold myself in check."

Now she cast her gaze down, a deep flush of shyness and desire rushing through her. The very passion in his voice and eyes heated her blood and brought a heavy wanting in her lower belly.

He whispered gently, "Have I shocked you too greatly, Rowena?"

Startled, she lifted her face, her unwillingness for him to think she did not want him overcoming her reticence. "I welcome you and your desire for me, Christian."

He groaned aloud, his mouth finding hers in a fierce kiss that left her head spinning.

She clung to him, relief and joy adding strength to her arms as she held his head to hers. She did indeed welcome him with all that was in her, with all her heart and soul.

Never had she thought to feel about another human being the way she did about Christian.

She was in love with him. She now knew she had been since the first moment of seeing him on the beach at Ashcroft. At the time she had convinced herself that her fascination with him was due to his being a noble like her father.

Now she knew it had only been her heart attempting to awaken.

What would have happened had he never appeared on that beach she could not even imagine. It was impossible, for as Isabelle had insisted and Rowena now saw, despite her reluctance, fate had decreed his doing so.

The realization of her love brought a new depth of wonder to her gaze as she pushed back from him and said, "Pray let me undress you."

Christian swallowed, leading her to the bed on shaking legs. He sat down on the edge and placed her hands on the hem of his tunic without a word.

She breathed in sharply and lifted the garment, drawing it up slowly. Her gaze feasted on the smooth skin of his chest, which was golden in the firelight. She tossed the garment aside, kneeling to press her mouth to that warm flesh.

Christian held her to him, reaching up to release her hair from its gold ribbons until it tumbled in a spill of fire down her back. His fingers tangled in the heavy fall of silk. It clung to his sweat-damp skin and he gloried in it and the fact that her sweet mouth was tracing a trail of desire over his chest.

Her lips moved lower, across his solar plexus and

belly, readying him, tasting him—Christian, the man she loved. Her tongue flicked out to trace his belly button, and she felt his stomach muscles clench, then quiver beneath her caress.

Hoarsely, he cried, "No more."

His breathing ragged, he pulled her up into his arms, laying her across his lap. He kissed her lips again, then drew back and set her on her feet once more before reaching down and grasping the hem of her shift. Her breath halted as his eyes held hers, then he lifted the fabric slowly, his gaze taking in each inch that was bared to him.

She held very still with both sudden shyness and anticipation, certain that he could hear the hammering of her heart in her chest as he lifted the garment free and allowed it to float to the floor. Her heart fluttered when he reached out to trace one unsteady finger over the upper curves of her breasts, his voice filled with awe as he said, "I told myself that nothing could be as soft and perfect as I remembered your skin being." His eyes met hers. "But I was wrong. You are even more so, for my paltry memory has no pictures or words that come close. Soft, luminous, the color of an exquisite pearl—none of these can quite capture the truth, though I have attempted to make them do so.

"Never could I even attempt to draw you this way with my meager skill. For the contours of your body are as God intended woman to be—even this delightful mark on your shoulder." He drew her forward, then leaned down to press a kiss to her shoulder blade. "My words, my thoughts, my hands, are too awkward and unworthy to form you."

Rowena would not have spoken in that moment had she wished to. She was overcome that the usually reticent and straightforward Christian would speak words that so plainly came from the depth of his being.

Instead she met his gaze with her tear-dampened one, feeling her love shining from the depths of her own being, uncaring if in that moment her heart was visible to him. She stretched out her arms.

He gathered her against him.

And then they were on his bed, his hose disappearing as if by magic, their skin touching without hindrance, their lips clinging without restraint.

Christian lay her upon the pillow and bent his head to nuzzle her breasts. His tongue flicked over a turgid peak and Rowena cried out, her breath coming quickly through parted lips as sweet honey pooled at the joining of her thighs. As if sensing her thoughts, her very feelings, Christian placed his hand over her there, holding her gently but knowingly.

And should he not know, after he had once before taken her to the very summit of ecstasy with his touch?

Rowena's thighs seemed to open of their own accord, inviting his hand to clasp her more fully. He did, his own manhood pulsing as he felt her damp and ready for him.

Gently his finger slipped into her, and Rowena sobbed with wanting. "Christian, please, I..."

He needed no more urging for he, too, had reached the limits of his control. He could think of nothing save being buried in those hot warm depths.

When he rose up above her she opened to him, offering her body without reservation. He was Christian, her joy, her pleasure, her beloved.

Her thighs were silken against his and he held his breath as he positioned himself over her. Never in his life had Christian wanted anything more than he wished to be lost in the sweetness of Rowena's body.

At the same time he knew that never before had he longed to make a moment last as he did this one. But he could not, not as he wished, for his body would not allow it. As he came to the door of her womanhood he grew still, realizing that he could not give free rein to his passion, lest he hurt her.

Rowena opened her eyes and looked into his, her gaze filled with longing and questions. He kissed her lips gently. "I would not cause you pain."

She kissed him back and rose up under him, pausing for no more than a heartbeat as her maidenhood was breached.

Christian shuddered as his straining flesh found its home, its rapture.

She held him to her, glorying in the tender way he took her. Rowena was woman and Christian was man as man and woman were intended to be—with no boundaries between them and limitless pleasure.

Slowly at first she began to rock beneath him, then gradually her body found a rhythm that she hadn't even realized she knew. She found it and urged him to join her, sighing as he followed her lead. She threw back her head, lost inside herself, beyond any thought of anything that was not the two of them.

He could not breathe, could not think past the power

of his need for her. His body pressed onward toward its own goal.

Hearing her hoarse cries of urgency and approval, he could not but revel in the fact that Rowena, too, was enslaved by the passion of their desire. He rose ever upward, carrying her with him as her voice became inarticulate with need.

Yet in some part of his mind he held on, knowing he must not reach that summit until the time was right.

It was not until she called out his name, arching up beneath him, that he gave in to the burning ache in his loins.

Christian drove forward in one last thrust before exploding in a show of sparks that seemed to shimmer all the brighter as she breathed her release into his neck, sighing with fulfillment.

He groaned, ''Rowena!'' then slumped onto his outstretched arms. Only after his heartbeat had come close to a natural pace did he roll to the side, pulling her into the circle of his arms, her head resting in the crook of his shoulder.

Rowena!

Even though his passion was spent he was lost in the scent and feel and intoxication of being here beside her.

Yet even as he realized this, he also realized that he had no right to these feelings, to this woman.

He owed his father, had pledged in good faith his intentions to be a better son. He would not break that faith.

Slowly he sat up and she raised up to look at him,

her eyes becoming confused as she took in his unrest. "What is it, Christian?"

"There is something we must talk about, something you must understand." She lay back, silent, watching him, her gaze now unreadable in the shadows of the bed.

Christian heard the strain in his voice as he sought to speak around the tightness of regret in his throat. "I can offer you nothing more than what we have just had. I must go home to Bransbury. My father and I...we parted on uneasy terms when I left for the Holy Land many years ago. I have been back less than a year. In that time I have spent very little of it at home, where I am needed."

She said nothing and Christian went on, trying to make her see reason. "My father has waited many years for my return."

"So you would live your life now for your father?"

"He is not well. Can you not see that?"

Lord Greatham seemed to have recovered fairly well for a man who had just undertaken a long and worrisome journey. "I see that he has a limp, but he is far from being a cripple."

Surely it was more than the state of his father's health that drew Christian home. It was his own guilt over staying away, over not understanding that his father was grieving the loss of the woman he had loved with all his heart. He had not meant to treat Christian unfairly, but in his boy's mind and heart Christian had not seen that.

He rubbed a hand over his face. "You will not even try to see it from my position. Jarrod and Aislynn leave for Bransbury come morning. That is not as things should be. Jarrod has his own duties, now that he has been named his brother's heir.''

Rowena glared at him. ''Why do you not go in their stead?'' When he did not reply she cried, ''It is only your determination to rid your conscience of another guilt that keeps you driving forward here.''

His lips tightened. He would not tell her how deeply he hurt at the thought of parting from her, of how it had kept him silent while others looked to his duties.

She held the cover about her. ''Please turn around.''

He groaned in frustration, but did as she asked. He heard the soft rustlings as she donned her clothing. Yet he did not look, allowing her the armor of her garments if she required them.

The next sound he heard was the opening of his chamber door. As he swung about, it closed behind her. He raced to the door and jerked it open, coming to a halt as he saw Isabelle standing in the doorway of the chamber directly across the corridor.

She raised her brows even as a deeply troubled expression darkened her lavender eyes. He bowed to her as he stepped back to shield his lower half behind his door, saying softly, ''Forgive me, Isabelle.'' At the same time he scanned the hallway.

Empty.

Isabelle nodded, her gaze remaining troubled, but she did not go back inside. As she continued to watch him he realized that she wished for him to do so.

Again he bowed and did as he was expected. He wanted to go to Rowena, make her listen, but he dared not do that this night. He had no wish to cause more embarrassment to her or any others, for Christian could not but wonder if Isabelle had seen Rowena leave his chamber.

His answer was not long in coming after he left his chamber following a long and sleepless night. It seemed almost as if Isabelle had been awaiting him, for she emerged from the opposite door in a long warm cloak and said, "Would you do me the honor of taking a walk with me in the gardens, Christian?"

"It is I who would be honored." He held out his arm, grateful that she was not too perturbed to take it.

Isabelle said nothing more until they were outside. There she paused beside him on the path and studied him closely. "I know not how to broach this subject other than to do so, my lord. I saw Rowena run from your room last night. I saw the state she was in."

Christian frowned. "The state she was in?" At her impatient expression he sighed. "I wondered if you had."

In spite of her obvious discomfort with the topic, Isabelle's gaze held his as she added, "Aye, I have thought that there was something going on between you for some time. I know when a man wants a woman. After last night I wish to know what your intention toward her might be, for it seems to me that did you wish to court her, to offer her your heart, you would not make such a secret of your meeting or your feelings. Nor would Rowena be crying as she left your room."

Christian watched her with a grimace of chagrin. "Are you asking me if I am considering taking her to wife?"

She nodded. "I am."

Slowly he shook his head. "Nay, I wouldst not have her to wife. I—"

Isabelle's expression hardened. "Then what, Christian, are you thinking?" Immediately she held up a hand. "Nay, tell me not, for I would save us both the embarrassment of hearing. Simply allow me to remind you that Rowena may very well be my sister, my only living kin, other than the madman who killed our father. Even if she were not, I would not have you offer her any less than the utmost honor. She is a good woman and has suffered much in her life."

She paused for a moment, then continued. "Even if it were true that she was the bastard child of some unknown knight, have you forgotten that I myself am a bastard?"

Christian would not stand by and be accused of this. "That is as far from being a factor in my thoughts as anything could be, Isabelle. I only…" He took a deep breath. "I do not know what to say."

Her fine black brows arched high. "I was afraid of that. Thus I must ask you to mind yourself where she is concerned. You will pursue her no more."

Christian bowed stiffly. "I had not intended to do so. What happened last eve was a mistake that will not be repeated."

With a jarring start, Rowena realized that their discussion was at an end, and she put her hands up to her burning cheeks. Dear God! That Isabelle and Christian would discuss her that way was mortifying, to say the least.

She had come down to the garden to think, to try to make some sense of the chaos of her life. Never had she expected to overhear this conversation when she had secluded herself behind a formal hedge. She had thought only of her privacy, of avoiding any chance meeting with Christian.

Once they had gone on she rose and hurried back into the keep, keeping a careful eye out for Christian and Isabelle. She would not have them see her coming in from the gardens.

Even as she hurried through the door of her own chamber she kept hearing Christian say, "Nay, I wouldst not have her to wife." Though he had said as much that day when he had carried her from the pond, the words hurt.

The fact that she would now not have him if he were the last man alive in no way lessened the tight, aching pain she felt in her chest. For Rowena did know that if things had been different, if he had wanted her, she would have gladly gifted him with her heart, her mind and her soul.

He simply did not want them.

She wanted to throw herself down upon the bed and sob out all the pain and loneliness inside her. She could not do that. She must hold herself together, must decide what to do.

For one thing she did know for certain was that she could no longer abide here. Nothing had been gained by her coming to England, not by her or by anyone else.

She must go home, back to Ashcroft and the life she

knew. It was the only hope she had of finding any semblance of peace in her life again.

However, Rowena knew that the last weeks had changed her. They had made the thought of living without Christian, no matter how much he had hurt her, so painful that it took her breath away.

Yet that was what she would—must—do.

She realized that one of the very things Christian held most dear in life, helping her to attain her father's land, was what made her untenable to him. He was convinced that he owed his future, his life, to his own father.

Thus he had nothing to give to her, even if he had wanted to.

Unfortunately, she had no way of leaving Avington without telling them. This would mean speaking to Christian, and to Isabelle, who clearly knew that she and Christian had...

Rowena drew herself up. It would simply have to be faced, and without delay. They would all be at table this morn. Telling them then would be easiest. She would not need to face either of them alone.

Holding her head high, she went down to the hall. Christian, Isabelle and Simon were already there.

She felt Isabelle's and Christian's close attention upon her as she seated herself next to the former.

While attempting to eat the meal that was placed before her, she cast a quick glance at their faces. They had become more dear to her than she would have imagined possible in such a short time, and she felt a deep ache of regret in her chest. Thus it was with a slight trace of huskiness in her voice that she said, "Your pardon. I would beg a moment of your time."

An expectant silence fell.

She especially felt the weight of Christian's blue eyes, eyes that had looked at her with such naked desire, but were now guarded.

Feeling even more uncertain with them watching her, Rowena took a deep breath. "I wish to tell you all that I have decided to go back to Ashcroft."

For a long moment the silence deepened. Then Simon said, "What has brought this about?"

Rowena dared not allow herself to even glance in Christian's direction as she replied, "I...it seems there is nothing more to be gained by my remaining here. No one has said a word of what was revealed by the man who arrived during the meal last eve. We are at a stalemate."

It was Isabelle who said, "But have you not been told? Christian's father has gone to a place called Brillington, to bring back a lady who knew Rosalind."

Rowena felt her eyes widen. "Truly?" Then she flushed, deliberately avoiding looking at Christian as she realized that he had said nothing of this when he had told her the previous night about Jarrod and Aislynn's leaving.

The shame of remembering their conversation and all that had led up to it made her shake her head. "But this may not prove of any help, at any rate."

Isabelle's lovely eyes pleaded with her to yield. "That need not mean anything. Even if we find out nothing more I would have you live here with us, Simon and me. Would we not welcome her, my love?"

He nodded, his gaze troubled as he took in his wife's sadness. Then he turned to Rowena. "Aye, we would be glad of your presence here."

Rowena was aware of that ache of regret in her chest again as she said, "Please, Isabelle, allow me to choose for myself. I do have another life, folk who love me and whom I love." Though she would miss this woman greatly, Rowena could not bear to be so near Christian even if she were willing to give up her other life.

Again silence descended.

Finally Simon said, "We must accept your wishes in this."

Rowena looked to him with gratitude. "Thank you."

Isabelle spoke softly, and Rowena saw that her lavender eyes were now damp. "I will not say anything more other than that I shall miss you."

"As I will you," Rowena whispered around the lump in her throat.

"When do you wish to go?" Isabelle asked.

"As soon as it can be arranged."

Isabelle sighed. "We must pack your belongings and ready an escort."

Rowena stopped her, shaking her head. "I shall take no more than I brought. Anything else I have attained here was given to the woman you hoped to learn was your sister."

Isabelle held her gaze. "And has been, be it only in my heart. I beg you not to cast my love back at me by returning my gifts."

Realizing that she could not hurt this dear woman, who had given so much more than garments, she nodded. "I—" Rowena could say no more, for her throat would not let go of the words without a sob.

Into the silence that fell came Christian's voice. "You will at least await my father's return."

She could avoid him no longer, but she was glad to see that that closed and unreadable visage helped her to hold her composure. "How long might that be?"

He spoke coolly. "Some four or five days."

Four or five days. It seemed an eternity.

The other faces about the table held expectation. How could she refuse? These people had been very kind to her, accepted her, wanted to believe in her, even if it were for the love of a man long dead.

"I will await his return."

There were sighs of relief and happiness from Isabelle. But only silence from Christian.

Facing him directly, Rowena said, "No matter what he might have discovered, I feel that I must go home. This life is yours, not mine, and I wish you well in your efforts to best Lord Kelsey, but I have no heart for it."

His lips tightened to a grim line. "As you will, Rowena. I did vow to return you home when you bade me. I will not break that vow."

"Thank you," she murmured amidst another heavy silence.

Without another word she rose and hurried from the hall. Her eyes stung with the tears she had not wished to shed before an audience. Tears that continued to run down her cheeks and spill onto her bodice as she slammed her door behind her, leaning against it for support as she sank to the cold stone floor.

Christian heard the hushed talk that followed Rowena's leaving the table. Yet it was as if he were listening to folk who spoke a language he did not understand. None of it penetrated one overwhelming thought.

Rowena was leaving.

Christian wanted to go after her to tell her she couldn't go. But he could not. It was as if he were riveted to his seat.

The ache he felt in his belly could only be caused by regret that he had failed. He had not proved Rowena's parentage. He had not avenged his foster father.

Yet as he watched her go, it was not The Dragon's face that came to mind, but Rowena's.

Christian looked up to see Isabelle watching him, her gaze dark with sadness.

After their earlier conversation he could not but think she was blaming him for this miserable turn of events. Truth to tell, he could not find it in him to think her wrong.

He also was certain that Rowena's decision was very likely brought on by what had happened between the two of them.

Simon asked, "Do you not think she will change her mind if Lady Jannelle can help to affirm her parentage?"

Again Christian felt Isabelle's gaze on him as she replied, "I think not."

Simon sighed. "We will ready an escort to take her back to her village with all honor."

Isabelle rested a hand upon her stomach. "Would that I could accompany her."

Christian frowned. "I brought Rowena here. I will be the one to take her home."

He felt Isabelle watching him closely once more. Again he knew she was thinking of their talk.

Given what had been said, he was not surprised, for she must wonder why he would wish to put himself to the test after saying that he would not make the mistake of being with her again.

Still, he knew he must accompany Rowena. He told himself that it was the right thing to do. He would not shirk his responsibility.

Chapter Twelve

It had been four days since Christian had spoken to Rowena, having avoided her as determinedly as she had him. He'd spent his time riding out with Simon, who, despite all that was going on, had his own responsibilities.

Christian sighed as he stroked the comb over Gideon's back. Though it had been a long day, which he had spent in delivering a message to one of Simon's smaller keeps some distance away, he did not wish to go into the castle. The only time he had seen Rowena in the last days had been at mealtime, and it was the most difficult hour of the day, in spite of, or perhaps because of, the fact that she had never once spoken to him.

So occupied was he with his thoughts that it was some time before the sound of raised voices penetrated. Yet as soon as the commotion did register, Christian knew without being told his father had arrived.

Even as a wave of unrest passed through him, he squared his shoulders with resolve. Either his father would have the lady with him and she would have some information for them, or she would not. What was done was done.

Truth to tell, unless the unknown Lady Jannelle had definitive proof for the maddening Rowena, whatever she had to say would likely make little difference. Rowena was determined to return to Scotland and her life there.

Was that not in great part his own fault?

Knowing there was naught to be gained in any of this, Christian left the stable. Determinedly he strode across the courtyard, meeting his father as he rode toward the keep. Beside him was a woman mounted on a white mare. Simon's men followed close behind.

So she had come. He could not forestall a momentary rise of hope, which he quickly tamped down.

They would see what she had to tell.

Rowena halted at the entrance to the small audience chamber. Although it was Christian whom she was most aware of, as always, it was his father she focused her attention upon. Her gaze swung from him to the slender, dark-haired woman of perhaps thirty years who hovered beside him, her gaze going often to his.

This could only be the woman Lord Greatham had gone to fetch. A quiver of nervousness passed through Rowena as she moved forward into the room, but she refused to acknowledge it. She could not allow herself to hope too greatly that this woman would be able to tell her who she was.

It was Christian who stood and motioned toward the stranger. ''Rowena, this is the Lady Jannelle. She tells us that she did indeed have occasion to visit the keep at Dragonwick when you were a child.'' She could read nothing in his emotionless blue eyes.

Rowena bowed. ''Lady Jannelle.''

The woman frowned, moving toward her, her heavily lashed brown eyes assessing each feature of Rowena's face. ''Lady Rosalind?''

Rowena shook her head. ''If they brought you here by telling you that I am indeed she, then I am sorry, for I have no memory of ever living at Dragonwick and have been told a different tale of my beginnings. Pray forgive me for being a part of your leaving your home and husband.''

Lady Jannelle's brown eyes softened and she placed a comforting hand upon Rowena's arm. ''Dear lady, worry not for my husband. I have been widowed these many months. And forgive me for seeming to question you, for all has been explained to me by a very kind Lord Greatham.'' She cast what seemed to Rowena a fond glance toward Christian's father. ''I was but questioning myself and my own recollection just now.''

Rowena did not want to ask, yet a voice that she knew was her own said, ''And what did you reply?''

She could feel the weight of the silence that followed, the weight of all their eyes as she was carefully measured by that assessing gaze. Finally the lady Jannelle, whose hair was as dark a brown as her eyes, shook her head. ''The truth is that I do not know. I do see that there is a similarity to The Dragon in your coloring and the way you hold your head. He had such a way about him, was regal as only kings have a right to be. You have that quality…''

Regal?

Rowena was amazed by this description of herself. She was one of the ordinary folk.

Lady Jannelle's voice drew her back.

"...yet I cannot be sure." Her gaze met Rowena's. "Are you completely certain that you recall absolutely nothing of your life before you were taken to Scotland? I know you were very young, but if there is anything, any small detail, I might be able to verify it."

Rowena tried not to allow the disappointment that washed over her to matter. She had known this would be for naught.

She told herself it was only her hope that she would at last have known her father that had been dashed. She had no care for being the heir to the lands that had caused so much misery for so many.

Not wanting any of them to see how she was feeling, especially not Christian, she raised her head. "I have two memories." Quickly she described what she recalled, though she knew there was little to warrant doing so.

Slowly Lady Jannelle shook her head. "It is so very little. I regret that I have nothing to add." Her sorry gaze found Lord Greatham's. "I did so wish to help."

Rowena watched as he came forward to take her arm in a gentle grip, the two of them with their backs toward the others as they faced Rowena. "You have done your very utmost, dear lady. None here would fault you."

Lady Jannelle's dark eyes seemed to hold his. "But I have disappointed you."

His tone was as gentle as his touch. "You have disappointed no one, me least of all."

Rowena, realizing that she was staring, looked down at her feet in the soft red leather slippers Isabelle had given her. Heavens above, what was going on between them?

It appeared that Lord Greatham had not given up on life as completely as Christian had imagined.

She sent a thoughtful glance Christian's way and saw that he was frowning darkly, clearly lost in his own thoughts.

He was very likely unhappy with Lady Jannelle's failure to identify her, Rowena thought. Resentment at his inability to see or care about anything but installing her at Dragonwick eased some of her own disappointment.

Yet it was with an undeniable ache in her chest that she realized there would no longer be any delay in her return to Scotland. She said to the lady, "You have my thanks for coming all this way on my behalf." She cast a sweeping glance over the others, being careful not to make eye contact for fear that any hint of sadness would make her waver in her resolve. "I thank you all for everything you have done." She allowed herself to meet Simon's gaze, for she knew that he was least likely to argue. "Now I would go home."

His dejected expression told of his regret, but he did no more than nod. "So be it."

She was aware of Christian's departure, but continued to keep her eyes averted even when the door slammed behind him.

Christian left the keep, going to the stables to fetch his stallion. He had a need not only for air, but for privacy, the privacy to think. To become accustomed to the fact that Rowena would soon be gone from his life without his having accomplished anything for their efforts.

As he rode, his frustration only grew. He took in the verdant fields, the well-fed folk who tended them, the peace that was such a contrast to his own churning emotions, with growing anger.

He could not help thinking of how different it was for the folk of Dragonwick and the surrounding lands. Not only was Rowena destroying his hopes of avenging her father, she was giving up on all the people whose lives would be bettered by her accepting her responsibilities.

He could not allow her to do that. Could he? Even if he had promised that he would not attempt to interfere in whatever decisions she chose to make in the matter.

Yet there had to be something he could do.

Suddenly he realized that it would not be coercion to simply attempt to show her how much her presence would mean to those at Dragonwick. Rowena was nothing if not giving. He had seen it in her work as a healer.

He would only show her what good she could do. Given who she was there was no way she could, or would, ignore that. With renewed hope, Christian turned back toward the keep.

He would convince her to give him the morrow. Surely he had a right to ask that much of her.

Deep in his heart he knew that if what he meant to show her was to matter, one day was all it would take.

If she did not respond immediately to what she saw, more time would count for naught.

The serving woman told him he would find the lady in her chamber. Christian did not allow himself to hesitate over going to her there.

The way Rowena had behaved this morn, he was unlikely to find an opportunity to speak to her alone, unless he make one. Her answer to his knock was slow in coming, but at last she opened the door. "Yes?"

Her expression grew cool as she saw who it was. "What do you want, Christian?"

Angered at her demeanor, he stepped through the door, forcing her to allow him entry. "To speak with you."

She stepped back, but her expression was tight. "I do not wish to speak with you."

He fought the anger and, yes, hurt, that rose up inside him. He had given her cause for anger.

Christian took a deep, calming breath. "I would beg a favor of you."

She looked at him, her brows raised in silent question.

Again he damped down his response. "I ask you to go riding with me in the morning."

She frowned. "Can you be serious? Why would I agree to ride with you?" She gestured about her. "I am preparing to leave."

He decided to be as honest as possible. "I know I have made you hate me. I cannot fault you that. I have made a jumble of it all. Yet there is something I would show you before you go."

She did not look at him. "I do not hate you, Christian. I..." She sighed heavily, closing her eyes.

"Then you will accompany me?"

"Will you then let it rest at last?" Her unhappy gaze met his.

He took a breath. "Aye."

She stood very still, taking a deep breath herself before she said, "Then I will do what you ask." But before he could even begin to experience the relief that rose up inside him, she said, "Will you please go now?"

He squared his shoulders and nodded sharply, then left her.

Rowena was confused, to say the least, unsure why she had agreed to accompany Christian on this mysterious ride. She had felt almost compelled to do so, driven by the quiet desperation she sensed in him despite the unease it caused her.

In the time she had known him Rowena had realized that three things mattered to Christian: His family, his friends, and avenging his foster father. Somehow she was sure that this outing was connected to his need for vengeance, else he would not have bidden her to come with him.

That certainty made her all the more uneasy about doing so.

Yet she had agreed. She did wish to admit that it was very likely because of the fact that she did not, as he imagined, hate him. Quite the contrary, in spite of all he had done to hurt her, she continued to love him with all of her wayward heart.

Thus she garbed herself in one of the gowns Isabelle had given her—a lovely, heavy garment of mauve velvet—and a dark blue cape, and met him in the courtyard. Christian wore a long black velvet cape over his own clothing, the front held together with his dragon brooch.

He bowed as the servant he had sent to fetch her led her out to him, but said only, "Good morrow."

She returned the greeting just as coolly.

It was the servant who helped her mount. From atop the mare, Rowena cast Christian a nervous glance.

He seemed to read her thoughts, for he said, "I will go slowly. I have not forgotten your inexperience with horses."

She did not welcome the rush of warmth this brought, and hurriedly looked away. Nothing had changed between them.

When he showed her how to hold the reins properly, asking if she thought she could manage, she nodded without looking at him.

Sighing, he said, "Have no fear. The mare is gentle and will follow Gideon."

Again she nodded. Frowning now, he mounted and nudged the stallion forward.

True to his statement, the mare did follow, and Rowena was forced to give her attention to riding. Although she had certainly had opportunity to grow accustomed to it when she'd ridden with Christian, riding a horse was still far from familiar.

In spite of his obvious distraction now that they were on their way, Christian clearly made an effort to keep his own restive stallion restrained. Because of this, Ro-

wena soon found that she was able to place less and
less of her attention upon riding.

Had she been less nervous, she might have enjoyed
the journey through the lush countryside. First they
passed through the village resting in the shadow of the
castle, then on into patches of forest and across now-
dormant fields.

Everywhere they went they came upon the people
who lived upon the lands, all busy with their own tasks.
As Rowena and Christian passed, hands were raised in
greeting, bows were exchanged and sometimes offers
of refreshment were made.

It went on like that for all of the morning, with Rowena and Christian exchanging few words between
them. Though she continued to puzzle over what they
were about, her curiosity grew with each mile they traversed.

Yet Rowena asked no questions. She would not give
Christian the satisfaction of questioning him, but
waited for him to talk to her.

They broke their fast with food Christian had
brought, each lost in thought. It was not until some
time after they started on again that Rowena sensed a
change in the man riding with her, a subtle tension that
put her on the alert.

She studied his mounted form ahead of her on the
trail, trying to determine what troubled him. There was
an even deeper rigidness to the set of his shoulders, as
if the muscle had hardened to the consistency of bone.
There was a faint air of distaste in the flare of his nos-
trils that had not been there before. And his hands on
the reins seemed to move less supply, his knees to grip

the animal beneath him more tightly as he scanned the countryside about them.

To one who was less attuned to him than she, Rowena realized, the changes in Christian might have gone quite unnoticed.

At the top of a hill she ran her gaze over the countryside spread out before them, trying to fathom what could have wrought this change in his demeanor. At first she could mark no reason as she eyed rolling hills with their fallow fields and tufts of green forest. Yet as she looked about, she realized that something was different. It was not so much visible as something subtle that left her feeling as if her former impression, of the fields lying in rest for the new life that would come in spring, had been mistaken. She now had a sense of bleakness, a barren chill that told her that sustenance would be coaxed from this earth with great toil and suffering.

Her mare followed Gideon down the hill and into a stand of forest. As they passed among the trees Rowena noted that the shadows seemed darker here and that their inky depths seemed to hold a lurking menace.

She found herself breaking her determination to keep from questioning him before she knew that she would do so, her voice husky with unease. "Where are we going, Christian?"

He slowed, dropping back to ride beside her, his gaze earnest. "Trust me."

She wet her lips with the tip of her tongue as she cast another trepidant glance about. Yet in spite of her anxiety, she nodded.

Soon they were out in the open again.

Rowena would have breathed a sigh of relief, but her feelings of unease continued to hover close as they rode across barren fields. The folk working there made no effort to greet them as people had throughout the morning. They kept their eyes downcast, most falling to their knees until the two of them had passed.

Finally, as they rode through yet another dark and foreboding stretch of forest, Rowena could stand no more, for a sneaking suspicion was beginning to creep into her consciousness. She urged her mount closer to Christian's, demanding, "What is this? Where have you brought me?"

His gaze met hers without apology. "Dragonwick."

She drew to an abrupt halt, as did he. "I thought as much. Did you imagine that I would somehow find it all familiar, that I would be able to tell you I remember any of this?"

He shook his head. "I thought it was possible, but that was not my true intent."

"Then why are we here?"

"Why? So you could see the state of things for yourself, of course. I thought…"

She put one hand to her hip. "You thought I would see that I must fight on. You thought I would do whatever I must to gain the right to take on the responsibility of all this." She gestured widely. "You thought I would want to make it better."

He frowned with obvious chagrin. "I did think that if you would only look about you you would see—"

She shook her head. "It is you who do not see. What could I do for them? If you could somehow prove that I am the woman *you* hope I am, I doubt any of these folk would thank you. For it would only mean war and more privation for them. You know as well as I that this man, this Kelsey, would not simply give up his lands to a mere girl, especially when he has the friendship of a king to bolster him. And what good would I be to them once they got me?''

''They would gain one who would care for their well-being.''

She threw her hands wide. ''I ask again, what good would I be to them? I know nothing of any of this. I know herbs and healing, not running great estates.''

''That can be taught.''

''I do not wish to learn.''

He sat there, his lips tight. ''Then there is nothing more to say.'' He bowed. ''Let us return to Avington.''

''Yes, let us.'' Forgetting her inexperience, Rowena jerked the reins to turn her mount, as she had seen Christian do. The mare, startled at this unexpected command, spun about too quickly.

One moment Rowena was in the saddle, the next she was on the ground.

So shocked was she that it took her a moment to realize that it was her pride that ached, more than her backside, though that portion of her anatomy had not gone completely unscathed.

Christian was on the ground beside her in an instant. ''God's teeth, Rowena, are you mad?''

''Yes, sir, I am. Quite mad. Else I would surely not find myself out here with you.''

When Christian reached out to her she scowled up at him. ''Pray leave me be. I can manage.''

With a thunderous expression he drew his hand back

and watched as she gained her feet. She wanted to rub her abused bottom but would not give him the satisfaction of knowing that it hurt.

Instead she raised her head high and felt she was completely successful in disguising her pain as she looked about for the offending mare. "What has happened to her?"

He spoke through tight lips. "She's run back to Avington in self-preservation."

Rowena refused to dignify the remark with a reply.

As he went on she could hear the barely leashed rage in his voice. "How can you ignore your responsibilities? Your birthright?"

Frustrated, Rowena turned in a circle, unable to fathom what she should do, knowing only that she wanted to be away from this man. How had her ordered and relatively happy life changed so very greatly in such a short period of time? For in spite of her sadness at not knowing her father, she had understood her place in the scheme of things.

Now she no longer knew anything about anything.

She glared at him. "You speak of your own version of my responsibility and birthright." She folded her arms over her chest. "You want to destroy everything I have ever known or believed in."

He glared back, his lips tight as he said, "What you knew was a lie."

She took a step closer to him, uncaring that she had to tilt her head back to look up at him. All she cared about was the fact that from the day she had first seen him washed up on the beach, Christian Greatham had brought her naught but confusion. That a good portion of her confusion was due to her own unresolved feelings of attraction for him was utterly irrelevant. She heard the harshness and uncertainty of her own anger as she exclaimed, "You cannot be sure of that. We have learned nothing that proves I am Rosalind of Dragonwick. You only wish it to be true so badly that you cannot see the lack of evidence as proof that I am not."

He groaned, balling his fists at his sides. "And you refuse to see anything we do know as proof that you are."

"You are impossible!" She turned her back to him, folding her arms across her chest as she stared down the path from whence they had come.

Chapter Thirteen

He was impossible?

Did the wench really imagine that he would simply allow her to walk back to Avington alone, even if she did know the way? Christian's mind whirled with rage and frustration.

He reached for Rowena, spinning her around to face him. She tried to pull away and he knew a renewed sense of frustration that made his body tighten as if a coiled snake inside him lay ready to strike.

He held her tight with a hand on each forearm, and she met his gaze with open challenge.

God rot his soul that he could still find her so beautiful, desirable, with that delicate nose turned skyward and her chin tilted with angry pride.

In spite of his fury, he tried for calm, knowing that his anger had never gotten him anywhere with her. "Where are you going?"

She did look at him then, but her green eyes were stormy as a wind-tossed sea and there was no yielding in them. "You broke your word to me. You swore that you would not attempt to force me to—"

Broken his word? Forced her? Christian had fought his every desire as far as this woman was concerned, and still she accused him.

Very well then.

If he was to be accused...

Without another thought, he pulled her forward into his arms as he had wished to do each and every moment since last he had done so. A soft gasp of shock escaped that sweet mouth, and he silenced it with his lips.

She struggled against him, but only for a moment, before her lips softened under his and she tilted her head back even farther, inviting an even deeper contact. Christian knew a brief instant of amazement at her reaction, yet he was happy to oblige her desire, kissing her with a thoroughness that made his own head spin with wanting.

Her response was to reach up, drawing his head down to her even as she strained against him.

Christian's arms tightened around her slender form. There was no mistaking her yielding, her need.

He lifted her in his arms and laid her down upon the ground. Her cloak spread out around her, creating a spill of blue in the bed of autumn leaves.

Rowena could not fight this, had no desire to do so. The moment his mouth found hers the fires that she had thought so carefully banked inside her burst into blazing life.

She had only been fooling herself to think she could resist her feelings for Christian. She would never stop wanting this man, loving him with every fiber of her being.

When he attempted to pull back, Rowena clung to him with her arms, her lips, her being. She could not bear for him to leave her now, not with this ache of desire so hot and wet inside her.

It must be slaked.

But when he leaned down to whisper, his breath hot and intimate against her ear, "I would free my flesh to better feel yours," she gasped with a renewed rush of passion and let him go.

Christian watched her as she lay there, her eyes hungry with desire, and his body ached all the more as he tossed his tunic aside. As he removed his hose, he found himself unable to look at her. He was afraid that her wanting would only unman him, when he so desperately wished to give both of them pleasure.

When he had shed the rest of his garments and turned back to her, he saw that Rowena was seeking to draw her gown up to her hips.

Moving to stop her with a hand that trembled with ill-suppressed longing, Christian held her startled gaze with his. "Nay, I would not let you rob me of the pleasure of this task."

Rowena gave a deliciously pleasurable shiver under that hot gaze. She caught her breath as a deeply arousing and lascivious smile curved those sensuous lips. She whispered, "As you will, my lord."

Christian watched as she slowly and deliberately pulled her gown back down so that it covered her all the way to the tips of her toes. Then she lay back, her hands behind her head, her eyes inviting his attention.

A thrill of desire shot through him and he surged forward to place his lips at the hem of her garment.

Then, with a delicateness born of his sheer pleasure in his task, he slipped her gown up to uncover a pair of red leather slippers. Slowly he slipped off one, then the other, exposing slender and shapely feet.

Rowena sighed as he uncovered her feet, anticipating the moment when she would be bared in preparation of their joining. But as his mouth touched her toes, her instep, her ankles, exploring skin she had never given more than a cursory thought, she found her breath quickening, and tremor after tremor raced up her body.

Christian had never kissed or explored a woman in this way, had never thought to do so. But something inside him made him long to know each and every inch of the woman before him as he had never known another human being.

He kissed her ankles, her calves, pausing at the lovely angles of her knees, removing her clothing from his path as he went. All the while he was aware of the way she quivered at every caress. Unexpectedly, her reactions seemed to dampen his own passion. For he found himself longing to give her the sweetest and greatest of pleasures above all else.

Yet when he reached the tops of her tights, it was his belly that spasmed, his breath that caught in his throat as she grew very still, her body rigid with expectancy. Nay, not yet; he could not cut their loving short no matter how the thought of her wanting enflamed him.

Rowena felt as if her body was a bow, pulled tighter and tighter with each kiss, each touch, each delicate flick of Christian's tongue on her eager flesh. When he hesitated there at the tops of her thighs she thought she might die of sheer anticipation. But he drew away, raising up to lean over her. Rowena's body seemed to cry out with aching disappointment.

Her disappointment instantly dissolved when his scorching mouth found hers, communicating his ardor. "Rowena."

"Christian." She surged toward him, inviting him.

He kissed her again and once more pulled away, urging her up with him. At first she clung to him, but when he put his hands on the hem of her gown she released him, not having to be told what he wanted. Eagerly she sat up, looking out from half-closed lids as she raised her arms and he drew her garments over her head.

Once bared, she lay back down, holding out her arms in welcome. For one long moment his gaze moved over her, his eyes darkening to indigo, before he came to her.

Christian had forgotten how exquisite she was, with her high firm breasts, narrow waist and perfectly proportioned hips. Yet, as he had told her before, how could any man be expected to recall such beauty from memory?

He kissed her once more on the mouth, then traced a trail of wonder down her throat, across her collarbone, until he at last found the rise of her breast. He lingered there, savoring the smooth softness of that curve, breathing in the warmth and womanly essence of her, which seemed both musky and fresh at the same time.

She gasped with new rapture as his mouth closed on her nipple and he suckled first one breast and then its sister. As he did so they seemed to harden and swell, as if bidding him to attend them further, to pleasure them.

Rowena had thought she burned before, but Christian's attentions to her breasts were as a spark to a keg of hot oil. She arched up beneath him, her hips seeming to search for him of their own accord. "I...oh, Christian, no more. I am afire."

Christian knew that he, too, could take little more than this. Her reactions to his loving were as heady, as passionate, as any physical joy he had ever known. Without even trying she had moved him to the brink of a craving that was so intense it left him quivering with need.

He rose over her, and found that there was no need to part her thighs, for she lay open and waiting for him. He slipped into that moist, beckoning darkness with a groan of elation and relief.

Then both those emotions were drowned in wave after wave of inexplicable delight. They crashed over him, through him, leaving him gasping at their intensity.

Rowena felt the rhythm of his body and responded in kind, eager to welcome him into her being. She was climbing ever higher on the wings of the passion Christian had awakened inside her. Because of their previous lovemaking, she knew what fulfillment could be, and fell into the joyous rise of her own desire eagerly.

When she rose to the crest that she thought she recalled so well, so vividly, she called out with amazement and wonder. For it washed over her in a feeling so intense and moving that its rapture was too great to hold in her mortal and all too fallible mind.

She was Christian and he was Rowena.

Only when the ecstasy had eased could she breathe once more.

But could she ever be separate from this man again? she asked herself as he rolled to the side. Sighing, she flung her arm across her eyes, her tongue flicking out to wet lips that were dry from the harshness of her breathing as he loved her. Would she ever again in her entire life feel complete without Christian?

Rowena did not think that would be possible.

The very knowledge of this seemingly inescapable truth rocked her to her core.

She looked over at him, her eyes hungry for the sight of his face, so dear to her. Even more dear than his touch on her body.

His eyes met hers. Shocked, she winced at the painful hopelessness in his expression. She wanted to close her lids, to block out the sight of it so soon after their loving, but knew she could not shield herself from what he was about to say.

His voice was filled with weary resignation. "Forgive me yet again, Rowena. I had no more right to touch you just now than I ever have. Would that there was something that could be done about the situation."

She returned that gaze for a long moment, feeling resentment rise up inside her. "What do you mean, would that something could be done? It is your own choice whether something be done about the *situation* or nay."

He frowned, clearly startled as well as displeased by

her anger. "You know how things stand between me and my father."

A wave of hopelessness washed over her. They were exactly where they had been.

She sat up and pulled her cloak close about her before standing. She then swung around to glare at him. "Oh yes, I know. But I am not sure that you do." She began to gather up her clothes.

"What say you?"

She cast him an assessing glance. "You insist that you are responsible for making life easier for your father. Yet I begin to wonder if what you do is based on your own need, rather than his."

"My own?" He was clearly incredulous. "How can you accuse me of that when you know I owe him so much after deserting him for so long?"

Having gathered up her garments, Rowena faced him again. "I wonder if you are not more attached to your guilt than to your father's well-being. Or perhaps it is fear that binds you, fear of giving too much of yourself away. Those are the only possible explanations I can find for such utter and complete blindness in an otherwise observant man."

"You speak in riddles."

She grimaced. "Do I? Convince yourself that this be true and you have no need to examine your motives."

She swung away and came to an abrupt halt as he grabbed her arm. She turned to glare at him, finding him gloriously naked and unashamed in his outrage. "You will tell me what you mean."

"You accuse me of not seeing. But there is so very much that you refuse to see. You see your father as a crippled, helpless man, because you wish to. See him through another's eyes. Perhaps the lady Jannelle's.''

"Lady Jannelle?"

Rowena simply stared at him. "Even if all you thought was truth, if your father was in need of your attendance upon him, you would also have a right to your own life. You left your father when he was grieving and did not respond to your grief. As you have come to realize, he is surely not an evil man for having made this error, but the error was his.'' She glared at him. "Children do not belong to their parents. Their lives are their own."

There was no change in his stubbornly set, yet frustratingly handsome features. "As yours belongs to you."

"Yes!" Rowena jerked her arm free. And ran.

He called out from behind her, "Rowena, don't...! It is too dangerous for you to go off alone here. You must stay with me."

But she would not heed him, could not. Her peace of mind depended upon her finding some measure of immunity to him and her love for him.

She ran on and on, his voice following her for a time before it died off. Yet she continued, desperate to get away from the man who could with a kiss sway her from the path of her own good.

It was only after she had come to the edge of the forest that she stopped to look out at the farmland spread before her as she hastily drew on her clothing. Where was she?

And how did she get back to Avington from here? A growing sense of unease gripped her.

She and Christian had ridden quite some distance this day. Now she was on foot.

Rowena decided to skirt along the edge of the wood. It would at least give her some cover to move. Though they had seen no one who had even attempted to speak to them, she was infinitely aware that they were on Dragonwick lands.

A part of her longed to go back the way she had come and find Christian. No matter how bad things were between them he would get her safely back to Avington.

Pride would not allow her to do so. It told her that she did not need Christian Greatham. She had roamed the woods about Ashcroft alone for years. She would simply call upon her wood lore to get her back. Once on Avington lands she would surely be able to beg aid from someone.

Allowing the position of the sun to guide her, she walked on.

Rowena only wished that she could stop thinking of Christian, of how good it had felt to be loved by him, of how painful it was to know that he could not be swayed from his determination to hold tightly to his guilt. Perhaps it was her preoccupation with him that made her fail to note the three men who rode out from the cover of the trees until one of them had actually dismounted and run toward her.

Rowena spun around and raced into the forest. For a moment she thought she had eluded him, but then she felt herself brought up short and realized he had grasped the back of her cloak.

Her heart rising up in her throat, Rowena cried out,

straining forward with all of her might, hoping the fabric might tear or his grip might slip. It did no good. The fabric was too heavy and the man's hold too sure.

Even as he read her fear, the fellow laughed, his blackened teeth showing. He motioned to the others, and one of them rushed to drag Rowena to the ground.

All she could do was scream in helpless terror.

Christian chased after Rowena for some time, calling out her name. Suddenly he stopped short, cursing as he stepped on a sharp twig. Looking down, he recalled his bare feet, his nakedness.

Hurriedly he went back to the place where they had lain, gathered up his discarded shoes and clothing. He dragged them on, then grabbed up the reins of his patiently waiting stallion.

Mounting, he rode in the direction Rowena had gone, still cursing under his breath, knowing he was going too fast for Gideon's safety. Yet also knowing that he must find her.

Damn her eyes. The things she had said.

Clearly Rowena was so angry and confused that she was not making any sense whatsoever. Her assessment of his motives was not rational.

He had chosen his future because it was the only thing he could choose with any honor. He had shirked his responsibilities by staying away from his home and duty for too long.

Yet the very thought of his life, his future without her caused a sickening ache in Christian's pounding heart. He knew he had to get hold of himself. He could not have Rowena see how truly devastated he was at the life he had chosen for himself.

He knew that she would say he was disturbed because he had not gotten what he wanted, had not avenged his foster father. Feeling that ache inside him, the sheer agony of it, Christian was not at all certain that this could explain his feelings.

Somehow he knew that whatever else might have caused him to hurt so dreadfully, it must be even more closely guarded than his disappointment over not convincing her to stay in England. For it was not The Dragon he thought of now, but Rowena herself, of the way he felt each time he held her in his arms, each time he saw her smile.

Again that ache rose up to roll over him.

It was into this state of misery that a sound intruded upon his consciousness. And it was because of his misery that it was a long moment before he realized the sound for what it was. A woman's scream.

Rowena!

Instantly he rose up in the saddle, pulling his horse around at the same time. The scream seemed to have come from behind and above him, where the cluster of trees marked the edge of the patch of forestland he had just come through.

He imagined that he must have passed close by her without even knowing he had done so. He galloped back, leaning low over the stallion's back.

He heard no more sounds—no more screams—but he did not try to tell himself that the scream had been other than what it was.

God rot him, he had been lost in his own selfish

thoughts. He did not know what had brought about the scream, but he did know that it was his fault. He should not have let her go off alone.

The fact that he had only stopped to clothe himself seemed unimportant in the face of the fact that Rowena might be hurt...or worse.

He had only that one piercing scream and nothing more to guide him to her.

It was not until he was nearly to the edge of the wood that he saw her and the disturbingly filthy man who held her, as well as the other two who stood by. And when he did the blood that had felt so hot in his chest only moments ago seemed to have turned to ice. The chill from it spread over his body, making his limbs feel leaden as he pulled the stallion up short only a few feet from where they stood.

His gaze found Rowena's even as the man who held her pulled her more closely against him. The gleam of a knife flashed out from the whiteness of her throat.

Her captor called out, ''Don't ye try to fight us, m'lord. 'Tis not beneath me to spit yer fine lady here and now.''

Christian heard the chill in his voice as he replied, ''Do you so much as prick her flesh you will wish you had never been born.''

Even though he held the knife against Rowena's throat the man and his fellows shifted slightly. As the knife wielder collected himself and went on, Christian could not help wondering if the words were more bravado than certainty. ''A fine threat. A fine threat indeed, m'lord, when ye've to get through her to get to me. Ye must give us yer sword.''

Christian cast assessing eyes over his opponents. They were a poorly equipped lot. Obviously they were displaced men from some army. Perhaps even Kelsey's, though Christian registered surprised that the motley crew would have the temerity to take their lives in their hands by preying upon those on the earl's lands. They could not know that he and Rowena were not riding upon Dragonwick lands by permission of their lord, and he was sure Kelsey preferred to do the preying if any was to be done.

All had swords, but they were of the quality carried by the commonest soldiers. Their filthy and tattered clothing had never been fine. All three were thin to the point of malnourishment, and dull of eye. They would offer him little resistance were he to meet them upon the field of battle.

Nonetheless he was frustrated by the leader's statement that Christian must go through him to get to Rowena. Therefore, in spite of his revelation that these men would not give him too great a challenge, he stood immobile. He could not take the risk that Rowena would be harmed or killed in a struggle against them.

Again the leader ordered, ''Give us yer sword.''

Reluctant as he was to turn over the weapon, Christian realized he would simply have to await a better moment for retribution and escape than this one.

Slowly, he unbuckled his sword belt and, holding it at arm's length, dropped it on the ground in front of him. The leader gestured to one of the other men, ''Fowler,'' who came forward gingerly, watching Christian warily.

Christian did not deign to inform him that he would

not try to thwart them at this time. He simply focused on Rowena's face as her horrified eyes followed the lost sword, and the man named Fowler looked to the leader. "I have it, Gorrel."

Seeing the sword safely in the hands of his companion, Gorrel eased his knife away from Rowena's throat.

Christian wanted to sigh in relief, for he realized that nothing was as precious to him as her life. He refrained from revealing the depth of his emotion for fear that it would only further endanger her. He spoke with deliberate calm. "Are you unharmed?"

She closed her eyes as she took a deep breath of relief herself. "I am."

Gorrel jerked her back against him, the knife pressing at her throat once more as he glared at Christian. "Did I say ye should speak?"

Christian raised a hand. "Nay, do not. I will say no more."

Pretending acquiescence was imperative no matter how it galled him. He dared not even risk attempting to reassure Rowena, even if it was only with a glance. Thus he avoided her questing gaze as he adopted a passive stance.

He held his breath until the knife was once again removed from her throat. His relief was short-lived, for their captor ordered his fellows, "Bring them."

Wherever he and Rowena were being taken, he could only pray that there were not more of them. Escaping would be made all the more difficult if he ended in fighting a greater number of outlaws, no matter how inept they might be.

He would get her free, no matter what the cost.

Chapter Fourteen

"It has proved a fine day indeed," the leader said to his fellows, who nodded with near idiotic enthusiasm. "We have not seen travelers of noble ilk upon these lands for some years."

He nodded sharply to one of them. "Take her, Carew." The third man moved forward and pulled Rowena back against him, his own knife now gleaming at her belly.

Christian closed his eyes and breathed deeply, forcing himself to remain calm even as his fear and guilt over what was happening to her threatened to overwhelm him.

"What have we here?" The words made him open his eyes.

Gorrel was so close now that Christian could smell the unwashed odor that emanated from him. His avaricious gaze was fixed on the purse at Christian's belt. He reached out and cut it free. He then hefted its weight with a black-toothed smile.

Watching this, Christian interjected eagerly, "There

is more where that came from if you do not harm this lady.''

The outlaw glared at him. ''And when I make to collect it I will be met with your army. Is that not true, me fine lord?''

Christian frowned. ''I assure you, sir, on my word, that if you do not harm her, you shall have your gold.'' His voice hardened as he felt a rush of uncontrollable rage inside him. ''But if you do harm her, make no mistake that it will be you who pays.''

Gorrel took an involuntary step backward, then quickly righted himself. ''Fine words.'' He gestured to the man he'd called Fowler. ''Bind him.''

Christian stayed acquiescent during this procedure. He knew he should not have threatened the man. His purpose was to convince the blackguard that they were no danger to him. No matter how great his rage he must control it for Rowena's sake.

When this was done to the leader's satisfaction, he ordered, ''We ride.'' As they moved off, Christian attempted to send a glance of encouragement to Rowena, who was forced to ride before one of the outlaws. It was difficult to catch her gaze, tied hand and foot to his own mount as he was.

What he needed was time to develop a plan to extricate them.

The three took them to a well-camouflaged cave in the forest, not far from where they had been captured. Carew took Rowena inside alone, while the other two stood watch over Christian after dragging him to the ground.

Unkempt and ill-spoken as the men might be, they

did seem to understand that their control of Rowena was their control of him.

Rowena appeared calm, and for that he was grateful. It would have been nearly impossible to bide his time if she had appeared more frightened.

In spite of this churning anger at himself and the three men, Christian remained passive as his feet were untied. He was then led through the narrow opening, his hands remaining tied behind him. He was pushed forward to where the still-bound Rowena had been left next to the cold fire pit.

Christian could not have articulated his relief at being positioned near her. Again he remained passive as they retied his feet, then looped the rope around the one at his wrists.

Obviously feeling quite secure in their control, their captors set about building a fire. When this was done one of them produced a bag of wine, which they began to pass back and forth with some enthusiasm as they prepared several hares for roasting.

Taking advantage of their preoccupation, Christian leaned as close as he could to Rowena. "Do not worry. I will get us free."

She looked at him with wide green eyes filled with trust, and nodded.

Far from making him happy, it only made him feel more a fool. He had gotten her into this by bringing her to Dragonwick.

Even as he turned away he met the scowling eyes of the leader of the little band. "What are ye over here whisperin' about, me fine lord?"

"I was telling her not to be afraid," Christian answered with careful civility.

"Oh ye were, were ye?" Gorrel gave a rough and scathing laugh as he raised the wineskin to his mouth. His companions followed his lead, each taking a long drink from the skin.

Christian nodded. "Aye. I judge you a clever man and believe you would never toss away the opportunity to gain riches that far exceed those you have already won this day."

Gorrel leaned over Christian threateningly. "I told ye I am not mad enough to fall into the trap that would be laid for me when I tried to get me reward."

Christian shrugged. "That could not happen if you planned well enough. I am sure that you already have begun to form a plan."

The other two had drawn closer to listen. Their leader, still leaning over Christian, cocked his head. "And what do ye think my plan might be?"

Christian was careful to keep his elation under control. "Why, I think you would send one of your men over to Avington. You would have him give a message to the first man he saw there, thus preventing your companion from having to go to the keep, where he might risk capture. The messenger would then be the one to tell Lord Warleigh of your demands, where you wished to have your gold delivered, and when, before you release your prisoners."

"Would I now?" Gorrel's tone was gruff, but Christian could see the wheels turning behind that increasingly bleary gaze. "I'd not be sharing such plans with ye, me fine lord, make no mistake."

Christian shrugged again with deliberate unconcern. He bowed. "I can see that you are indeed too clever to confide in me."

His captor nodded and went to his companions. The three of them moved off, talking animatedly amongst themselves.

Not wishing to draw their attention, Christian said nothing more to Rowena. He sent her a glance of encouragement and she nodded, her gaze filled with faith and gratitude.

Christian had to turn away. Her confidence in him was painful. When they were able to gain their freedom he would return her to Ashcroft without another word. He had made far too much of a disaster of things to try ever again to interfere in what she wanted for herself.

Their captors continued to converse in hushed tones, still drinking from the skin, until the rabbits roasting over the fire began to give off an acrid odor. The leader cuffed one of the other men, who raced to rescue their meal.

There was no more private talk between them as they began to consume the meat with great enthusiasm, despite its charred condition.

They shared some of the rabbit with their captives, feeding them with their own dirty fingers. Christian noted that Rowena declined after only one bite, but he forced himself to consume the burned meat, as he wished to keep up his strength in the event that an opportunity to escape presented itself.

After they had eaten, the leader pointed an unsteady finger from where he sat on the other side of the fire, the wineskin on his lap. "Ye get yerselves to sleep now."

Christian shrugged his cloak close about him as best he could with his hands tied. He then lay down where he sat. He watched as Rowena did the same.

It was impossible to find a comfortable position, but he finally managed to fall into a restless sleep.

Rowena lay down, as Christian had, but she was unable to sleep. She did make a pretense of having gone to sleep, however, in order to keep from displeasing their captors.

She was not truly afraid now. When they had captured Christian she had known that he would be able to think of some way out. Though the men had not acted on his obvious suggestion to ransom them, she had some hope that they would do so.

She heard the sounds of the men passing the wineskin among them. Eventually they began to talk quietly once more, congratulating themselves on their good fortune, their tongues obviously having been loosened by the wine.

Yet when Carew spoke up in the midst of this talk, saying, "Aye, but what I would give to have things the way they were when The Dragon was alive," there was a long and decidedly painful silence.

Into that silence Gorrel said, "There is no sense in thinking on such things. 'Tis passed." In spite of his words there was a naked yearning in his voice.

"Aye." Carew spoke so quietly that his voice could barely be heard. "But do you never remember those days when we were men respected by those we knew?

It was a great good The Dragon did us to give us a place when we came back from fighting in the east. The things we had seen and done there... 'Twas enough to turn my own blood cold when I thought on it. I never felt such worth as a man except in the years he led us.''

Gorrel groaned. ''I said enough of this talk.''

It was Fowler who sighed. ''I remember, on the nights when my belly is empty and my bones ache from sleeping on the ground. And when I long for the company of a good woman.''

Clearly emboldened by his companion's lack of heed for their leader's direction, Carew continued as well. ''We should not have stayed on at Dragonwick when The Dragon was killed. We should not have remained here under Kelsey.''

Gorrel seemed to take offense at this, forgetting his own directive. ''We did what we knew. We were fighting men and he offered us a place, if we would follow him.''

She thought that it was Fowler who answered, ''But following him meant that we had to put all thought of right or wrong aside. And we knew that within the first few months.''

Gorrel's own voice was filled with regret. ''But no other lord would have us, after we'd served him.''

Another silence ensued.

Rowena held her breath, realizing the pain these men felt, and she suddenly understood that they had been given a direction in life when they had someone of good character to lead them.

Perhaps she was right in her belief that it would be

reasonable for the common folk to lead themselves in a world where there were no men like the earl of Kelsey. Unfortunately, there were such men. Without other strong and honorable men to protect them, they were subject to the unscrupulous rule of the former.

How could she, a woman with no experience in leading anyone, let alone the needy of a whole earldom, help them? If she had someone, someone who would stand by her side and be a helpmate, then perhaps…

Christian's face came into her mind.

With self-derision, she dismissed it. Christian wanted no part of Dragonwick. Or her.

Heaven help her, she wished she had the ability to prevent herself from thinking. From hurting.

The best thing she could do was go to sleep. And finally she was able to.

When Rowena opened her eyes she was glad to see that the sky beyond the narrow mouth of the cave was finally lighting. With the morning came her realization that her anger toward Christian was pointless. In spite of his stubborn insistence that he owed his father his future, he was a good man.

Although she was quite aware that they would never have been captured had he not brought her to Dragonwick, she was not angry with him for that. His obvious self-castigation was far more than sufficient punishment. He had, despite the fact that it clearly chafed him, submitted to the outlaws in a meek and respectful manner. It illustrated for her so very well that Christian was willing to do whatever he must when he felt he had done wrong, as he did in relation to his father.

What did hurt, though, more than she could say, was

the knowledge that he did not love her as she did him. For clearly, if he had, that love would be able to break through the wall of guilt he had erected around his heart.

Rowena fought and conquered the tears that threatened to spill, telling herself there would be time for self-indulgence when they had gained their freedom.

The unmistakable sounds of wood being thrown on the fire behind her indicated that at least one of their captors was awake.

She wondered what this new day might bring. Hopefully, they would act on Christian's proposal to ransom their captives. She realized that had the three been cleverer villains they would surely have realized what he was about. But if they were cleverer they would certainly have thought of it themselves.

She heard Christian shift.

A voice she recognized as Gorrel's said, "So ye've decided to rise, me fine lord. Ye must be on the ready to ride."

Rowena sat up and wiped the hair back from her brow as Christian replied carefully, "Ride where?"

"Ye'll find out soon enough."

Rowena saw the way Christian's gaze swept the cave several times as they were talking. And suddenly she realized what he had noted. Carew was missing.

She met Christian's triumphant gaze. What...?

Then suddenly she knew. They had sent a man with a message for Simon, as Christian had suggested. Her own hopes soared. They would soon be free, for there was no doubt in her mind that Simon would indeed pay whatever sum these outlaws demanded.

No morning meal was produced. In some distant part of herself Rowena felt a further sense of pity for these men, as she recalled their talk of hunger and despair.

Her pity did not fill her empty belly, which cramped with hunger.

Last night she had been unable to consume more than a bite of the burned rabbit, when she had seen how filthy were the fingers that held it to her lips. Now she felt she might not be so squeamish.

Yet she was not able to dwell on her hunger for long. Carew returned when the morning was still quite young. He called his fellows to the side and muttered to them in an excited whisper that would have been quite intelligible if he had not rattled on so quickly.

Gorrel stepped back with a smile of triumph as he looked at his captives. "We ride."

Before she had time to think, Rowena was mounted before Fowler, as she had been the previous evening. She tried to be calm, to really believe that she and Christian would soon be free.

The three outlaws were in obviously fine spirits. They did not discuss where they were going or why, but they held their shoulders erect as they rode toward their destination.

Looking about them, Christian stated, "You are not taking us to Avington."

Gorrel, clearly pleased with himself, replied, "Nay."

Christian said, "But you have sent word to Lord Warleigh."

Gorrel watched him for a long moment, then shrugged. "It matters not if ye know now. The meeting is ta be at Dragonwick. 'Tis what we know best. And now that Lord Kelsey's men no longer have a care as to our doin's hereabouts, we'll not be troubled until yer friends bring the money.'' He scowled at Christian. ''Lest ye are not as worthy to them as ye say.''

Rowena noted that Christian grimaced at this, but he said, ''Lord Warleigh will come.'' He then fell silent once more as he scanned the area around them uneasily.

She tried not to be concerned about his disquiet. As long as Simon came with the ransom, surely all would be well.

It was with a sinking feeling in the pit of her stomach that Rowena saw the group of mounted men come from a stand of trees some distance ahead of them not more than an hour later. There were at least eight riders. They displayed some measure of surprise at coming upon Gorrel's little band and their captives, for they did not react for some moments. Then one of them raised his hand and shouted as he urged his horse forward. The others followed.

Rowena did not require Christian's shouted curse to know that this was a most dreadful development. He cried to their captors, ''Untie me and I will assist in warding them off!''

Whether or not they would have heeded him was lost in the fact that the men were upon them too quickly.

Both Carew and Gorrel were dispatched without compunction or great effort, leaving Rowena gasping with horror and shock, even as one of the soldiers jumped down to grab the head of Christian's mount.

Having seen his fellows fall with such lack of regard,

Fowler cowered behind Rowena, begging, "Do not kill me, Sir Fredrick. We was bringin' them to ye at the castle."

Rowena's horrified gaze went to the man who answered, "Were you? Then perhaps I should not have been so hasty." It was quite clear that in spite of his words he had no regret at having killed the other two, for his cold gray gaze swept their bodies with complete unconcern. "I shall be happy to relieve you of the trouble," he added coolly, as his hate-filled eyes ran over Christian, who sat tall and proud on his horse in spite of his bound state.

"Surely, sir." Fowler pushed Rowena to the ground. She stumbled, righting herself immediately, and turned to run, though her legs were shaking with fear.

Sir Fredrick caught her up easily, jerking her across the saddle in front of him. Rowena struggled, and he slapped the flat of his sword over her backside.

"God rot you." Christian's voice drew her gaze, and she saw that his eyes were also filled with hatred as he watched Sir Fredrick. "You don't want the woman. She is nothing to you."

Sir Fredrick smiled. "You are correct in that she is nothing to me. But her clear value to you precludes my setting her free. Gilbert." He motioned to one of his soldiers, who jumped down and came to take her.

She realized that further struggle was useless, thus Rowena submitted as he lifted her onto his horse and climbed up behind her. She did not wish to be placed facedown across Sir Fredrick's lap once more.

Christian spoke in a voice so filled with hate that it made the hairs stand up along her spine. "If you harm her, I will kill you. And if I die in the process, Simon and Jarrod will hunt you to the ends of the earth.''

Sir Fredrick laughed. ''Jarrod, the half-heathen whelp. He's weak. He had me right in his hands and let me go.''

''Jarrod is not weak. What he granted you was mercy, something you have never given another in your life. But you will not be so fortunate a second time.''

Rowena felt a chill run down her spine at the ice in Christian's voice, and thought she saw a brief glimmer of uncertainty in Sir Fredrick's gray gaze. But it was gone so quickly she was not sure.

He ordered roughly, ''To Dragonwick.'' They started off, leaving the fallen men where they lay.

Rowena suddenly felt a new wave of anxiety wash over her. At Dragonwick dwelt the man who had murdered his own brother and a helpless child. A man who would kill her without compunction if he had the least reason to believe she was a threat to him.

She was not sure that Christian, determined as he was to protect her, could conquer these men alone. Her anxiety was not lessened when Fowler was forced to reveal his true plan to ransom them to Simon.

They were taken to Dragonwick Castle, but Rowena's fear and anxiety kept her from clearly noting her surroundings. She had an impression of bleakness and deterioration. The few castle folk she saw as they made their way through the courtyard, then the castle, seemed morose and dejected, carefully avoiding Sir Fredrick's path.

They were taken to a large stone chamber with an

enormous bed and heavy oak furnishings. For a moment Rowena thought the room was vacant, but then a man rose from the high-backed chair that sat before the fire. He seemed to lean heavily on the arms of the chair as he faced them. "Why have you intruded upon me this way?"

Sir Fredrick hurried forward, falling to one knee. "We have captured Christian Greatham and a woman, my lord Kelsey. This man—" he indicated Fowler "—and his now dead fellows had intended to ransom them to Lord Warleigh."

"Greatham?" Lord Kelsey moved closer. When the light from the wall sconce fell across his face, Rowena had to fight to withhold a gasp.

The earl was a mere skeleton of a man, his cheeks sunken, his dark eyes burning with malevolence in a gray face. If Christian was right, this man had killed her father, and believed he had killed her. But seeing him, she felt no sense of recognition or antagonism. She felt nothing but fear of what he might do with them, for she could see that he was indeed a man capable of great ill. Clearly, hatred had eaten him from the inside, leaving nothing but a brittle shell.

As he made a harsh gasping sound and moved toward them, a sharp fit of coughing took him.

Sir Fredrick rose and reached out to hold him upright as he crumpled. The earl continued to cough until he had no more breath and his emaciated frame seemed to fold in upon itself.

Sir Fredrick picked the sick man up with surprising gentleness and took him to the bed. Carefully he laid him down upon it.

The earl rose up weakly on one elbow. "Take them to the tower. We will see how much Warleigh is willing to give for them. Mayhap he will exchange my Isabelle for his co-conspirator."

"Are you mad? Simon would never make such a trade." Christian fought the hands that restrained him.

Sir Fredrick, who had moved toward them at his master's command, slapped him full across the face with the back of his hand. Christian's head snapped backward, but he bent forward immediately, breaking the hold of his captors as he thrust his head into the belly of the man who had hit him. Sir Fredrick staggered back, groaning with shock and obvious pain.

The guards grabbed at the rope that ran from Christian's hands to his feet. They pulled him up short even as he moved to go after his prey once more. Bound as he was, Christian had no way of retaining his balance. He fell backward, hitting his head upon the floor, then lay still.

When the door closed behind Sir Fredrick and his men, Rowena scurried across the floor to where they had tossed Christian on a filthy pallet in the corner. "Christian! Christian!"

He groaned, straining at his bonds with all his might. To her amazement, and clearly, to Christian's as well, they parted. The men must have loosened the rope when they pulled on it, she realized. "I thought... Are you all right?" Rowena whispered.

He reached up to rub the back of his head. "I am fine. God, what a mess I have made of things." He reached down to untie his feet, then turned to her. "Let me free you.

When he had finished, Rowena knelt on the pallet beside him. "Don't blame yourself for what has happened. You did warn me not to go off alone. They could never have taken me if I had been with you. Aside from that, you could not have known this would happen when you suggested we come to Dragonwick. I understand that your motives were good ones."

He did not look at her directly as he shook his head. "No. I have interfered in things that were none of my concern. It was all a mistake from the very beginning."

Before she could tell him that he had been right about the people of Dragonwick needing someone to care for their well-being, he vowed, "I will take you back to Scotland as soon as I can get you out of this." His lips twisted ruefully. "*If* I can get you out of this. If it is Kelsey's intention to demand Simon hand over Isabelle to gain our release, the plan will fail. Simon will never do so." Christian struck his fist against his palm. "I should have left you in Ashcroft when you told me how you felt about nobles. I have managed to make a mess of all our lives by bringing you here."

Rowena shrank away from him, but Christian did not seem to notice.

Her realizations about Dragonwick were irrelevant. She was not the one to change things here. She knew nothing of leading men. She had not been able to convince the one man who mattered to her that he need not live his life for others.

She could not have him take responsibility for her decisions. "You may keep your guilt. I have no need of it. I should never have come to England, but the choice was my own. The choice to go back to Scotland is my own.''

Christian stiffened, his eyes appearing haunted. ''So be it.'' He drew himself up. ''Our only hope is escape.''

She nodded, gratefully taking his lead, for she would not discuss the matter further. ''How are we to do that?''

He took a deep breath, his gaze taking in the light streaming through the cracks in the shutters that covered the only window. Rising, he went and opened them, looking out. He closed them again, turning back to her. ''There is no hope of leaving by that route. We shall have to go through the keep.''

She gazed at him in surprise. ''Through the keep.''

''Aye, there is no other choice.''

''But how?''

''We must rely on stealth and good fortune.''

''But the guard. I heard Sir Fredrick tell one of the men to stay outside the door as he brought us here.''

Christian took a deep breath. ''Let me worry on that score.'' He sat down on the floor across from her. ''Try to rest now. We leave under cover of night.''

Rowena did not know how much time had passed when she felt a touch upon her arm. Opening her eyes, she realized that she must have been asleep for some time, for the chamber was now shrouded in darkness.

Christian leaned close and whispered, ''Please lie still until I tell you otherwise. Can you do that?''

She nodded. Then, realizing that he would not be able to see her, she whispered, "Yes."

Christian patted her arm. "Remember now. Don't move until I tell you." Then he was gone.

She heard his voice from the direction of the door. "Guard! Guard! The lady is sick."

From outside a voice answered, "What say you?"

"The lady is ill. I cannot wake her."

The bolt grated as it was drawn. The door opened and a brawny man in mail stood in the opening, a torch blazing from a wall sconce behind him. He held his sword ready. "Bring her here."

Christian stood back from him, offering no threat. "I am fearful of moving her."

Slowly the man came into the room and halted. "You've removed your bonds!" He motioned to Christian with the sword. "Against the wall."

Holding up his hands, Christian moved back.

The soldier moved toward Rowena. "Lady?" She made no reply, closing her eyes tightly.

"Lady?" She could feel him leaning over her.

The next thing she heard was a muffled grunt, then the man's weight was on top of her, crushing her. Rowena's scream of shock was lost in his chest.

The weight was lifted from her before she could even move to push him away. Christian took her hand and lifted her to her feet. "Are you all right?"

She gasped out, "Yes. I was just startled."

He bent and took up the sword from where the guard had dropped it as he fell. "We must go now."

With a nod, Rowena followed Christian out the open door of the tower room and into the hall. He shot the bolt home, then ran down the steps leading from the landing outside the room.

At the bottom of that flight, he hesitated, looking right then left. Rowena started to the right without thinking.

Christian came after her. Rowena led him to the stone stairway at the end of the dark hall and down the steps. At the foot a burning torch cast a dim glow over a fork in another narrow hallway. Again Rowena strode forward, taking the right fork without hesitation.

She was so very terrified that they might be caught before they would be able to make their escape from the castle that she gave this no real thought. It was not until they came to a chamber at the end of this passage that she stopped. Rowena put her hand to her mouth to stifle a gasp of shock as her gaze came to rest on the crest that dominated the far wall. Yet it was not the crest, with its dragon bearing raised talons, that had frightened her, but the banner that hung above it. Slithering across its length was a serpent, its tongue extended.

Christian's voice, harsh with excitement, whispered in her ear, "You are recognizing things!"

Rowena shook her head. "I do not know. I..." It was true. She did not know if she was recognizing anything. What she did know was that the sight of that banner filled her with a sickening horror.

He came around her to take her shoulders in a tight grip. "What is it, Rowena?" When her attention continued to be fixed on that banner, he demanded, "Look at me."

Her gaze focused on his and he spoke more gently. "Tell me."

"That banner. It frightens me."

He cast a disgusted glance at it. "It is Kelsey's. It is the banner he carried the day he attacked Dragonwick. The day he killed your father."

Rowena shuddered as her own gaze flicked to the banner and away. She then looked into Christian's eager eyes, raking her hair back from her brow with a trembling hand. "It proves nothing. I am...frightened of snakes." Her eyes held his. "As you know well. It could be because of that fear."

He shook his head. "Still you persist in this ridiculous denial of the truth. You know the twists and turns of this keep even in the dark. Does it not make more sense that the fear of snakes was brought on by what happened the day you saw this banner come to your keep?"

"I..." Again she raked a hand through her hair. Was he right? Was she simply refusing to see the truth because she was afraid, as he had insisted all along?

The very sight of that banner filled her with such revulsion and terror. Her young mind had not remembered what had occurred that day. Her body had.

Rowena looked up at him in indecision and misery. Perhaps she was also afraid because she did not know how to accomplish what must be done if she were the heir to these lands.

The loud cry that sounded from the darkness behind them stopped her from thinking further.

Christian grabbed her by the hand and started toward the opening across the chamber.

Rowena resisted. "Not that way. This way leads out." She led him toward another door. This time she was fully conscious of the fact that somehow she knew.

Christian did not question her, but moved to lead the way. He kept his ears peeled for sounds ahead or behind them, gliding his fingers along the rough stone wall in order to mark his passage. By doing so he was able to keep up a pace that would otherwise be dangerous in such darkness.

Thus it was likely only Rowena's voice saying, "We should be coming to a door," that alerted him to slow down in time to keep from bumping into the portal.

Reaching out, he felt along a narrow but heavy wooden door secured by a wide iron bar. Hurriedly, he lifted the bar and pulled.

The door swung open with a soft but shrill creak.

Christian stepped out onto a narrow ledge and gazed about, searching for some landmark that would tell him where he was in relation to the rest of the castle. The silhouette of a lone tower told him that he was facing the back portion of the curtain wall. Again a shout sounded, this time from behind them.

Rowena started toward a narrow opening in the crenellations. "There is a stair."

Following, he looked down. There was indeed a tight, circling stair, so narrow as to be barely passable by a man. Rowena sighed as she started down them. Could she have finally accepted the truth, that she was Rosalind? Christian wondered. Yet what did that matter when she wanted nothing but to go home to Ashcroft?

Just a few steps ahead of him Rowena suddenly halted on the narrow steps, crying out. Before he could even react, she disappeared around the next curve in the stair.

Rushing forward, he stopped short as he saw Sir Fredrick, his sword drawn. In the light of the torch the man behind him held, Christian could see that the knight held Rowena in his arms. Christian could hear the clatter of more booted feet coming up the stairs behind him.

Rage and frustration made him call out, "Let her go." He lunged forward.

The other knight laughed. "Drop the sword."

Desperately Christian turned to go back the way they had come. If he was free, perhaps he could help her. But he immediately noted in the flickering light of several torches that more soldiers looked down from the battlements above. With a shout of despair he threw the sword out into the darkness.

Chapter Fifteen

They were taken back to the earl's bedchamber.

Rowena felt Christian's agitation and knew that they were in dire straits indeed, for never in all that had occurred over the weeks she had known him had his blue eyes shone with such anger and desperation.

She tried for calm, somehow knowing that any sign of fear on her own part might make him act, no matter how hopeless his chances of overcoming these men. She knew that it would mean his death. And that she could not bear.

The earl lay in his bed, propped up on a pile of pillows. The fire blazed high, and in spite of the chill outside, the room was uncomfortably hot. His face was as shrunken and hollow as it had been earlier. Weakly he gestured to Sir Fredrick. "Bring them."

Both she and Christian were led forward. The sick man's gaze moved over Christian, who was bound once more. "Why have you come to Dragonwick?"

Christian said nothing.

"Why must you fight me, Greatham?"

Christian shrugged. "I do not want to be used in your vendetta against Simon."

He reared up in the bed. "Used in my vendetta? He has taken what was mine." And suddenly he was choking again, gasping for air as blood tinged the sheet, which he had held up to his face.

Sir Fredrick started forward, as did Rowena.

The earl's knight blocked her path. "What do you think you are doing?"

Rowena peered around him at the man in the bed. A part of her wanted to deny any ability to help him. Another part—the part that took her abilities as a healer as a sacred honor—could not do so.

She looked at Sir Fredrick. "I am a healer. I can help him."

"Rowena, are you mad?" Christian cried.

She did not face him. "I...perhaps I am, but he is very ill."

"Let him die."

"I can no more let him die than you can set aside your own duty." Her voice was calm with resignation.

Sir Fredrick swung around. "Take him away to the tower and do not open the door until I come."

When four guards grasped his arms, Christian fought them. "I will not leave you...."

Sir Fredrick started toward him, drawing his sword.

"No!" Rowena called out. "Do not harm him or I will let your master die." The knight swung around to glare at her, and she returned that look without wavering as she said, "And mark me well, he is not long for this world lest something is done for him." She did not add that he might indeed die no matter what she did.

Without another word, Sir Fredrick motioned to the men. Though Christian fought them with every ounce of his strength and will, they dragged him away.

Rowena worked throughout the night.

In one part of her mind she was aware of the fact that this man, who she now believed was her uncle, had murdered her father. He had in fact also attempted to murder her in order to gain the lands that he was now too physically debilitated to hold.

Sir Fredrick came and went, ever watchful, as the castle women fetched the things Rowena needed to tend the earl. At first Frederick kept a careful eye on her, but as he saw that the potions she gave him seemed to ease the earl's breathing, his expression became less suspicious and more openly fearful for his master's life.

The earl himself spoke to her very little. Even when the medication began to alleviate his suffering she saw in those burning eyes the knowledge that the end was near.

Not long after dawn Sir Fredrick and his men returned with Christian, who was held tightly as before. Her anxious eyes ran over him and she saw that in spite of his continued anger and frustration, Christian had not been harmed. He said, "Are you well, Rowena?"

Before she could reply, Sir Fredrick roared, "Do not speak!" He motioned two of the men forward to where she was clearing away the clutter from the latest dose of medication for Lord Kelsey. "Take her."

They grabbed her arms as Lord Kelsey said, "What are you doing, Fredrick? I need her."

They released her.

Fredrick frowned. "Warleigh has arrived with his army."

Rowena heard Christian's indrawn breath of surprise and looked up to see the satisfaction in his blue eyes as they met the earl's.

The earl took a deep breath, visibly collecting himself as he gasped out, "It will avail you nothing, Greatham. I shall fight him."

Christian cast a scathing gaze over him, then the men who held them. "With what army? These few fools who have remained loyal to you in spite of your inability to lead them?"

Rowena gasped as Sir Fredrick's hand went to his sword hilt and he took a step forward.

Christian smiled, his blue eyes cold with contempt. "The only reason you would even consider coming near me is that these men are holding me."

Knowing that it was nothing short of suicide for him to taunt the other man, Rowena moved toward him, but halted, swaying, as a wave of weakness took her. The last days had left their mark.

Distantly she heard Christian cry, "Something is wrong. Rowena? What have they done to you?"

She wiped her hair back from her brow, attempting to meet his anxiety with reassurance, yet her voice was husky with exhaustion as she said, "Nothing. They have done nothing. I am only tired."

Wildly Christian strained against the men who held him. He broke loose, but they caught him before he could reach her. Christian's eyes burned with hatred as he looked down at the wasted man in the bed. "You are evil, evil in flesh. Sick as you are, all you care for is the need to hurt others.''

Sir Fredrick made a curt motion and the soldiers dragged him back from the earl. Unheeding, Christian looked at Rowena. "You are unworthy to breathe the very same air as this woman whom you have used so callously. No matter that she has every reason to hate you and wish you dead, she labored to save your miserable life. She has done so in spite of the fact that your minions continue to treat her as if she were nothing.''

Ill as he was, Kelsey spoke with confusion. "You question the loyalty of those who love me. Yet this girl—" his watery gaze swept her "—has no reason to hate me beyond the fact that you do.''

Rowena could bear no more. Her own anger and frustration rose inside her, giving her strength. "I have every reason to hate you. You have let your knight beat and hold Christian prisoner without compunction. You killed my father and thought that you had killed me, too.''

Christian cried out, "Nay, do not—''

Even as he did so the earl waved a weakly dismissive hand. "I have never laid eyes upon you, girl.''

She leaned over him. "You have indeed, Uncle, you have indeed. The last time was the very night you took this keep.''

"Are you mad, Rowena?" Christian cried, again breaking free. Yet even as she turned to him, Sir Fredrick brought the butt of his sword down on the back of his head.

Christian crumpled to the floor.

She cried, "Nay!" running to fall on her knees at his side. As best she could, Rowena gathered him into her arms, her heart aching at the sight of his still white face. She closed her eyes with relief when his breath stirred the hair that lay across her cheek.

From the bed came the earl's faint protest. "It is not true. I watched my brother's daughter fall down the stair when I…"

Still holding Christian close against her, Rowena looked around at the earl, who had risen up on his elbow, his face the color of whey. "It is true. 'Twas not me you killed but the nursemaid's little one. You would never have noticed her, for she was beneath you, but we both had red hair."

He nodded to Sir Fredrick. "Bring her."

Sir Fredrick grabbed her arms from behind, and though she struggled with all her might to keep her hold on the man she loved, he pulled her roughly to her feet. She continued to struggle as he forced her back to the bed. For a moment she did manage to break free, and he grabbed her shoulder, tearing her gown as he dragged her to his master.

"Release her. She can go nowhere," Lord Kelsey instructed his knight. "They are helpless."

In spite of the fact that this was all too true, Rowena held her head high.

The earl's eyes bored into hers, his gaze wild. At last he said, "Aye, there is the look of The Dragon about you, so overtly proud, yet—"

Sickened at his assessment of her father, Rowena turned toward the wall, and heard the earl gasp. With surprising speed he rose up, gripping her with talonlike fingers, and pulled her toward him as he stared at her bare white shoulder, making her skin crawl where his gaze touched her.

The next thing she knew she was being pushed away. The earl sagged back against the pillows. "Dear God." He wiped a shaking hand over his face.

It all happened so quickly that Rowena did not know what to make of it as she sought to hold her torn gown over her.

It was Christian's voice that questioned, "What is it, Kelsey? What have you seen?"

Her heart soared with the knowledge that Christian was all right. Yet she could not acknowledge her joy, for she realized that something of great import had just occurred. "What indeed have you seen?" she asked the earl.

The old man's gaze met hers. "The birthmark. The one on your shoulder. Your father had one…. It is very distinctive."

Rowena staggered with shock, even though some part of her had known what he would say. Dear God, it was true. She was Rosalind of Dragonwick.

Christian felt the same shock that held the others immobile, but knew he could not afford himself the luxury of indulging it. He rose up from the floor and fell upon Sir Fredrick, grabbing the sword from his belt. He held the blade to the knight's belly. "You will release us."

Sir Fredrick recovered quickly, calling to his fellows. "Do not let him go, no matter what he threatens to do to me."

It was the earl who held up a trembling hand. "Nay, do not thwart him. They are to be released."

"But my lord!" Fredrick pleaded.

His master looked at him with unseeing eyes. "I said let them go."

Rowena moved closer to the earl, her gaze questioning. "Why? Why would you do this? Surely it is not for love of either me or my father."

He looked up at her, his expression empty, his voice weak. "Because even whilst you believed that I had killed your father and attempted to kill you, you helped me. Tended me with care and gentleness."

"You were helpless and ill. How could I do anything else?"

"And that is why you shall go free." His voice grew stronger then. "Not only will you go free but you'll receive what is rightfully yours. Dragonwick and all that came with it shall be yours."

"What of Isabelle?"

His face crumpled. "Isabelle would have nothing from me. And I have only myself to blame." A fit of coughing took him then and he reached up to claw at his chest in helpless misery.

Rowena took up the bowl of medication that still sat beside the bed. She tipped the bowl to the earl's mouth.

"Rowena?" Christian questioned, still keeping his hold on Sir Fredrick.

She sent him a look that pleaded for understanding. "It is my duty."

He sighed. Would he love her as he did if she were other than who she was? For he knew that he did love her, as the night loved the stars. He had always loved her. What this meant he was not sure, for he knew that he deserved no love in return from her. He had hurt her and used her most ill.

All he could do for Rowena was give her what she desired most. Her old life. He addressed Sir Fredrick. "You will give entry to Lord Warleigh and his men."

The knight cried, "You have no say here!"

The earl gasped out, "Do as he bids you." He looked at Christian with tormented eyes. "If she will but come, pray beg Isabelle to attend me this one last time. Though I will not blame her should she deny me." Again that skeletal frame was wracked with a fit of coughing.

"Let us go, Sir Fredrick," Christian ordered. Again the knight hesitated, and Christian raised his brows in warning. He was prepared to use the sword if he did not comply.

Casting another sullen glance at the man in the bed, the man he had always obeyed without question, Sir Fredrick swung toward the soldier who stood beside him and grabbed the sword from his belt. "I cannot obey. Cannot give the keep over to them."

Still holding the sword he held at the ready, Christian prepared for a descending blow. The clash of steel on steel rang out even as the earl called, "Nay," then fell back in a spasm of coughing.

Christian ignored everything but his opponent, who came at him like a man possessed. To say that Christian was sorry it had come to this would be a lie. Sir Fredrick had indeed harmed many he loved, and would continue to do so if he was given the least opportunity.

He could not be given the opportunity.

Christian fought carefully, conserving his strength as the other man launched attack after attack. Christian knew that though rage fueled him, he had twice taken heavy blows to the head in the last hours.

In the end Fredrick's will to destroy was his undoing. Christian took a side step to avoid a double-handed stroke that was clearly meant to cleave him in twain. As he did so he realized the other man had left his side completely exposed. He brought his blade up and around. It bit deep.

His eyes growing round in shock, Sir Fredrick dropped his sword. He clutched at his side, then fell forward and lay still.

For a moment, Christian could hardly believe he was dead. And unexpectedly, he felt no rush of satisfaction or triumph. He felt nothing but pity.

"Dear God, Fredrick..." the earl murmured. "Why would he not heed me?" He sounded weak and plaintive.

Christian looked to where Rowena was watching him with relief and concern. He turned away from her, for he suddenly longed for more. Yet he knew he was not entitled to more.

He motioned to the guards. "Take him." He glanced toward the earl, who lay silent, his face shrunken with grief and illness. "He will be given a proper burial."

Even as they moved to obey, he called one of them to him. "Come with me." They went to the castle gates. The man in the tower seemed shocked at the command to open, but when the guard nodded, he did as he was told.

Within minutes Simon and his men were pouring

onto the castle grounds. Seeing Christian, who had moved to stand upon the steps of the keep, they galloped forward, drawing up their mounts at the last moment.

Christian's father was with them, and ran an anxious gaze over him. "You are well, my son?"

"Aye, I am fine, Father."

Simon glanced about them warily. "What has happened?"

"Kelsey has identified Rowena as Rosalind and named her as his heir. I have just fought Sir Fredrick and won." He was in complete empathy as he saw the disbelief not only on Simon's face but on his father's. Christian could hardly credit what had occurred, and he had been present.

"Good St. George!" Simon exclaimed.

"Aye, and what is more, Kelsey may be dying at this very moment. He is asking for Isabelle."

Simon frowned. "I do not…" His gaze met Christian's. "Think you he means her ill?"

Christian thought for a long moment, then shook his head. "I think not. He is…changed."

"Kelsey?"

Christian nodded.

He thought of Rowena and his realization that he loved her. He had no right to speak of that love. He had treated her so badly, telling her over and over that his guilt over his father was more important to him than was she. To declare himself now would only make matters worse, for any affection she might have ever felt for him was certainly crushed.

It was impossible.

"Christian?"

He collected himself with some difficulty. "You must decide what you will do, but I think there would be no harm meant Isabelle. She may well regret it if she is not given the opportunity to decide if she will or will not come."

Simon nodded. "I will go for her myself. You and your father will see to things here?"

They both bowed. Christian then ordered Simon's men to take up positions about the keep, including the gate and the watchtower. They met with little or no resistance.

He also sent two of Simon's men to watch over Rowena in the earl's chamber. He did not go there himself, for he knew not what to say to her now that all had been revealed. He did not wish for her to imagine that he expected anything of her.

It was because of his thoughts of Rowena that Christian took his father aside to talk with him for a moment in one of the vacant bedchambers. "Father, I have something to say to you. I know this will come as a shock but I feel I must do this in spite of my promise to be a better son."

His father frowned.

Christian took a deep breath. "After I have taken Rowena back to Scotland I mean to stay on here for a time. Once things have been set in order I will then be free to come to Bransbury, but this is something I feel I must do, not only for The Dragon, but for Rowena."

His father shook his head. "Why would this interfere with your promise to be a better son?"

Surprise made Christian hesitate, but only for a moment. "Because you need me at Bransbury."

"I would love to have you at Bransbury. You have been sorely missed in the past years, but I do not need you."

"I thought you were disappointed with me for staying away for so long. For neglecting my duty."

The elder Greatham sat down heavily, his eyes tearing. "I have not been angry with you, my son. I thought that you were angry with me for not preventing your mother's death."

Christian put a hand on his shoulder. "I never blamed you for that. It was she who did not heed your warning about the dream you had had of her death. I only wished that you could have comforted me, as I missed her so very dreadfully."

His father sighed. "It seems we have both been mistaken in the other's thoughts. Let us not make such mistakes in the future." He stood. "I bid you do as you need in the matter of Dragonwick. There is much to do here."

Christian embraced his father, and was embraced in return.

Rowena had told him that he did not owe his life to his father. He should have set aside his guilt and spoken of this from the beginning. What a fool he had been!

Now it was too late. She would never forgive him for the way he had treated her. He had no right to expect it.

When Simon returned he not only had Isabelle with him but Lady Jannelle as well. Now that Rowena had pointed out that something was going on between his father and the dark-haired lady Christian felt a fool for not having seen it.

His father fairly hovered over the gentle dame, seeming far more vigorous than Christian had thought. Though his limp was as evident as ever, there was a virility in the way he carried himself that Christian had not noted before. And she seemed to hang on his every word, her concern for his worry over Christian's capture most apparent.

He had indeed been a fool.

From beside the bed where the dying earl labored for each and every breath, Rowena watched as Isabelle approached. Though her head was held high, there was obvious trepidation in her gaze. A wave of love came over Rowena and she held out her hand. "My sister."

Isabelle's lavender eyes lit with happiness for one brief moment as they joined hands, then her attention fixed on the man in the bed. Rowena continued to hold her hand as Isabelle looked down into the face of the man who had brought them both such pain.

Yet all Rowena could feel was pity for the earl. Because of his greed for power and wealth he had hurt and betrayed the very person who had meant him only good.

Isabelle's face registered shock and horror as she looked into the sunken, gray countenance. She whispered, "Fa—Lord Kelsey."

He opened his clouded eyes and they filled with tears the moment he saw her. "Isabelle."

Rowena began to back away, to give them a moment

of privacy, but the other woman held tightly to her hand and she grew still. Isabelle swallowed hard. "You sent for me."

He drew a deep breath, though it obviously pained him to do so. "I...thank you for coming. I deserve nothing from you. I want only to say that I am sorry for what I have done—" his gaze flicked briefly to Rowena "—to all of you. You who were my brother's heir shall have what was rightfully yours. But as you seek to rebuild these lands you will not think of me. It is only now that I am dying that I realize the only thing that would have mattered was to have someone nearby who would grieve my passing."

A single tear slipped down Isabelle's cheek. "I did love you. I wanted nothing more than for you to return my love."

He fought for breath as he clutched his chest. "And I was unable to do that." His eyes grew desperate. "There is but one thing I would have, though I have no right to ask... But it is all that could give me some measure of peace now as I prepare to leave this world." His eyes closed as he sucked in harsh, ragged breaths.

Isabelle leaned close and whispered, "I forgive you."

Never opening his eyes, the earl heaved a great sigh, then fell still.

It was a moment before Rowena realized what had happened. She reached out to place her free hand upon that sunken chest. "He is gone."

Isabelle put her hands up to cover her face before running to Simon, who waited beside the fire with Lord

Greatham and Lady Jannelle. He enfolded her in his arms.

Rowena stood there, feeling confused and uncertain. Everything had happened so very quickly.

She wished that she, too, had somewhere to go for comfort. But when she risked a glance toward Christian, he was looking out the window, his back to the chamber.

It was as if he had forgotten her. He was very likely reveling in the fact that it was all over. He had accomplished the task of seeing right done by the foster father he had loved.

He could now go home to Bransbury with a clear conscience.

She tried to calm her painfully pounding heart, but could not seem to do so. It was all so overwhelming. How was she to take the chaos that existed for the people of Dragonwick and make it right?

Christian had taken charge this day, securing the entire keep with the loss of only one life, and that had been Sir Fredrick's choice. How different things would be if she had him at her side. But that was not to be.

Rowena felt dazed with confusion, unhappiness and exhaustion. Suddenly she had to be alone with her churning thoughts. She turned toward the door, knowing not where she would go, only that it must be away from Christian.

Yet the tension and fatigue of the last days and weeks had taken their toll. She had barely gained the door when a wave of dizziness washed over her and she swayed. Rowena reached out for something solid to cling to, desperate for her spinning world to right itself. Then it all went black....

"Rowena!" Christian heard Isabelle's alarmed exclamation and spun around. His gaze immediately took in the fact that Rowena lay crumpled on the floor, even as his father, Simon and Lady Jannelle also cried out.

Heaven help him, he had allowed her to push herself too hard! Before any of the others could react, he ran across the room, gathering her into his arms. "Rowena, my beloved."

Her lids fluttered and she whispered, "Is this Christian?"

"It is me, love." He was driven beyond his fear of rejection by his concern for her.

She opened those lovely green eyes. "Am I dreaming?"

Feeling the eyes not only of his father, but of all the others upon them, he picked her up and carried her out into the hall. He would not bare his soul in that room.

He tried the door across the hall and entered when he saw that the room was comfortably furnished. Settling her upon the bed, he sat down next to her, watching her face. "Do you want to be dreaming, Rowena?"

Her expression was guarded now. "Why are you asking?"

He paused for a long moment, then said, "I have told my father that I mean to stay on here at Dragonwick for as long as I am needed."

She looked away. "Is it because you have realized that managing Dragonwick will be a great task for me?"

He grew very still. "What are you saying? Are you telling me that you have changed your mind, that you are considering staying?"

Rowena's lovely green eyes met his with challenge. "I...yes. I have realized that the people here need someone, as you said all along. Those men who took us prisoner yesterday would have been so very different with someone strong and caring to lead them. Yet I pray you do not offer your aid out of guilt. I do not want nor require your guilt."

Christian took a deep breath, knowing that no matter what pain a rejection might bring him, he could not hide his love for her another moment. "I love you, Rowena. I have loved you from the first moment I saw you. It is why I was so determined that you had to come to England with me, even though you were obviously less than eager. How could I fail to love you? You are beautiful and kind, and wise beyond your years. And if you are angry with me for saying so I am sorry."

"Angry?"

"Yes. I know how I have hurt you." He looked away. "I don't know how you can ever forgive me."

"Forgive you?" She rose up and put her hand to his face. "Forgive you, Christian? I would forgive you anything."

He looked at her then, seeing the tears of joy in her lovely eyes.

"I love you, Christian, I have and will always love you."

"You love me?"

"To echo your words, how could I not? Fate has decreed that we be together."

His own eyes grew damp. "And I love you, Rowena."

There was a hint of sadness in her voice as she said, "Rosalind, now."

He shook his head. "You will always be Rowena to me. The years since you were Rosalind are part of what has shaped you to be the woman I love."

Happiness rose up inside her like a blazing light, which she could feel shining from her eyes. She never wanted to forget her life as Rowena, for it had indeed made her who she was. Christian was even more dear to her for having realized it. "I do love you, Christian, more than you will ever know."

He took her in his arms, where she had always longed to be.

Epilogue

R owena heard booted feet coming down the corridor to her chamber and leaped up, dropping her sewing to the floor. Knowing that step well, she ran to the door to greet him. "Christian!"

They had chosen their rooms at the opposite end of the keep from what had previously been the lord's chamber. Rowena had taken part in the cleaning and provisioning herself, wanting their life together to begin with as little of the past to remind them of the pain they had experienced as there could be. The heavy green brocade draperies, the linens and tapestries, as well as the thick carpet that Christian had brought back from the Holy Land, were all new.

The door burst open just as Rowena reached it. And then she was in her husband's arms, held close against his heart. For one precious moment she breathed in the scent of him—cool wind, perspiration and horse, and underneath all that, warm man.

Then she pushed away, feeling with joy his reluctance to release her. She looked up into those blue eyes. "What said the king?"

He pulled her back against him. "He said that you may hold the lands."

Again she pushed away. "Truly? As simply as that?"

Christian frowned. "I have missed you so. I would hold you for a moment."

Rowena placed a hand upon his chest. "As I have you, but you have been privy to all that I have not. And I would know what has gone forward, not only for myself but for all who abide here."

He sighed. "Aye, I know that, love. I am only feeling selfish after my time away. As to your question, nay, not as simply as that. Because my father and Simon both gave witness that Kelsey confirmed your identity before he died, as well as naming you heir, John has confirmed your position. Yet he does have his own conditions. Because you are a woman, he has agreed that you may hold, with my aid, only until you have a son who reaches the age at which he might do so. If you die without issue—" a tender expression softened Christian's face as he moved his hand down to cover her belly "—the lands will revert to the crown. And we have already begun to assure that does not occur."

Rowena felt a thrill of longing at that touch. He had been gone such a long time and their bed was so near.

But she still had questions—questions that had burned in her mind these two long weeks. "Did you tell your father of our news? I have, of course, informed Isabelle.''

He ran a hand through his dark hair, seeming overwhelmed for a moment before he said, ''You will not believe what news I have. 'Tis difficult to credit such a possibility, but not only is Aislynn breeding, but Lady Jannelle as well.''

''Both of them?''

''Aye. He is pleased about Aislynn, of course, but he is ecstatic about his own child. He is as a young man again. He is concerned for his bride, as she is in her thirty-sixth year, but he tells me that she assures him of her good health hourly.''

''I am so very glad for him, Christian, for them. I know how you worried about taking on Dragonwick rather than helping him at Bransbury.''

He grinned. ''It seems he only needed someone to share his life and dreams with. Not to mention his passion. It is thus with all men.'' He nuzzled her nape.

Rowena closed her eyes as a delicious shiver raced down her spine. They flew open immediately and she said, ''Aislynn as well?''

''Jarrod's letter to Father said that she is near as round as she is tall, but bounds about as if it were nothing.''

Rowena shook her own head. ''I would dearly love to know your sister better. Isabelle has become so very dear to me. And little Simon. I have twice picnicked with the two of them whilst you and Simon have been off at court. 'Twas more a joy than I would have imagined. We have been so busy here at Dragonwick these past six months. We do not have enough opportunity to see our loved ones.''

They had indeed worked hard in their six months at Dragonwick. The coming harvest promised to be a good one, and Christian and Rowena planned to leave the greatest share of that bounty for the hungry mouths of their folk.

He hugged her. "Do not worry on my behalf, beloved. My father knew that it would be difficult at the start, as did the others. Time is changing that even now.''

She asked him again, "Did you tell them of our news?''

He kissed her mouth, grinning at last. "I did. Neither were surprised, and Father intends to inform Jarrod and Aislynn when he reaches Bransbury. They have been there with his lady wife whilst he was at court, since Jarrod's brother Eustace's condition has improved somewhat of late. They will write the moment the babe arrives.''

Her eyes grew round. "I nearly forgot. I have had word from Hagar. She took my letter to the monastery as the messenger instructed, and they read it to her, then wrote back to me. She says all is well, though I am missed and that Sean, though he is sad, has begun to get on with his life.''

"I am happy to hear it,'' Christian answered. "I find it easy to pity the man who had to give you up.''

She shook her head. "Though I loved him dearly I was never his.'' Her green eyes were filled with adoration. "'Twas always you, my love, even before I knew."

He held her to him, his voice tight even as he teased, "Where are the kisses I have longed for?"

She lifted her mouth, kissing him with fervor as she felt the familiar rush of longing in her blood. "I love you, Christian, with all that I am and ever will be."

He slipped his hands down her back, making her shiver with wonder and need. "I have missed you so, missed…"

"As have I, dear heart." Then there were no more words as he picked her up, kicking the door closed behind them as he took her to their bed.

When at last she drew back, her body sated, she held his hand against her still-flat belly. Tenderly he whispered against her ear, "He shall be a great man, as his grandfather was, just and wise and full of life."

She lifted her lips to his throat, her heart aching with love as she said, "I honor your love for my father, and his memory, yet I would have you know that our son will gain all those qualities from his own father."

Christian swallowed hard around the lump that rose up in his throat. "I…I didn't know that it was possible to love anyone as I love you."

She touched his face with wonder. "I was only surviving till you came to fetch me, though I knew it not. I thought it was my father and my past that I must search for, but it was you and your heart all along."

"And I learned the same of you, Rowena." He kissed her deeply, thoroughly, and passion stirred inside her once more. But the sensation was tender and gentle, requiring no haste, for they had their whole lives ahead of them.

She sighed, placing her hand over his on her belly. "I am so pleased that the babes will be of an age to be friends, as you and Jarrod and Simon have been. Life and the continuation of it is the purpose of love."

He shook his head, his dear gaze holding hers. "Nay, beloved. Love has no purpose but to be given away."

* * * * *

From Regency Ballrooms to Medieval Castles, fall in love with these stirring tales from Harlequin Historicals

On sale March 2003

THE SILVER LORD by Miranda Jarrett

Don't miss the first of **The Lordly Claremonts** trilogy!
Despite being on the opposite side of the law,
a spinster with a secret smuggling habit can't resist
a handsome navy captain!

BRIDE OF THE TOWER by Sharon Schulze
(England, 1217)

Will a fallen knight become bewitched with the
mysterious noblewoman who nurses him back to health?

On sale April 2003

LADY ALLERTON'S WAGER by Nicola Cornick

A woman masquerading as a cyprian challenges a
dashing earl to a wager—with the stake being an island
he owns against her favors!

HIGHLAND SWORD by Ruth Langan

Be sure to read this first installment in the
Mystical Highlands series about three sisters
and the handsome Highlanders they bewitch!

  Harlequin Historicals®
Historical Romantic Adventure!

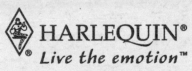
PHAS

Steeple Hill Books is proud to present
a beautiful and contemporary new look
for Love Inspired!

As always, Love Inspired delivers
endearing romances full of hope, faith and love.

Beginning January 2003
look for these titles
and three more each month
at your favorite retail outlet.

Steeple
Hill®

Visit us at www.steeplehill.com

LINEW03

SAVOR THE BREATHTAKING ROMANCES AND THRILLING ADVENTURES OF THE OLD WEST WITH HARLEQUIN HISTORICALS

On sale March 2003

TEMPTING A TEXAN by Carolyn Davidson

A wealthy Texas businessman is ambitious, demanding and in no rush to get to the altar. But when a beautiful woman arrives with a child she claims is his niece, he must decide between wealth and love....

THE ANGEL OF DEVIL'S CAMP by Lynna Banning

When a Southern belle goes to Oregon to start a new life, the last thing she expects is to have her heart captured by a stubborn Yankee!

On sale April 2003

McKINNON'S BRIDE by Sharon Harlow

While traveling with her children, a young widow falls in love with the kind rancher who opens his home and his heart to her family....

ADAM'S PROMISE by Julianne MacLean

A ruggedly handsome Canadian finds unexpected love when his fiancée arrives and he discovers she's not the woman he thought he was marrying!

Harlequin Historicals®
Historical Romantic Adventure!

HHWEST24

COMING NEXT MONTH FROM

HARLEQUIN HISTORICALS®

- **THE SCOT**
by **Lyn Stone,** author of MARRYING MISCHIEF
After overhearing two men plotting to kill an earl and his daughter,
James Garrow, Baron of Galioch, goes to warn the earl. Instead, he
meets the earl's daughter, freethinking, unruly Susanna Eastonby.
Despite the sparks flying between them, James and Susanna enter
into a marriage of convenience. Will this hardheaded couple realize
they're perfect for each other—before it's too late?

    HH #643 ISBN# 29243-0 $5.25 U.S./$6.25 CAN.

- **THE MIDWIFE'S SECRET**
by **Kate Bridges,** author of LUKE'S RUNAWAY BRIDE
Amanda Ryan is escaping her painful past and trying to start a new
life as a midwife when she meets Tom Murdock. As Tom teaches
Amanda to overcome the past, they start a budding relationship. But
will Amanda's secrets stand in the path of true love?

    HH #644 ISBN# 29244-9 $5.25 U.S./$6.25 CAN.

- **FALCON'S DESIRE**
by **Denise Lynn,** Harlequin Historical debut
Wrongly accused of murder, Count Rhys Faucon is given one month
to prove his innocence. In order to stop him, the victim's vengeance-
seeking fiancée, Lady Lyonesse, holds him captive in her keep and
unwittingly discovers a love beyond her wildest dreams!

    HH #645 ISBN# 29245-7 $5.25 U.S./$6.25 CAN.

- **THE LAW AND KATE MALONE**
by **Charlene Sands,** author of CHASE WHEELER'S WOMAN
Determined to grant her mother's last wish, Kate Malone returns
to her hometown to rebuild the Silver Saddle Saloon and reclaim
her family legacy. But the only man she's ever loved, Sheriff
Cole Bradshaw, is determined to stop the saloon from being built
and determined to steal Kate's heart....

    HH #646 ISBN# 29246-5 $5.25 U.S./$6.25 CAN.

KEEP AN EYE OUT FOR ALL FOUR
OF THESE TERRIFIC NEW TITLES

HHCNM0103